Fre~~ddy~~
~~pulled~~ Millette close.

P ...ing rapidly, she rested her cheek on his
ε~~ and he bent to kiss her crown, his own
...hing none too steady.

'...wouldn't do to be caught out again,' he
...d gently.

'...o,' she agreed, much to his body's painful
...sappointment.

...he placed a hand on his lapel and stroked
...own the fabric. Delight with her response
...o his touch was a wild beat in his blood.
...his attraction was a positive sign for their
...arriage. There was much pleasure to be had
...etween them, as long as he made sure not
...o let things go too far. Not to get too out of
...ontrol.

'...e really should go before someone misses
...,' she said, not moving an inch. She sighed.
'...e don't want to set tongues wagging again.'

...agging tongues were the story of his life. He
...d told himself a long time ago that he didn't
...are. But he didn't want her hurt by vicious
...ossip.

'...es, we should.' He kissed her forehead and
...nked his arm through hers, feeling for the
...rst time in a long while a sense of hope.

AUTHOR NOTE

I hope you enjoy this offshoot of the Beresford Abbey stories: *Haunted by the Earl's Touch* and *Captured Countess*. When we first met Freddy and Minette I could not understand why they seemed to dislike each other when they would be perfect together. I have enjoyed finding out what was keeping them apart.

Another fun part of researching this story was learning about Mr Brummell's game of cricket in 1807. Like Minette, I was surprised to see the Beau engaging in anything so active—and with an audience too!

I love to hear from readers, so feel free to email me at ann@annlethbridge. If you would like to know more about my books or sign up for my quarterly newsletter go to my website at annlethbridge.com. And if you are a history buff, you might enjoy my blog: regencyramble.blogspot.com

THE DUKE'S DARING DEBUTANTE

Ann Lethbridge

Published in Great Britain 2015
by Mills & Boon, an imprint of Harlequin (UK) Limited,
Eton House, 18-24 Paradise Road, Richmond, Surrey, TW9 1SR

© 2015 Michèle Ann Young

ISBN: 978-0-263-24790-9

In her youth, award-winning author **Ann Lethbridge** re-imagined the Regency romances she read—and now she loves writing her own. Now living in Canada, Ann visits Britain every year, where family members understand—or so they say—her need to poke around every antiquity within a hundred miles. Learn more about Ann or contact her at annlethbridge.com. She loves hearing from readers.

**Visit the author profile page
at millsandboon.co.uk for more titles**

Each book has a life of its own and is influenced by many people, but I would like to dedicate this book to those who serve their country in whatever capacity they choose—as my dad did in the army.
I believe he would have liked my foray into authorship, since he was a dedicated Georgette Heyer fan and loved reading about history.

Chapter One

⚬⚬⚬

The foul stench coated Minette Rideau's throat. With her skirts held high in one hand and the other clutching Granby's arm, she focussed on taking only tiny sips of air as she picked her way over Bridge Alley's slimy cobbles. One of many narrow passages in the reviled district of St Giles, it led to London's most infamous hell. The only one owned by a duke. Falconwood. The man she now risked her reputation to track down in his lair.

Ancient tenements crowded in on both sides, the glimmer of lanterns behind oilpaper giving them menacing aspects. All around, noises of a seething mass of humanity pierced the darkness. Shouts and curses, music from the tavern on the corner. A child crying. A woman coughing.

So very different from the elegance of Mayfair, but not the worst she'd seen.

Granby halted before a low wooden door

bound with iron and set with studs. The lantern above the door cast an oily gleam in the slime oozing along the alley's central runnel.

'This is it?' she asked. 'The Fools' Paradise?'

'It is,' Granby croaked as if his throat was parched.

It had required all of Minette's powers of persuasion to convince Lieutenant, the Honourable Laurence Granby, to be her escort when she'd named her destination. Now he was peering over his shoulder with the expression of one who had regained his sense of self-preservation and feared for his life. Finally he had realised that if this little adventure ever came to light, he was destined for a wagonload of trouble.

He cleared his throat. 'You can't want me to take you in there.' Begging her to change her mind.

An unpleasant sensation squirmed behind her breastbone. A guilty conscience was an uncomfortable companion, but not unfamiliar. Guilt lay behind this expedition to London's worst slums. Even as the idea had germinated, she'd known her escort hadn't deserved to be placed in such an awkward position. Honour balanced against gentlemanly conduct and no way to reconcile either. He was a nice young man. Open. Honest. And too terribly susceptible to female manipulation. For all that her conscience pricked her, in the end she'd been unable to come up with a better alternative.

Worse, it might all be for naught. The man she'd come to for help had been going out of his way to avoid her for years, hence this charade. For all her careful scheming, he could easily turn her away and report her to Gabe, her sister's husband.

If so, she'd have to think of another way to achieve her ends and avert disaster.

A disaster she'd set in motion years before. When she'd been young and exceedingly reckless. Not to mention in love.

She patted Granby's arm. 'Surely you aren't going back on your word?' She put a full measure of disappointment at his lack of courage into her voice.

The young man straightened his shoulders. 'Certainly not. Gentleman, you know. But really—'

'*Courage, mon ami.* Knock. It will be *très amusant, n'est-ce pas*? No one will ever know.' She cast him a blinding smile.

Predictably dazzled, Granby rapped on the door with the head of his walking cane.

A square peephole opened. A glimmer of light quickly blocked by an eye peering out. Pah. Men and their dramatics.

'Ah, 'tis you, sir,' a gruff voice said from behind the door. The peephole snapped shut, and the door swung inwards. The porter's glance slid over her without interest. Unlike proper gentle-men's clubs, here there was no ban on admitting females. It was part of the hell's attraction, along with wickedly deep play. Hopefully there would be others of her gender present tonight. Creating a stir was not her aim. A simple word with the club's owner, His Grace, the Duke of Falconwood, was all she wanted.

Granby tucked her arm under his in a rather sweet gesture of protection and escorted her along a short, dimly lit passage to a red velvet curtain drawn to cover a wide doorway. A liveried lad of about fifteen pulled the curtain aside, and they entered the low-ceilinged subscription room. The smell and haze of cigar smoke hung so thick in the air that Minette struggled not to cough as she gazed at men of every age and social class seated at green baize tables. Games of chance occupied their full attention. Pharo, deep basset, dice, to name but a few. Sovereigns and scraps of paper littered the tabletops. The bowstring-taut atmo-sphere reeked of both triumph and despair.

No sign of her quarry. The elusive Duke of Falconwood, Freddy to his friends, though she did not rank among their number. Anticipation tensed her shoulders, her stomach fluttering with the hope he wouldn't turn her away mingled with the expectation he would. The unpleasant churn-ing brought bile rising in her throat.

A stocky, pugnacious-looking young man in

his thirties, neatly dressed in the style of a butler, his light brown hair fashionably dressed, stepped forward to greet them. 'Lieutenant Granby. What is your pleasure tonight?' The maître d'hotel, then. His gaze focussed on Minette, and she read surprise in his narrowed blue gaze.

She held her breath, waiting for him to turn her away. Instead, he gave her escort a look of enquiry and she let her breath out.

'*Vingt-et-un*, if you don't mind, Barker,' Granby said, as agreed earlier in the evening.

The maître d' settled them at a table and snapped his fingers for a waiter to take their orders while Minette casually glanced around, trying to spot her man. The back of her neck prickled. Awareness. Someone watching.

The suave-looking gentleman seated at the next table leaned back in his seat. His heated gaze took in her face and the low cut of her gown. 'Welcome, lovely lady,' he said, eyeing her escort in the way of a male prepared to compete.

She merely inclined her head and leaned closer to Granby. The gentleman shrugged and turned back to his game.

After an hour of play in which Granby lost a great deal of money to her and there was still no sign of the Duke, she decided her quest was hopeless. So disappointing. And irritating. She'd been certain she would find him here tonight after trying for days to catch him at his lodgings. Now she'd have to think of a different way to meet him. She was running out of ideas.

'Why am I not surprised?' The familiar deep male voice struck a chord low in her stomach. He'd always had that effect on her, though she'd tried to ignore it. As she did now. Slowly, she put her cards face down and glanced up to meet a pair of dark, insolent eyes set in a lean, saturnine face.

A face of pure male beauty, his eyes of the darkest blue ringed by grey. He'd changed since she'd last seen him. His expression had grown colder, harder, more remote. More darkly fascinating. And while his form remained elegantly slender, he'd broadened across the shoulders to match his six-foot frame, which he now used with great effect to loom over her with all the menace of a greater physical force.

Not that she was surprised by the anger smouldering in his dark eyes. She'd invaded his very masculine sanctum.

'Good evening, Your Grace,' she said coolly, the daringly low cut of her gown seeming far more outrageous than when she'd left home. *Nom d'un nom*, she would not give him the satisfaction of feeling embarrassed. She lifted her chin. *'Quelle surprise.'*

His intense dark gaze shifted to her companion. The cold, hard scrutiny of an offended aristocrat.

'Your servant, Your Grace,' Granby said, rising to bow, colour flooding his face.

A dark eyebrow lifted in question. 'Hardly the place to bring a lady, Lieutenant.'

Granby tugged at his neckcloth. Perspiration popped out on his brow. 'A wager,' he choked out. 'Lady wanted to see the inside of a hell. Debt of honour and all that.'

'Naturally you are not one to argue with a lady.' The Duke's narrowed gaze flicked down to the cards and the guineas on her side of the table. 'Your companion has the devil's own luck, I see.'

He was being careful not to use her name. She couldn't help but be grateful for the courtesy. She offered him a sweet smile. 'Don't you mean skill, Your Grace?'

'A newly won skill, then.'

As she had hoped beyond hope, he hadn't forgotten her or their card games aboard ship some two years before. While she had played off her feminine wiles to get his attention, he'd treated her as little more than an annoying child. Brat, he had called her on the last occasion he had visited Meak, or any other of her brother-in-law's residences.

'Unfair, sir,' she said, keeping her expression flirtatious. 'I learned from the best.'

His lips quirked at the corners, his eyes glinted, the brief smile making him appear less austere. And more devastatingly handsome. An unwelcome pang pierced her heart. As if she had missed his smiles, which back then had been wickedly teasing. Oh, of a certainty she had missed him. The way one missed a stone in one's shoe.

The maitre d', standing at a little behind him, gave an impatient cough.

The flash of amusement on Freddy's face vanished as quickly as it had appeared. He turned his chilly gaze on her escort. 'Lieutenant, may I offer you a parlour where you can continue your game in private?'

The commanding tone of his voice was something she certainly didn't miss. His attempts to act like her older brother. To take charge, as if he had some authority over her actions. She damped down the instant raising of her hackles. After all, this was the reaction she had set out to achieve. His wanting to protect her from her own folly. Not that she would let him know the full extent of her error.

Granby's expression collapsed into something like relief. He gulped. 'Very civil, Your Grace. Perhaps…' He gave Minette a pleading look. 'Perhaps we should leave?'

Several nearby patrons, including the man who had inspected her when she'd first arrived, had paused in their game to watch the unfolding drama.

'Oh, no,' she said, rising to her feet. 'We should accept His Grace's kind offer.'

Granby's face crumpled. 'Really?'

'*Naturellement.*'

Freddy bowed, his expression mocking. 'Be so good as to follow me.'

He led them through a door in the back wall of the subscription room. As she passed him in the doorway, Freddy leaned close and murmured in her ear, 'I wonder what Gabe is going to think of this piece of mischief?'

She cast him a glance from beneath her lashes. 'I didn't take you for a tattletale, Your Grace.'

Granby gasped.

His Grace glowered.

Minette gave him her brightest, most innocent smile and breezed past him. Her gamble had paid off. She had his full attention.

Now came the most difficult part of her plan.

Following in the wake of the shamefaced Granby and the clearly recalcitrant Miss Rideau, Freddy curbed his ire. The attraction he'd always felt towards the stunningly beautiful French girl, with her velvety brown eyes flecked with gold and her deliciously creamy skin, of which he and everyone else in the club had seen far too much this evening, had nothing to do with his anger.

He was a normal, red-blooded male, and she was a lovely young woman.

No, it was Minette's lack of respect for the feelings of his friends, Gabe, the Marquess of

Mooreshead, and his wife, Nicky, that had him clenching his jaw to the point of cracking his back teeth. How could she be such a little idiot as to come to a place like this? 'Heaven', as his customers like to call his establishment when in the throes of their disillusion. For he had no doubt this was all her doing.

Fortunately for her, Barker, his maître d', knew a member of the Quality when he saw one. The moment Freddy had come in by way of his private entrance, his man had brought him the news that the wrong sort of woman had strayed onto the premises. She wasn't the first lady to wander through his portals. Usually they were older, married, matrons looking for a bit of excitement after doing their marital duty. As long as they were discreet, no one paid them any mind. However, never did freshly minted debutantes like Minette Rideau darken his disreputable door. Neither did he want them to. He liked his women as dissolute as he was, when he bothered with them at all.

She was lucky no one had recognised her. If they had, not even Gabe could save her reputation.

Minette was trouble. Reckless. Heedless. Things the male predator within him had recognised at their very first encounter on board ship. Apparently, she had no more idea than a baby about the harsh truths of the world in which he resided. The need to beat a little sense into the baby-faced Granby pulsed in his blood. How could the man have let her inveigle him this way?

He escorted the pair along a carpeted passageway, the salacious pictures on the walls advertising the purpose of the rooms at the back of the house. Some of his customers preferred their amusements out of the public eye. Such as those who held political positions, where deep play would cause a raised eyebrow or two. Others demanded more carnal forms of entertainment.

Minette carefully kept her eyes lowered, but he knew she saw them.

He opened the door to a room set up for gentlemen who took their cards seriously to the point of utter ruin. Windowless, panelled in dark wood, the only ornament a marble fireplace and mantel.

Once the pair were inside, Freddy closed the door and turned the key. Granby started.

Freddy put up a hand. 'To ensure we are not interrupted.'

The lieutenant nodded and looked relieved.

Freddy fixed him with a look designed to freeze. 'Are there maggots in your brain, Lieutenant? What do you mean by bringing a gently bred girl to a hell?'

'*Pardonnez-moi,*' Minette said, her voice equally icy, 'I do not believe what I do is your concern.'

'Well, you believe wrongly,' Freddy said. 'Well, Granby? Are you indeed so bacon-brained you did not realise that any one of your friends might have walked in and recognised Miss Rideau?'

The poor tongue-tied lad gulped and shifted on his feet. 'Told you. Debt of honour.'

Freddy leaned against the doorjamb and crossed his arms over his chest. 'Tell me about this wager of yours.'

'Lady Cargyle's *al fresco* breakfast,' he blurted in a rush.

Freddy waited for the next burst of words. If memory served, the young man had a bit of a stutter, which he manfully controlled by these staccato deliveries.

'Croquet,' Granby choked out. 'Wager. Ball through three hoops with only one knock of the mallet.' He blushed. 'Not possible.'

'So did she?'

'Kicked it through the last one.' He looked at Minette with a wan grin. 'Fair. No rule about kicking.'

Minette lifted a defiant chin.

Unwanted laughter bubbled in Freddy's throat. With great effort he managed to hide it. The girl was a minx. As smart as paint and always got what she wanted—by fair means or foul, according to a harassed Gabe.

Too bad she wouldn't want— He cut the thought off before it fully formed. He wasn't interested in respectable young females and if he had been, she had certainly never masked her dislike of him from the very first. Intelligent woman.

Now she was staring at him in that direct way she had, as if daring him to criticise.

He focussed on Granby. 'What on earth made you agree to such a hen-witted wager?' He waved a hand to encompass the club.

Minette bridled, her brown eyes flashing sparks of gold. Saints, in a temper she wasn't just beautiful, she looked like a goddess of war. Gabe really needed to take a firmer hand on her bridle or the girl would find herself dished before she had time to make an eligible marriage.

The thought of her married painfully pierced the wall of ice he'd built around his emotions. Really? Mentally, he shook his head. It wasn't possible. He didn't care what she did, as long as it didn't ruin his friendship with Gabe. One of the very few people he valued. He focussed his attention on her young idiot of an escort.

The boy looked as if he wanted the floor to open beneath his feet. 'I didn't know. Secret wager. Written on paper. Held by the judge.'

'I can imagine what you wrote on yours.'

The blush turned fiery. That was the trouble with fair hair and skin—there was no hiding your embarrassment. Freddy felt a grim sense of satisfaction as the discomforted young man swallowed hard. 'Nothing terrible. I swear.'

The fact that Freddy had sympathy for Minette's victim didn't mean he would be let off the hook. 'What? Are you a sheep to be led by the nose?' Some other part of his anatomy more like. 'You are fortunate I do not intend to report you to your colonel for conduct unbefitting.'

Resentment flared in the boy's eyes at the slur. No doubt he was thinking his tormenter was a pot calling the kettle black, but Freddy held his gaze and knew he'd made his point when the lad's shoulders slumped. 'Yes, sir.'

'You can go. As a family friend, I will see Miss Rideau home.'

Granby looked at Minette in question.

An expression flickered over Minette's face. If he had to guess at the meaning of that brief flash in her eyes, he would have said it was triumph. It didn't make sense. Chagrin more likely. Annoyance at being stuck with him as an escort. She knew very well he'd not put up with her nonsense.

She gave Granby the nod of acceptance. He felt as much relief as Granby clearly did that she'd decided not to refuse or make a fuss.

He really ought to tell Gabe about this little escapade, but he wouldn't, as long as she was reasonable. It would only worry Nicky, who he had heard was in a delicate condition. No, Miss Rideau would have to endure a lecture from him instead.

Freddy unlocked the door and opened it wide. 'Lieutenant?' he said softly, making sure the other man heard the authority in his voice. 'Not a word of this evening to anyone. Do I make myself clear?'

The young man snapped a quick salute in reply. 'Wouldn't dream...' he blurted. 'Mum's the word.' He scuttled out.

Freddy closed the door and turned to face the real villain of the piece.

Taking in her false expression of innocence, something inside him snapped. Fear for what might have happened had she chosen some other club in which to exercise her need for adventure. 'What the devil did you think you were doing? Did you want to marry the fellow, or simply ruin his career?'

She recoiled, the colour draining from her face, but, pluck to the backbone, she recovered in a second, squaring her shoulders. 'I wanted to see inside a hell.'

He narrowed his eyes, instinctively sensing dissembling. 'Why?'

The defiant gaze met his square on and, like the first time they had met, he was struck by her fragile beauty and the shadows in those beautiful doelike eyes. Secrets and pain. Once more, he was aware of a very real desire to shield her from a harsh world, even knowing she'd seen far more of it that any gently bred girl should have to witness during the years she'd wandered revolutionary France.

He gestured for her to take a seat. When she did so, he strode to the decanter of brandy and the two glasses on a side table. As was usual in the presence of a beautiful woman, he was aware of his awkward gait. He carried the glasses back to the table, taking care not to spill the contents yet not showing he was in any way conscious of making an effort. He'd had years to practise what other men took for granted. And while the slight halt in his left leg was so much a part of him it rarely discommoded him, it did demand more care in some of the simplest actions of life.

She looked at the glass he set in front of her with an expression of surprise.

'You will find it to be the finest cognac,' he said.

'Smuggled, no doubt.'

He shrugged and sat down in the seat on the other side of the table. 'Naturally. How else is one to obtain French brandy?'

Her shoulders relaxed. She sipped and nodded her approval. 'Excellent.'

'I am glad you approve.'

Her gaze shot to his face as if she suspected him of sarcasm. He was careful to show nothing of what he was feeling. Anger that she'd risked her reputation on a whim. The wish that she'd chosen some other club in which to play her games. No. He was glad she had come to Heaven. At least here she was safe. He took a mental inventory of those present in the subscription room who might know who she was and spread gossip. None sprang to mind.

'What do you think Gabe will say?' he asked. 'Or your sister?'

His jab clearly hit home. Though she disguised her reaction well, the winding of the strings of her reticule around her fingers gave away her nervousness. She had small hands, neat and quick as they knotted and unknotted the delicate cord. Hands that would feel wonderful on his body, stroking and caressing— He cut the thought off, dragged his gaze from their restless twisting. He hated it that he'd made her nervous, but it was as he had intended.

'Does Gabe know you own such a wicked place?' she asked.

Wicked. His body tightened at the image of the sort of wickedness he'd like to engage in with this girl who had become a woman since they'd last met. A beautiful desirable woman he had no right to be near. But, of course, it was the gambling she was talking about, not the other vices rampant beneath his roof. He considered the other import of her words. 'What makes you think I own it?'

'Bah. I'm not a fool. The pugilist dressed as a maître d' went to fetch you and stood back as if you were in charge.'

No, she wasn't a fool. 'I own a part share.' He wondered what she'd think if she knew who owned the other share. Sceptre had thought it a grand joke.

Her head tilted. 'An odd enterprise for a duke.'

He'd inherited his title a little over a year ago, six or seven months after he had invested in the Fools' Paradise. He still had a nasty feeling in his gut it had been the last straw for his father. The last straw in a long line of them that had caused the apoplexy that had taken his life. He took a long pull at the warming liquid in his glass. 'Why are you here, Minette? If you think I am fooled by that tale of a wager, you can think again.'

Women never did anything without an ulterior motive. Not the intelligent ones. And he had no illusions about the sharpness of her mind.

A crease formed between her straight brows as if she was trying to make up her mind about something. Probably whether she could trust him with the truth. She couldn't, of course, but that was something he didn't intend to point out.

'Tell me,' he said. 'Or explain it to Gabe later. Your choice.'

Looking down at her hands, she slowly unravelled the twisted strings.

Not going to trust him. The hollow ache of disappointment in his gut was a surprise. Perhaps it was merely because he was left with no recourse but to force the issue. He tossed back the balance of his brandy and went to pull the bell.

'Wait,' she said. 'I need to locate someone. I thought you might help me.'

Yet another surprise. His breath caught in his throat. She'd come to him for assistance. The cold inside him seemed to melt a little. As if he liked the idea she'd turned to him for aid. Not good. Not good at all. He was the wrong man to be offering his help to a woman with a reputation to protect. He strode back to the table and looked down at her. 'Who?'

A defiant lift of her chin. 'You must swear to say nothing of this to Gabe or Nicky.'

'Not tell them verbally, or in writing, or both?' Two could play at the game of cheating. She needed to understand that, unlike Granby, he was nobody's fool.

She glared at him. 'Not to tell them in any manner, shape or form through your own actions or that of any other person.'

Another bubble of laughter fought for escape. It was so long since he'd wanted to laugh, no wonder it hurt. But this was no laughing matter. 'You would have made a good lawyer, I think.'

'Women aren't allowed to be lawyers. They are not allowed to do anything useful.'

Oh, was that was she thought? 'Oh, believe me, they have lots of uses.' He let the wicked ideas in his head show in his eyes, echo in his tone of voice.

Undisturbed by the innuendo, she lifted one shoulder in a very Gallic gesture of disdain. 'Men.'

Not a blush in sight. His blood heated. Was it her boldness that attracted him, when most debutantes had him running for the hills? 'So jaded?'

A flash of pain in her eyes, followed by an acceptance he didn't understand, robbed him of amusement. He should not have resorted to idle teasing. They weren't on those kinds of terms. 'I beg your pardon, but that is the sort of male jocularity you exposed yourself to by coming here.'

'Thank you for your concern, but I am perfectly able to take care of myself.'

'Are you?' He pulled her to her feet, tilting her chin with one hand to look down into a stormy gaze that reminded him of trees in autumn lashed by the wind, pulling her hard against his body with the other. Her sweet curves were an aphrodisiac in his blood. His body hardened as he took her mouth in a punishing kiss. *Show me, sweetheart*, he willed. *Resist me.* His heart thundered and blood roared in his ears.

For a satisfying moment he felt her tense, but even as he prepared to force himself to let her go, she melted sweetly, kissing him back with a passion that would have seared his soul. If he'd had one.

His mind blanked of everything except the sensations scorching through his body, the feel of her softness melding into him, the taste of brandy on her silken tongue sliding against his, the scent of her, jasmine and hot summer nights. Delicious. Tempting.

Luscious and…not for him. He pushed her away before he forgot himself entirely.

Twin spots of colour blazed on her cheekbones. Embarrassment. Shame.

Self-loathing burned like acid in his throat. 'See how vulnerable you are?' he said harshly, all too aware of his raging desire and uneven breathing. 'No woman has the strength to prevent a determined man from taking what he wants. Dressed as you are, you told every man in the establishment that you are available and willing.'

Her eyes widened as if he'd wounded her feelings. Good. Perhaps she had learned her lesson. He'd certainly learned his. Keep his distance. 'Give me your word you won't try anything like this again and I'll take you home.'

He reached out to take her arm.

She jerked away. 'If you promise not to tell Gabe about this evening, I will not tell him of your insult to my person.'

Though he showed nothing on his face, he was surprised to discover her words hurt more than a slap would have done. Yet she was right. It had been an insult. Deliberately so. Outcast by the more respectable members of the *ton*, his attentions should be unwelcome. He'd used his reputation for vice to gain the trust of the dregs of society, the informants, the spies, and earned the scorn of his peers. He raised a brow. 'Blackmail. How unworthy. And what do you think Gabe would do? Call me out? He'd be more likely to insist we marry.'

A strange look came to her face. Yet another one he couldn't read. She shook her head. 'No, thank you.'

He did not bother to keep the bitter edge from his tone. 'My sentiments exactly.' He intended never to marry, and certainly wasn't going to let a little chit like her change his mind.

'I wouldn't have had to come here,' she shot back, 'had you responded to my notes.'

Notes he should have returned unopened, instead of stuffing them in his desk drawer. 'A young lady doesn't demand a gentlemen wait on her. It is not good *ton*.'

'Oh, and I suppose you are good *ton*,' she muttered, then lifted her gaze to meet his face. 'You avoided me on purpose.'

He'd been avoiding her like a man avoided the hangman's noose. She was too damnably attractive. 'Well, here I am now.' He poured chill into his voice. No easy task when his body burned with lust. 'Tell me who it is you want found and then I'll take you home.'

'You've no doubt heard that Moreau is back in England.' Clear, velvet-brown eyes met his in challenge.

A spy placed in England by Fouché, Moreau had very nearly succeeded in a plan to assassinate King George. He had used Minette to lure her sister Nicky, now Gabe's wife, into helping him. He'd almost captured Gabe into the bargain. It had been a near-run thing, but ultimately Nicky and Gabe had outwitted him. Moreau's spectacular failure had resulted in him being relocated to Madrid, where he must have helped Napoleon's brother gain the throne of Spain. No doubt back in favour, he was once more assigned to help in the downfall of the only country stopping Napoleon from ruling the whole of Europe. Britain.

'Nothing I didn't already know,' Freddy said. 'And not your concern.'

Her eyes darkened. 'Is it not?' She took a deep breath. 'What if he goes after Nicky? After the way she tricked him...' The slight gesture of her hands encompassed the enormity of what a man like Moreau could do to an enemy.

Admiration caused something in his chest to expand. She looked like such a fragile creature, with her glowing skin and fine bones, while the blood of a Valkyrie ran in her veins. The understanding shook him to the core. He forced himself to focus on the very real danger within her words.

'He will be found and dealt with.'

'Like you dealt with him before? You don't even know what he looks like. I do. And if you won't help me, I will find him by myself.'

The challenge in her voice, her manner, raised his hackles. The Frenchman had a network of informants all over England. One hint that he was at risk of discovery and he wouldn't hesitate to kill.

Anger at her bravado chilled him to the bone. He kept his voice was calm. 'What have you heard?'

'You have to let me help in his capture.'

He almost laughed. But that would have hurt her feelings. And, besides, it wasn't the least bit humorous. 'Do not be ridiculous.'

Her chin went up. 'Someone I know has seen him. I thought you would want to know. If you won't let me be part of it, I will seek his aid.'

His blood ran cold. Moreau was a dangerous man. A killer when cornered.

'Why this renewed interest in Moreau?' he asked.

Shadows skittered across her face. 'He tried to use me to harm Nicky. I need to know first-hand he is no longer a threat.'

Sincerity shone in her gaze. She'd given him the truth, but only part of it. He'd spent too long working for Sceptre not to recognise a half-truth. 'Trust me to do my job and I will let you know when he is taken care of. Come, I will take you home.' And in the meantime he'd have to discover what she was hiding.

When she hesitated, he gave her a glare that

would have turned Granby to a pillar of salt. On Minette, it had no effect.

She glared right back. 'You always did treat me like a child.'

To stop himself from treating her like a desirable woman. Not something she needed to know. 'My carriage awaits us at the back.'

'Would you mind dropping me off in the mews?' she said airily. 'I left the gate open before I left, since no one knew I went out this evening.'

Thus embroiling him deeper in her scheme. He bit back a curse.

Chapter Two

Seated in his curricle, Minette watched Freddy leap nimbly aboard to take the reins. He showed no sign of discomfort or awkwardness. She'd noticed that, although he limped, he did not seem to find whatever ailed his leg an impediment. Except when people offered him a seat as if he were some sort of invalid. Then he looked ready for murder.

The horses' hooves ringing on the cobbles, they turned onto Broad Street. The roads were quiet at this time of night and, in this quarter of Town, ill lit. Ruffians lurked in shadows, watching their passing with keen eyes. It said something about the dangerous air of the man beside her that their carriage suffered no interference and they soon reached the well-kept streets of Mayfair.

'Why do you never come to see Gabe and Nicky?' Minette asked. 'Are you too good for us now you are a duke?'

The streetlight caught his grim expression in

stark relief. 'Gabe has moved on. It is better if no one knows of our prior…association.'

Gabe had once worked as a spy, too. 'He saved the King's life.' The attempted assassination had never been mentioned in the newspapers, and Moreau remained at large. The sound of his name in her head left a bitter taste on her tongue. A vile concoction of betrayal, regret and guilt.

'If you would accept my help, I am sure we could find him more quickly,' she said.

'You need someone to put you over a knee and give you a spanking,' he muttered.

She swivelled in her seat to face him and traced a fingertip along the length of his thigh. 'Is that your idea of fun with a woman?'

He turned a choke into a cough, and she smiled innocently up at him as the next streetlamp caught her full in the face.

'You little minx,' he said, when he finally caught his breath. 'You should know better.'

Since Gabe had first warned her and Nicky that Moreau had been recalled to France, she'd been expecting him to show up in England. He wasn't one to leave unfinished business. She'd had her French maid, Christine, ask discreetly among the *émigrés*. Moreau, as he'd called himself in England, had destroyed more lives than the English could even guess at. The families of those people had long memories. 'I have a con-

tact who will give us the name of someone who
has seen him.'

'Us.'

He made a sound of scorn, the kind one's el-
ders made when one said something stupid. Apparently her kiss— she resisted the urge to touch
her lips where the heat of his mouth on hers still
lingered—hadn't convinced him he was dealing
with a woman grown. If he knew, if any of them
knew what she'd done…

She should never have allowed Nicky to bring
her out, as they called it here in London. They all
thought her so sweet and innocent. How could she
reveal the truth when Nicky had given up her own
dreams to protect her little sister? Nicky had married the brutal Count Vilandry to keep Minette
safe and she had thrown that sacrifice away. So
now she faced the prospect of refusing any and
all perfectly acceptable offers of marriage. And
there would be offers. She wasn't an antidote, as
Gabe called ladies lacking in charms, and the
dowry Gabe had so generously bestowed on her
made her a very eligible *parti*.

But that was mostly her problem. Worse was
the weapon she had given Moreau. He could,
whenever he wished, destroy her and Gabe and
Nicky with the gift she had given him. He would
have no hesitation to use it against them. It did
not bear thinking about. 'I won't get in your way.

I would help identify him and ask him one question. Nothing more.'

'No.'

Men. They never listened. 'As you please.' She folded her hands in her lap in a parody of innocence.

Freddy shot her an exasperated glance mingled with something she could not quite read. 'If there was any possibility at all of you being able to accomplish the matter alone, you would not have come to me for help.'

The man had a brain. Gabe had said he'd been brilliant at university. Too clever by half, she'd always thought, when she'd tried to cheat him at cards. And he knew it, which was worse. 'It needs money to get my informant to give up what they know.'

He pulled the carriage into the alley behind the mews in Grosvenor Square. Relief shot through her. Until that moment she'd half expected he would give her away to Gabe. At least he wasn't going to give her up tonight. Perhaps she was making some headway.

'You want money.' He sounded aggrieved, as if she should have wanted something different. 'Who is this contact you speak of?'

'Why would I tell you when you won't help me?' Her maid, an *émigrée*, had been given only a titbit of information. 'Please, Freddy.'

'You picked the wrong man for your games.

Tomorrow I will have the truth. Or I will reveal the whole to Gabe.'

He tied off the horses' reins, jumped clear and helped her down. He gazed at the garden gate she'd left ajar. 'Bolt that behind you.'

She stepped inside and then turned to look up at him, put her hand on his arm and felt him tense. 'I don't care how much you and Gabe badger me, I will tell you nothing unless you involve me in the plan for Moreau's capture. It is of the utmost importance.' It was the most she dared say and she was surprised she was trusting him this much. Except that he had never made her feel unsafe. Irritated, yes. Annoyed, yes. But never in any danger.

He put his hand on the brick wall and loomed over her. 'Why?'

'I told you. I was his victim. I need to know he can never harm me or Nicky again, even if it means killing him.' She held her breath.

His eyes widened. 'You will not approach him.'

'Not if you agree to my involvement.'

A frustrated growl issued from his throat.

'Don't call in the morning,' she said. 'I will know more tomorrow night. Meet me at Gosport's ball and we can talk again.' She whisked inside and shut and bolted the gate behind her.

A fist slammed against the wood.

'Hush,' she whispered. 'You'll wake someone.' She fled down the garden path in case he should decide to break his way in, but as she slid through the French doors into the breakfast room she heard the sound of his carriage moving off.

Everything depended on the slim chance she'd told him enough to stop him from exposing her visit to Gabe in the morning.

Nicky's future depended on it.

She touched a finger to her lips, remembering their kiss. How quickly she had responded, how good it had felt. The intensity, almost as if he, too, had felt something deeper between them than passing lust.

Ridiculous. It was his attempt to scare her, that was all. There had never been any doubt in her mind that he disliked her. Probably because she was French. His whole purpose in life was to defeat her countrymen.

'Now, don't you look as fine as fivepence? Bang up to the knocker, you might say.'

Freddy met Barker's gaze in the mirror and grinned. '*Sartorial elegance* are the words you are seeking.'

Barker liked to pretend he came from the stews rather than a respectable merchant family. 'Unlikely.' He narrowed his eyes. 'Pity you can't do something about your expression. You look like a man walking up the steps to the nubbin' cheat.'

The gallows would be preferable to what he

had planned for tonight. 'Are you sure no one has seen him?'

'Nary a peep, but we'll find him, given time.'

Freddy cursed. With Minette on the rampage, he didn't have time. Neither did he want to play foolish games with manipulating little baggages like Minette Rideau. He should have gone to see Gabe this morning, but that would have finished any hope he'd have of getting her to talk. He'd recognised the signs. He certainly didn't want her going off half-cocked and ruining any chance they had of finding Moreau before he did any damage. She was as stubborn as she was beautiful. He closed his eyes briefly as the recollection of their kiss flooded his mind. The feel of her soft body pressed against his own. His blood heated. Damn it all, that was the last thing he needed.

He gave one more twitch to his neckcloth and turned from the mirror.

Barker held up his coat, fingering the cloth. 'As fine a bit of yardage as I've ever seen. Weston, did you say?'

'Yes.' He slid his arms into the sleeves, and Barker eased the coat over his shoulders.

It was like slipping into a disguise. The persona of aristocrat, rather than that of owner of a hell-cum-brothel. It was the latter part that stuck in the craw of the *ton*. A gentleman might not mind enjoying its offerings but they didn't want their wives near the owner of a bawdy house. Not that a truly ambitious mama would care if she thought she had a chance at the title.

The main reason he never went to balls and such.

Hopefully, the Gosports wouldn't throw their uninvited guest out on his ear. While the ducal title trumped a mere baron any day of the week, likely his host wouldn't be pleased at such a disgraceful duke darkening his doors.

Freddy grinned at the alliteration. It would make a good title for one of the romances the ladies like to read.

'Is the carriage ready?' he asked.

He'd had his mother's town carriage dragged out and dusted off. Lord, his father must be turning in his grave right now, given the path his heir had decided to follow. As if he wasn't disappointing enough as it was.

'Ready and waiting, guv. Er...I mean, Your Grace.'

'No need to stand on ceremony, Barker. You know me too well for that.' Barker had dragged him home half-seas over too many times after long nights of talking to his eyes and ears in London's lowest taverns to scrape and bow to his title.

Barker grinned. 'Right you are, then, guv. Time we were off.'

Freddy grinned back. Whatever happened, tonight was going to be unpleasant, but at least it wouldn't be boring. Minette Rideau was never dull.

When he arrived at Gosports' house he saw

that he had timed his arrival to perfection. The receiving line had already abandoned its post at the head of the stairs, his host and hostess off enjoying their party. He slipped the butler a coach wheel. The man closed his fist over the silver coin and agreed there was no need to announce a latecomer, particularly since he'd come at the behest of another guest.

Following the sound of music, Freddy ascended the stairs to the first floor and located the ballroom. A large drawing room with the furniture removed and a three-man orchestra at one end.

Minette, in proper debutante white, looked glorious, her face flushed, her eyes sparkling as she pirouetted beneath the arm of a fresh-faced youth. This was what a girl like her should be doing. Dancing. Flirting. Establishing herself in society. It would be a shame to spoil all that, but if he had to he would tell Gabe what she'd been up to and have her sent to rusticate at his country house until they had Moreau firmly in their grasp.

Her glance met his across the room. He stilled. Caught by the laughing brightness of her face. His chest tightened. She wouldn't be smiling at him by the end of the evening. Most likely she'd hate him. The thought made him feel colder than usual. He scanned the room, found Gabe and

Nicky standing with a group of friends. He took a deep breath and straightened his shoulders.

'Freddy. I didn't know you would be here to-night.' Arthur Stone's cheerful greeting at his back had him spinning around.

Arthur, his cousin, put out a hand to steady him. Freddy gritted his teeth, avoided the clutching hand and smiled. 'A surprise to me, too.'

The slow-top frowned his puzzlement. 'It is good to see you, Freddy.' He winced. 'I suppose I should be calling you Duke now or Falconwood.'

'Freddy will do, cuz. Falconwood sounds too much like Father to me.'

His cousin's open countenance cleared of worry. He had a naturally cheerful disposition and a dullness of intellect Freddy found hard work, but he was a nice enough chap. 'It's hard to believe the old fellow's been gone more than a year, isn't it?' His cousin glanced about him, pity in his eyes. 'There are some chairs over there by the wall if you need to sit down. I'd be more than happy sit and keep you company.'

Pity for Freddy's lame leg. Along with the un-ease people generally felt around someone less than whole. Not to mention a man whose mother had accused him of making a play for the duke-dom. A charge levelled behind his back but never laid to his face. Fratricide. The unspoken word lingered in the air like the smell of rotten eggs.

Rather than offering to plant the man a facer,

Freddy ignored the suggestion that he sit, along with those other unspoken sentiments. 'How is the family?'

'The boys are just like me at their age, full of pluck.' His face beamed with pride.

Freddy liked that most about his cousin, his love of his boys. 'I imagine they have grown a great deal since I saw them last.'

'You really ought to pay us a visit. I'll have Liz send you an invitation.'

He couldn't think of anything worse. If Arthur was oversolicitous, his wife vacillated between offers to help the poor benighted invalid and the secret worry that he might yet marry, beget a family of his own and cut out her sons. He had the feeling she agreed with the old duke, his father, that if his older brother had to die in the accident, when they had been little more than boys on the cusp of manhood, it would have been better if Freddy had found the decency to accompany his brother to the pearly gates.

The old man was likely right. And if Freddy had been a kinder man, he would set Liz's mind at rest. He had no intention of passing on what his father had called, on good days, the taint in his blood.

He watched Minette chattering to the woman beside her in the set and found the tension in his shoulders easing. 'Perhaps I'll come down during hunting season.'

'Hunting?' Anxiety creased Arthur's brow. 'It's rough country, you know.' His brow smoothed out. 'Shooting, you mean. The very thing. We can carry a chair out with us in case...' He seemed to realise his words were not going down all that well. 'See how you feel on the day, what?'

Such a dolt, his heir who would one day inherit the dukedom. Biting back the words, he bowed. 'If you will excuse me, I need a drink.'

He found his way to the refreshment table and had the lackey pour him a brandy. A few minutes with Arthur always left him ready for murder. Guilt pushing to the forefront, no doubt. Glass in hand, he watched Gabe and Nicky chat with friends, but could not bring himself to join them. He hated to break up what looked like a merry party. Such a handsome couple and the darlings of the *ton*.

Three years ago he would have wagered his best horse that Gabe would never marry. What must it be like? Marriage? And now incipient fatherhood. The emptiness inside him seemed to expand at the reminder of his vow. He downed the brandy as the group around his friends dispersed and walked over to join them.

'*Quelle surprise,*' Nicky said, greeting him with obvious pleasure. 'I thought you must be hibernating somewhere in the country it is so long since we saw you.'

Gabe rolled his eyes. 'Stop prying.' He gave Freddy an intense look. 'Everything all right?'

'Perfect.'

They both knew it for a lie, but there were too many ears in such a public place to say more. Gabe was no longer involved in espionage. He was part of the establishment now. It was certainly not the right place to reveal what his ward had been up to. Indeed, Freddy hoped that tonight's conversation with Minette would put a halt to any need to do so. The set came to an end and Minette tripped back to her sister, her lovely face radiant. She dipped a curtsey to Freddy. 'Your Grace. How unexpected.'

Minx. She knew he'd have no choice but to gather the information she'd promised. He forced himself to ignore the way his blood stirred at the saucy look she cast up at him from beneath thick russet lashes. Somehow she managed to convey all manner of wickedness with a glance beyond any demure English miss. The French called it *je ne sais quois*. Whatever it was, it exuded from her skin like sensual perfume.

But he was not completely lacking in the charm department, as more than one woman had told him. Though he suspected it was his title they found alluring. 'Miss Rideau. May I compliment you on your appearance? The other ladies present are no doubt gnashing their teeth.'

Her amber eyes danced with laughter, while

her expression remained innocent. 'Or perhaps they are jealous because I am the only unmarried lady such a great personage has deigned to speak with this evening. You only have to dance with me to completely ruin their night.'

Beside him, Nicky shifted. She knew he could not dance and was tender-hearted enough not to want him embarrassed. Strangely, though, Minette's words warmed him deep inside. It was as if she had not noticed his halting gait. Or thought nothing of it. The girl certainly had a way, like no other, of catching him off guard. He kept his face impassive. 'I do not dance, but let us take a stroll about the room, unless you have another partner waiting for this next set?'

'Oh, pooh. 'Tis only Granby and he is nowhere to be seen.' She placed her hand on his arm. 'He must have forgotten.'

The young idiot was probably somewhere hiding behind one of the potted palms strategically placed around the room, in case Freddy was inclined to tell Gabe about his lapse in judgement.

'Run along,' Gabe said, smiling, but with puzzlement clear in his eyes. Not surprising when he and Minette usually traded nothing but barbs.

Gabe turned to Nicky. '*Madame*, may I have this next dance?' His voice was a caress, and Nicky blushed like a girl.

'*Certainement.*'

They strolled out onto dance floor.

Their happiness filled Freddy with gladness for his friend but, damn it, he missed Gabe. They had worked well together.

He guided Minette in a gentle stroll around the dance floor, not bothering to smooth out his gait. When he'd been younger he had spent a great deal of time in front of the mirror, trying to appear normal. It had been a complete waste of time.

'So,' she said, sotto voce, 'you have considered my proposition?'

'The answer remains the same. And in case you have forgotten, it is no.'

Her chin went up.

'Also,' he continued, 'if you even think about going after Moreau yourself, I'll have you arrested for treason.'

Her eyes widened a fraction, something dark skated across their gold-flecked depths that had him tensing. What the hell wasn't she telling him?

Her smile turned mischievous, a feminine sideways glance that had his blood running hot. 'You'd have to catch me first,' she murmured in velvet tones.

God, it sounded salacious, a challenge of a very different sort.

'Stop it,' he said, keeping his voice cold with some effort. 'Keep your tricks for the likes of Granby.'

She laughed. 'If I didn't know better, I might think you were jealous.'

Something like a growl rose in his throat. He stopped it dead.

'My informant discovered someone who has seen Moreau. Knows the name he is using,' she said, as lightly as if she'd passed a comment on the weather.

He only just stopped himself from grabbing her arm and spinning her around to face him. It was the information he and his men had been seeking for weeks. 'Who is this informant?'

She dipped a curtsey at a passing matron of obvious consequence. 'I won't tell, unless you agree to let me speak to Moreau before you arrest him. I have a plan. Bother, here comes Granby. We can't talk here. I'll make an excuse and meet you in the library in a few minutes.'

'Minette—'

But she was already moving towards the lieutenant, who had halted a few feet away, his expression wary.

Damn it. He should leave. See her tomorrow in Gabe's presence. But he had the feeling that if he did not talk to her tonight, she might not be at Gabe's house in the morning. Why the hell did she want to speak with a man who had held her prisoner for several weeks? There was something she had not told them when she had been rescued. Something he had the feeling he needed to know before he went after the man.

He strode out of the ballroom, heading for the library.

* * *

Men, Minette thought darkly as she moved down the set with a smile pinned to her lips. They always thought a woman needed protection from the least little thing. She glanced around and didn't see Freddy. Either he would meet her in the library or she would find him on Gabe's doorstep in the morning.

Then how would she get her property back before Moreau was taken?

She should have known Moreau would find a way to get back in favour with Napoleon's spymaster, Fouché. But what was his purpose here in England? If she'd learned one thing about him, it was that he did not like to be crossed. People paid for it, in blood. A shudder ran down her spine.

If only Freddy trusted her enough to know she would never ask for such a concession if it wasn't vital. And trusted her enough not to ask why. Then again, she didn't trust him, either. Men like Moreau and Freddy used people to get what they wanted.

She glanced around. If she was going to meet him before he got impatient and left, it would be best to go before Nicky and Gabe left the dance floor. She smiled at Granby, took his hand for a backward pass across the set and deliberately stepped on her gown's train. The hem tore beautifully.

'Bother,' she said.

Granby stared at her blankly.

'I tore my lace,' she explained. 'I'll have to pin it. Excuse me.' She dived through the other dancers, making for the door, in her haste brushing the arm of a tall girl in regulation white.

The young woman gave her a hesitant smile. 'Is something wrong?'

Nom d'un nom, now she'd have to be polite or risk causing a stir. 'Someone stepped on my gown.' She pulled at her skirt. 'I can't see, but I think the lace is torn.'

The girl stepped closer, peering down. 'Yes. There is a long strip hanging by a thread.'

Minette gave a theatrical sigh. 'I thought so. I was on my way to pin it.'

'Would you like help?'

Oh, now one of these snooty English *mademoiselles* decided to be kind. They usually ignored her as an upstart *émigrée* trying to steal all the best men on the marriage mart. This one looked a nice young woman, like someone she might have liked to know better. Too bad circumstances demanded she turn her offer down. '*Merci*, but I think I can manage.' She hurried on her way.

The library was only a few doors down from the ballroom, according to a footman, and it wasn't long before she was slipping inside a room lit by one candelabrum on the round central table.

Standing beside it, Freddy's lean, almost saturnine face looked thoroughly devilish. A very handsome if austere devil. Her heart gave a little kick. Most unnerving, when he always seemed so utterly indifferent. Except when they'd kissed. Heat rushed upward, engulfing her face. Thank goodness for the gloom.

She closed the door.

'Well?' he said, his voice low and menacing. 'Who is this person who knows of Moreau's new identity?'

The demand in his voice brought a hot rush of temper to the surface. 'I will tell you when you agree to let me question him.'

'You can do so and welcome, once we have him in chains.'

She folded her arms over her chest. 'If you capture him, you mean. You let him get away once. And without my help you will lose him this time, too.'

His face became even more haughty. 'Are you proposing that I drive you around London chasing shadows? Gabe may be my friend but he isn't a fool. He won't allow his ward to be seen alone in my company.'

'We could pretend to be engaged.' It was an idea she'd had in the night when she'd recalled his words at the hell about Gabe insisting they marry. It had seemed like the perfect answer. Then. Now, from the look of horror on his face, she wished she hadn't mentioned it.

'Have you lost your reason?' His expression

changed, became harder. 'Or is it a title you are after?'

Hot anger raced through her veins. As if she would do anything so dishonourable. She struck out at those dark, mocking eyes, her fingers curled into claws, and found her wrist caught in long, strong fingers. Slowly, inexorably he forced her arm behind her back and loomed over her, forcing her to bend back. His breath was a harsh sound in his throat. Her heart raced wildly as she gazed at his beautiful, cruelly smiling mouth inches from hers. 'No?' he murmured with soft menace. 'Then perhaps it is another kiss you seek.'

She froze. Lord help her, but she did want him to kiss her. And more. She swallowed against the dryness in her throat. As if sensing her weakness, her racing pulse, he brushed his mouth across her lips. Recklessly, she kissed him back, twining her free hand around his neck, though she had no need for balance he held her so firmly, so powerfully within one arm. She could not resist the hard, strong feel of his chest against her breasts or the pressure of his thigh between her legs. Such a sweet, painful ache.

She parted her lips to the flick of his tongue and revelled in the way he stroked the inside of her mouth. So stirring, so exciting. So achingly perfect.

He released her wrist and held her close while his mouth and tongue worked their magic. His hand went to her breast, his thumb seeking the hardened peak. A groan rumbled up from his chest.

She made a small sound of longing, knowing the pleasures he could bring with his touch. Her head spun with the sensation of the kiss, the sensation of his hand languorously learning the shape of her breast and teasing at her nipple through the thin layers of fabric. Her insides became all liquid fire and exquisite tension.

She wanted…him. His hardness, inside her. She wanted the vast pleasure a man could bring to a woman, not the pale imitation she achieved in her lonely bed.

As if he knew her inner thoughts and needs, he backed her up until she was pressed against the book shelves. The hand at her back slipped down over her buttocks, his fingers rucking up her skirts, while his other hand continued to caress her breasts, attending to each in turn.

She trembled at the promise of delight. Shook with need as the cool air in the room hit her naked flesh above her stockings. The gown now bunched high behind her back, his fingers, those long clever fingers dipped into the crevasse between her buttocks, tickling and teasing and promising. He withdrew his tongue from her mouth, and she followed it, licking and tasting, tangling with his tongue. And then he sucked.

Her knees gave way at the salacious sensation rippling through her body. Her inner muscles clenched, squeezing and begging for the bliss his body could bring.

She wanted all he could give her and he knew it.

He widened his stance. Unable to resist, she reached between them, cupped him between the legs, found the hard ridge of his arousal and the softness beneath. She caressed him with all her skill, squeezing and rubbing until he groaned into her mouth.

Heady triumph shot through her as he broke free, his breathing as loud and uneven as hers.

He pushed one hand deep into the neckline of her low gown, his warm palm meeting bare, hot flesh, grazing across her thrusting nipple.

His other hand brushed her questing fingers away and cupped the hot flesh between her thighs. She rocked into his palm, increasing the pleasure of his touch tenfold.

So delicious. So unutterably, exquisitely pleasurable. Yet not nearly enough. She wanted him as she hadn't wanted any other man since Pierre's betrayal, perhaps even more. *'S'il vous plaît,'* she whispered in his ear, and felt him shudder at the whisper of her breath across his skin. And the words. The words had such meaning. They spoke of mutual pleasure. Of pleasing. Of wanting.

And how she did want. It had been so long.

His hand left her body to tear at the buttons on his falls. 'I want your breasts,' he said thickly, as if he, too, warred with a hunger so great it could not be denied.

'Ties at the back,' she gasped, longing to feel his mouth and tongue hot and wet on her nipples.

He spun her around, his arousal now pressed against the dip in her buttocks, rocking into her, making her moan with each forward push of his hips, while his hands dealt with the laces of her bodice and then her stays. She reached behind her and cupped him, making him draw in a hiss of breath that caused her insides to quiver with blissful anticipation.

Bodice undone, he brought her around to face him, stepping aside to let the subdued light of the candle play over her breasts. Full and proud, the nipples, dark rose and hard with excitement, jutted towards him, seeking his touch. His gaze travelled to the juncture of her thighs. She knew he must see the evidence of her desire, even as she gazed in longing at his own readiness.

'Lovely,' he said, hoarsely.

She licked her lips.

He covered her with his body and kissed her full and hard, while he took himself in hand in preparation for entry.

'Oh,' a female voice cried.

Freddy cursed, froze, looking down into her

face. His eyes widened as if with realisation. He shook his head in disbelief and horror. 'You little fool,' he whispered. 'What in the devil's name have you done?'

Chapter Three

Why the hell hadn't he locked the door? He should have guessed she'd do something to force his hand. A typical female trick. Freddy fastened his buttons and turned to face the intruder, shielding Minette from view as much as was possible. Behind him, he heard the rustle of the adjustment of clothing.

He glared at the young woman in white hovering on the threshold, light spilling in a wide arc into the room. A woman he didn't know, of pale complexion and mousy brown hair. Fortunately the light from the corridor did not reach fully across the room, though the candle gave enough light to reveal their embrace, if not the details. 'You required something?'

The girl, whose pallid face was clearly visible, gulped, her eyes round. 'Oh, no. I was looking for someone. Miss Rideau. She had torn her gown and I thought to offer my pins. Someone said they saw her enter the library. Please, excuse me.'

She started to close the door. God. They were going to get away with it. He moved towards the door to lock it.

'What are you doing here, Priscilla?' A male voice. 'The ballroom is at the other end of this corridor.'

The young woman turned to look at whoever had spoken. 'I was looking for the withdrawing room, Papa. I missed my way.'

'Not meeting someone, are you, my girl?' The door swung back.

Freddy swallowed a curse as he faced an irate-faced gentleman. Lord Sparshott, if he recalled correctly.

'Good God,' the other man said, his face turning turkey red. 'Priscilla—' He halted, and Freddy knew the man had no illusions about what he was seeing.

Sparshott grabbed his daughter's hand. 'Come away. This is no place for a decent gel.'

'I don't see why not,' Freddy said, hoping like hell Minette had herself decently covered. 'I am sure you and your daughter would like to be the first to congratulate Mademoiselle Rideau and me on our betrothal.'

The other man snorted and bowed stiffly. 'My commiserations, *mademoiselle*. Come, child.' He stalked off with his daughter in tow. Just before she disappeared she glanced back over her shoulder. Freddy had the distinct impression there was regret in her eyes.

He closed the door. Hell and damnation, there was no key. Had she planned that, too? He swung around to face her, to assess the full extent of the damage. Thank God she was decently covered, if a bit dishevelled. At a quick glance one could assume it was no more than a kiss they had been sharing in the dark. The dull throb of an arousal denied served to increase his fury.

'You did it on purpose.' He kept his expression cool, his emotions under guard. Now was not the time to express his anger.

'I did not,' she snapped back, her eyes flashing fire.

A fire he would like to have put to better use than an argument, but it was far too late. He was dished. Done up. Betrothed, when he had planned never to marry.

'Turn around.'

Her jaw dropped. 'Are you going to—?'

'No, I'm bloody well not. I'm going to see you properly laced and back into the ballroom. We have to break the good news to Gabe and Nicky before the gossip gets out of hand.'

'Oh.'

Damn it, had that been disappointment he'd heard in her voice? That they wouldn't finish what they'd started? His body twitched appreciatively at the very idea as she turned around and let him fix what he had undone. Hell and damnation, the girl had made him lose all sense of civility and reason. He should never have met her alone. It had been far too long since he'd taken a woman to his bed. Surrounded by women in the brothel had given him a distaste of coldly commercial transactions. And, if he was honest, seeing Gabe's marital happiness had made him want more. No wonder the first brush of Minette's skin against his palm had sent all his good intentions going up in the flames of lust. Because she was the one woman he had always wanted and could never have for the flick of a finger.

And now he was trapped. After years of him denying his unwanted attraction out of respect for Gabe, who knew of his vow never to marry. Who knew dalliance was all he ever wanted or needed. As Gabe's ward, Minette deserved far better than he would ever be. And a far better life than he could offer. Finished with the buttons and lacings, he spun her round to face him. 'You and your little friend have properly put us in the basket. There's no backing out of this, you know. We are shackled for life.'

She lifted her chin, her eyes huge and roiling with emotion. 'I didn't plan it, you idiot. You kissed me, remember? And, besides, it will be forgotten in a week.'

'It won't. Of all people, you had to pick Sparshott's daughter to help in your schemes. He's one of the biggest sticklers I know. You can be sure he won't let people forget, even after we tie the knot.'

'*Mon Dieu*. You will stop saying I planned this. She saw my hem was torn and offered to help. I said no. She followed me of her own accord.'

'A happy coincidence, then,' he said, trying to bury his frustration. There was no sense in being angry. What was done was done.

She eyed him speculatively, as if she didn't believe his resignation to his fate, and dug in her reticule. 'You had better pin up my hem before we go back.' She handed him some pins.

Grimacing, Freddy fell to one knee and worked on reattaching the delicate flounce.

The door opened to admit a grim-looking Gabe.

'How very touching,' he drawled, his expression as hard as granite.

'Don't be an ass,' Freddy said, placing the last pin. He leaped to his feet, grabbed Minette's hand and gave his friend a smile he did not feel. Although there was something satisfying in the feel of that small gloved hand within his palm, as if it belonged there. 'We were about to come and find you and share our good news. You can be the first to congratulate us on our betrothal.'

The grimness around Gabe's mouth did not ease. 'I gather, then, that Sparshott did not offer his felicitations.'

Sarcasm. From his friend. They'd often dis-
agreed, but they'd always had mutual respect. 'It
was a rather awkward moment.'

Minette's hand quivered in his. His spine stiffened, the tension growing second by second as
he prayed her temper wasn't such that she would
deny their engagement and send Gabe's anger
over the edge. He was a good friend, but when it
came to his women he was very protective. Renewed anger simmered in his own veins. At her
role in driving a wedge between him and a man
he'd come to think of as a brother. He held Gabe's
gaze without flinching. 'Well, aren't you going to
wish us happiness?'

Gabe blew out a breath and stuck out a reluc-
tant hand. 'Congratulations.'

The tension in his neck eased as he shook it. He
glanced down at Minette and realised she wasn't
looking any happier than he felt. He pulled her
close and kissed her cheek. 'I'm sorry, Gabe. Our
passion got the better of us when we realised we
both wanted this. We should have come to speak
to you and Nicky right away.'

'We will talk more in the morning. You will
both come with me now.' Gabe shot a glance at
Minette. 'We need to look like a family with joy-
ous news.'

A bright smile appeared on Minette's lips.
'Bien sûr,' she said gaily. *'Très heureux.* Is it not
so, my dearest Freddy?'

'Without question,' he replied, with an equally false smile.

God help him, what a mess.

To Minette's acutely sensitive emotions, it seemed as if the buzz of conversation ceased when she and Freddy entered the ballroom. But it resumed too quickly to be sure. She held her head high, showing not a scrap of shame on her face. The heat she felt on her cheeks was caused by her anger at Freddy's assumption that she had intended to trick him into marriage.

Why she would care so deeply about what he thought she didn't know. This engagement was the perfect answer to her conundrum, so why did she feel so uncomfortable inside? The answer struck her in one of those odd flashes of realisation. Freddy's reaction. His horror. Pain stabbed behind her breastbone. The pain of betrayal.

Nonsense. The whole thing was a horrible accident. One she'd find a way to put right.

Shackled for life, he'd said with such cold remoteness. Hardly. She would cry off after a time and that would be that. Not even a duke could force a woman into a marriage she didn't want. This wasn't the Middle Ages. And certainly she wouldn't marry a man who thought he'd been tricked. A girl had her pride.

Sweet smiles and blushes were to be expected from a newly betrothed debutante, so all she needed to do at this moment was curve her lips and fool the world. The anxious look from her sister said it wasn't working, so she surged forward and took both of Nicky's hands in hers. 'Wish me well, sister. His Grace has done me the honour of asking for my hand.'

If anything, Nicky looked even more concerned, but a warning glance from Gabe had her lips curving in the well-practised smile of a politician's wife. 'Dearest,' she said, leaning forward to kiss each of her cheeks. 'Are you sure?' she whispered.

Always Nicky offered her support. And always Minette felt as if she'd let her sister down. She threw her arms around Nicky's neck. 'Positive.' Later would come the recriminations and even later the disappointment of an ended engagement, but right now they would show a united front.

She stepped back and received Gabe's blessing, a formal kiss on each cheek.

Her brother-in-law then shook hands with Freddy.

Nicky also held out her hand, and Freddy bowed over it with the manly elegance that always stole Minette's breath.

'You will be good to her,' Nicky warned.

He nodded and looked perfectly content, as if he really did want this marriage. The man was an excellent actor, easily able to hide his true feelings. He wasn't the only one. She kept her smile bright.

The musicians struck up the opening bars of the next set and everyone's attention drifted slowly away. A quick scan of those about her assured her no one really cared. Her gaze met that of the girl who had accidentally given her and Freddy away. Priscilla.

Seeing that Minette had noticed her regard, the girl offered a tentative smile and mouthed, 'I'm sorry.'

Minette waved an airy hand of forgiveness. Not that she had anything to forgive. This was the outcome she'd wanted. Almost. Freddy's agreement to her plan without all the scandal would have been a hundred times better than what had occurred. She'd seen Lord Sparshott's face as she'd peered around Freddy. He'd definitely realised things had gone quite a bit further than a peck on the cheek or even a passionate kiss. He'd be quick to express shock when she cried off.

A pretend engagement agreed to by both parties in private, as she'd suggested, would have been a much better idea.

Tiens. It was far too late for remorse. What was done was done. But Freddy was wrong about one thing. The situation was not irretrievable.

Freddy left Gabe's study reasonably satisfied with the settlement he had reached with his future wife's outraged brother-in-law. At first, Gabe's attitude had bordered on starchy, but once he realised Freddy had no intention of being anything but generous, and that he intended to observe all the courtesies with regard to his prospective bride, he'd mellowed. They'd even managed a cordial glass of brandy and a toast to the future. Indeed, Freddy had the very real hope he might one day regain the trust of his once best friend.

One thing he had not done had been to relay his suspicions about Minette's entrapment of him or her reasons. That concerned no one but the two of them.

Good God, he was actually going to be married. To a little spitfire who heated his blood beyond reason. Heaven help him. The thought of having her in his bed almost made up for how she'd got him to the sticking point. And the thought of Liz's anger when she heard the news of his engagement was almost worth the price. Not that he intended to do his nephews out of their inheritance. He didn't want children any more than he had wanted a wife.

And that was going to be a problem, based on what he'd learned in Gosport's library. He found Minette's boldness practically irresistible. Before coming to England, she'd not led the innocent, protected life of her peers. And if during that time she'd used her feminine wiles as a means of defence he would not blame her one bit. The fact that she also used them as a weapon, against him, gave him pause. And sent blood racing south.

There were ways to prevent the arrival of children that did not require forgoing mutual pleasure. He certainly wasn't going to let her cry off, as she had suggested.

He would not permit another scandal in his family. Particularly one easily avoided.

And now he would have yet another responsibility he had never wanted. A wife.

No doubt this one would be troublesome. Demanding. Wily. Untrustworthy. Utterly, deliciously sensual. Hell, his mind was wandering again. Theirs was going to be a marriage of convenience. With added benefits. The coldness inside him prevented any deeper feelings. As long as children didn't ensue, everything would be fine.

He headed for the drawing room, where Gabe said Minette was waiting, knocked on the door and entered. She was standing at the window, looking down into the street, standing to one side so she would not be seen.

As always, her feminine allure called to his baser urges.

But it wasn't that alone, it was her audacity, her passion, the energy she exuded. Dangerous attributes to a man in his line of work.

Slowly, she turned to face him. 'Is it done?'

The calmness in her face troubled him. Their

dealings had never been calm. No doubt she was trying to hide her triumph at the success of her little plot. He would do well to remember how she had tricked him.

'The terms are agreed upon,' he said.

She nodded.

For some reason, he wanted more than cool looks and calm acceptance. He crossed the room and took her hands in his. They were cold. As icy as her expression. Was she suffering qualms? Too bad. It was too late for second thoughts. He lifted first one hand to his lips and then the other. A formal acknowledgement of their future. 'I will inform my mother of the good news and arrange for an engagement ball at my estate in Kent at the end of next week. That will be time enough to send out invitations. The wedding will take place in three months. After the banns are called.'

She lowered her lashes as if to hide her thoughts, but her gaze was clear when she finally looked at him. 'Engagement ball? Is it really necessary?'

'Gabe insists. And I agree. A ball will confirm our assertion that what Sparshott saw was a congratulatory kiss, as well as uphold your virtue and put paid to some of the gossip. An event attended by all the right people showing their approval will do the trick.'

She looked far from happy. 'What about our other plans? Won't it interfere?'

'I thought this was what you wanted. An engagement, so we can go about together without engendering comment.'

'It was, but is it necessary to involve so many others?'

Could it be that while she wanted the title, she was ashamed of the owner? Or had she been truthful all along and it had been nothing but a dreadful coincidence? None of it mattered. 'We have no choice but to go through with it in proper style.'

'You are right. We will deal with the engagement part later.'

Deal with it? He eyed her narrowly as with quick, short steps she headed for a chair by the hearth and perched on its edge. She gestured for him to sit on the sofa. 'We need to arrange our meeting with the person who can help us find Moreau.'

The reason for this whole fiasco. 'So it was not some Banbury tale?'

A slight shake of her head, a puzzled frown. 'Banbury? I do not understand.'

'It means lies.'

Her face cleared. '*Mon cher* Freddy, you misjudge me but then, you always have. There is a woman who lives in Southwark who can tell us what we need to know. For a consideration, as I mentioned.'

'Us? I wouldn't take a dog of mine to South-wark, let alone a young lady.'

The determined chin came up. 'If you go alone, she will tell you nothing. Women talk to other women. And she is French.'

'There are other women I can use.'

She shrugged. 'But you do not know her name. Come tomorrow at nine in the morning. I will guide you to her door.'

With a glare, he rose to his feet. 'I will take you driving tomorrow. In Hyde Park. It is impor-tant that we be seen together. But we will not be going to Southwark, *je vous assure.*'

'How prettily you speak French,' she said with a catlike smile. 'So perfect. So very English.'

He cursed under his breath. God preserve him from stubborn women. As he saw it, he had two choices. Refuse her request and risk her going off half-cocked without him, or give in.

'Nine tomorrow morning,' he said through gritted teeth.

Surely by then Barker could find this woman, now he knew where to look.

Minette tried to sit still while her maid fin-ished dressing her hair. Anxiety gnawed at her belly. What if Madame Vitesse was lying about her knowledge of Moreau? What if it was a trap? Freddy would be so angry. He would certainly never give her a second chance. No. She had been so very careful. Things had to go according to plan. They must.

'All done, *mademoiselle*,' the maid said, eyeing the effect of her handiwork in the mirror. Curls framing her face. Her hair piled on her crown, ready to receive the straw bonnet whose plumes matched her form-fitting carriage dress of pale blue sarsenet.

Minette rose from the rosewood dressing table and took the bonnet from her maid's hand, placing it on her head, just so. The maid tied the blue velvet ribbon under her left ear. 'You look beautiful, *mademoiselle*. The Duke is sure to be pleased.'

Unlikely, but that was no reason not to look the part.

'Christine, you must promise not to breathe a word of our intention to visit Southwark today to anyone.'

'*Mais, non, mademoiselle.* Your secrets are safe with me. Always.'

Minette believed her. The maid, too, had lost innocent family in France's grand experiment and had been embarrassingly grateful when offered this position. She would not lie to Minette about anything.

Nicky breezed in looking very matronly in a pale green morning gown that clearly showed her expanding waistline. 'Freddy's phaeton is outside the house. He sent his tiger to the door, since he won't leave the horses. Are you ready?'

'Oh, yes.' Ready for battle. She kissed her sister on the cheek and hurried down the stairs. If there was anything to put a man in a temper, she'd learned since coming out, it was keeping his horses fretting at their bits. And an irritated Freddy would only compound the difficulty of her task.

The butler bowed her out of the door with a warm smile. At the kerb stood a shiny black vehicle with wheels picked out in navy and gold, drawn by a pair of matched black horses with white stars on their foreheads. The phaeton had attracted the rapt attention of the street sweeper, who had left his customary post on the corner to stand mouth agape.

Helped up by the waiting footman, Minette bestowed a smile on Freddy. 'Good morning, Your Grace.'

The dark look he gave her did not augur a better mood than yesterday. Fa-la. No more than she'd expected.

He gave the horses the off and the tiger jumped up behind.

When they entered Hyde Park she glowered. 'We were to go to Southwark.'

He reined in the horses. 'Jimmy,' he threw over his shoulder, 'go and find some violets for the lady.'

'Wot, at this time of year, guv?'

'Violets,' Freddy said firmly. 'Take them to

Barker. He will arrange for their delivery upon my return.'

The tiger muttered something under his breath and jumped down.

'If you wanted us to be alone, you could have sent him home, instead of on a wild-goose chase,' she said.

'I could. But then I wouldn't have had a reason why we were driving alone.'

'Ah.'

He set the horses in motion. 'Now I'll have the whole of it.'

'I do not understand your meaning.'

A brow shot up. His lips pressed together as if he was seeking to contain words he did not think he should say. After several long seconds he spoke. 'Who is this woman in Southwark and how do you know of her?'

She gave him a glance full of sympathy. 'Your men didn't find her, did they? When we get there you will learn all you need to know.'

He muttered something under his breath. A curse, no doubt. 'I hope you don't live to regret this, Mademoiselle Rideau.'

'Should we not be on a first-name basis now we are betrothed?'

He glanced over at her, his lips eased very slightly, and was that a twinkle in his eyes? 'Minette.'

Yes, indeed, his voice had laughter at the edges.

She smiled at him. 'Come, it will not be so bad, Freddy. We will work together to put Moreau in the ground.'

He gave a slight shake of his head. 'I do not like this game you are playing and, believe me, I'll not be giving you a free hand, my sweet.'

My sweet. Her heart gave an odd little flutter. Too bad he did not mean it. She smiled coolly. 'Naturally not. But there are some things I must insist upon at the outset.'

'We'll deal with those later. Right now I need to know where I am going.'

'We cross the river at London Bridge.'

His expression darkened. 'So I am to follow your directions street by street. You do know Southwark is a hotbed of unsavoury types, do you not?'

'*Naturellement*. But, then, I have you to protect me.'

His jaw flexed, his expression became thoughtful. 'So you do.'

Chapter Four

The drive to London Bridge remained starkly silent, with Freddy apparently too engrossed in managing his team in the press of traffic for conversation. Or too annoyed with her prevarication. Not that the streets were quiet. Indeed, they bustled with people and carriages, assaulting hearing, sight and each indrawn breath. The cacophony of colour, noise and smells became more intense as they drove east. A stench of manure, rotting vegetables and overcrowding battled with the noise of street vendors and vehicles of every kind.

It took more than an hour to reach London Bridge and make their way to Southwark.

'Now where?' he asked, with his usual chilly reserve and an expression she was sure was designed to keep her at a distance. Her and the rest of the world.

'Aren't you going to ask for the address?'

'I have no doubt you will tell me when you

are ready. I have no doubt that it will be located among the worst of the slums. You have a penchant for going where no lady should tread.'

A jibe at her presence at his club. So there was to be no quarter given between them. Not that she had really expected it. Not when he still thought she had trapped him on purpose. She almost wished she had, then she wouldn't feel quite so aggrieved, since she could not deny that this engagement suited her purpose admirably. But his anger and distrust gave her a miserable feeling. They had never been friends, but now they were going to have to spend a great deal of time in each other's company, and it would be better if they could at least be cordial.

'The house we seek lies behind St George's Church,' she said.

His mouth tightened but he continued along Borough High Street. As they proceeded, the buildings on either side of the street became meaner and the road muddy and ill maintained.

'When we arrive, let me do the talking,' she said.

'So I am to remain silent and pay the bill.' He sounded less than pleased.

She turned in her seat the better to see his face. 'This family has not been well treated since their arrival in England. They are bourgeoisie. They gave up much to follow the king and feel they have been abandoned.' There were a goodly number of French families living in Southwark who were scratching out the most meagre of livings in the worst of circumstances. 'They no longer trust the English to treat them right.'

'And you think they will trust you?'

She gripped her hands in her lap. 'I don't know. I do know they want their king back in France so they can return home. If they believe this will help, then perhaps, yes.'

'Very well, I'll remain silent. As long as you don't promise them the moon.'

It was a warning he would not let her make promises he could not keep. Fair enough.

'Turn onto Mint Street.'

'You may as well give me the address,' he said, throwing her a glance of suppressed anger.

He was right to be angry. She could not continue to treat him as if she didn't trust him, even if good sense advised caution. She needed his help. 'Well's Court. They are expecting us.'

'How do you know people living in Well's Court?'

She winced at his harsh tone. 'Through my maid, who I found by talking to the parish priest. We *émigrés* help our own whenever possible.'

He halted at the entrance to a small alley. He glanced up at the surrounding buildings and around at the loiterers in the street. He gestured at one of them who lounged over to them. *'M'sieur?'*

He tossed the man a silver coin. 'Mind the horses. There's another for you when we return.'

The man's eyes brightened. He touched his forelock and went to the horses' heads.

'Will they be safe?' she asked.

'It's a little late to be thinking of that.'

Freddy guided Minette through the narrow entrance to the court, surreptitiously checking the small pistol he had tucked into his waistband at the small of his back. He also had a dagger in his boot. Barker, who had been instructed to follow them, would be somewhere nearby. He doubted all these precautions would be needed—it was, after all, broad daylight—but it didn't pay to take chances. Not if he wanted to survive. The contrast between the wealth of Mayfair and the poverty of this area was a stark reminder of the desperation of some of London's people. He placed his hand in the small of her back, ensuring that anyone watching would know he took her safety seriously.

A pang of guilt twisted in his gut. Minette thought she was in control. In the not-too-distant future she was going to discover he had no intention of involving her in the capture of Moreau. If Gabe knew he'd gone this far, bringing her to such a dangerous part of town, he'd be stringing Freddy up by his thumbs. No, after today, she would discover herself on the sidelines. He would not let her put herself in danger.

A small, ragged boy sitting on a step in front of one of the tenements leapt to his feet the moment they set foot in the courtyard at the end of the alley. He approached warily.

'You are here for Madame Vitesse?' His English was carefully spoken. Not the accent of the local people, but that of a well-tutored boy.

'We are,' Minette replied.

'Follow me, if you please.' The boy led them into the building and up a set of rickety stairs to the third floor. On the landing he opened one of several doors. He reverted to his mother tongue as he spoke to the occupant. 'Maman, they are here.'

A woman of about thirty with hard eyes and a careworn face appeared in the doorway. The look she gave Freddy reminded him of an animal preparing to defend its young, then she turned her attention to Minette. 'You are Christine's mistress?'

'I am.'

'This is your fiancé? The Duke?'

'I am,' Freddy said.

'Come in. We will discuss the matter between us.'

They sat down on a pair of rickety wooden chairs, while their hostess took a stool. She glanced up at the boy. 'See we are not disturbed.'

The boy closed the door, shutting himself outside.

'Christine said you might be able to help us in our search for a certain man,' Minette said.

'For a price,' the woman said.

'How much?' Freddy asked. 'And how can we be sure you have the information we need?'

Minette glared at him. He ignored it. If she thought he was going to sit here like a bump on the proverbial log, she should have known better.

The woman rolled her shoulders. 'You cannot be sure, but this man you seek is as much my enemy as he is yours. If not for him and his like, my husband would be alive and I would be living in Paris.'

'We understand, *madame*,' Minette said gently. 'You have lost much. I would like to help you as well as find the man we seek. We will pay what is reasonable for the information.'

The woman's expression contained resentment. 'I am not asking for charity, *mademoiselle*. The chance to make a decent living, to bring up my son in a good home, not this...' she shuddered, glancing around her '...this rat-infested room, surrounded by criminals who are allowed to wander the streets.'

Many of the criminals were debtors, allowed the freedom of Borough as long as they did not step outside set boundaries, but there were other sorts of criminals here, too, as there were in all the poorer neighbourhoods of London.

'Name your price,' Freddy said. 'And we will see if the information you have is worth it.'

'I personally do not have the information you seek,' the woman said.

Freddy looked up at the ceiling, a plea for divine intervention. None came. 'Why am I not surprised?'

'Freddy,' Minette said in a warning. 'Who does, *madame*?'

'My brother. He hides where you will not find him until our demands are met.'

'Your brother,' Freddy said. 'His name is Vitesse?'

'No.'

Of course not. The woman was a widow, using her married name. To find her brother he'd need her maiden name. No doubt the Alien Office would have collected that when they had permitted her to take up residence in England.

Minette also looked unhappy with the woman's reply. 'You told Christine you had information about Moreau.'

The woman tensed. 'Henri is afraid. He wants to help, but if this man finds out...' She pressed her lips together. 'He needs to know, if anything happens to him, that I will be cared for. It is his duty as the head of our household. It is a small thing to ask.'

'What is it you want?' Minette asked with a very practical tone to her voice.

'Christine says you are to be married. To this

Duke.' She nodded at Freddy. 'You will need a trousseau of the finest.'

Freddy frowned, but Minette was smiling. 'You are a seamstress.'

The other woman nodded. 'I do fine work. You will see.' She raised her voice. 'Lilly!'

A girl of around eight peered around the open door. *'Oui, Maman?'*

'Bring them,' the woman commanded.

The child disappeared and returned a moment later, struggling to carry in her arms what looked like three dolls. Madame Vitesse took them from the girl and stood them up on the table. 'This is my work.'

Dolls?

'Oh,' Minette breathed, fingering the fabric of the doll's gown. 'This is beautiful. I have seen nothing like it in London. Look, Freddy, isn't it exquisite?'

Really? He narrowed his eyes at the doll. The dress was some fancy silky stuff, and it revealed quite a bit of the doll's shape above the neckline. Revelation came like a flash. He'd seen something like it in his mother's drawing room as a boy. 'They are dressmaker's dolls.'

Both women looked at him as if he was a dolt.

'You see, *mademoiselle*,' the woman said, 'I was just beginning my business in Paris. I had left my old mistress to start on my own. I had one very important client, a woman at Court. She would have made my name but—' She made a chopping motion with her hand. 'There was nothing. No work. No food. Everything we had we left behind.' Tears welled in her brown eyes. 'Family. Money. Everything. Henri was positive we could start again. But for that I need a patron. I have no contacts here in England. No money for a shop. For fabric.'

'So if we give you money to open a shop, you will tell us what we want to know.'

The woman's face hardened. She shook her head. 'That is only part of it. You will wear the gowns. Go to parties. Talk of my work. Then I will give you the information you seek.'

She was using them. Imposing on Minette in the worst possible way. Anger surged in Freddy's veins. He rose to his feet and glared at the woman, who seemed to shrink in her chair. 'That will take weeks. I am sorry, *madame*, but there are other ways to obtain this information.'

'Freddy is right,' Minette said also rising. 'We do not have time—'

'Two weeks,' the woman said, her face white, her voice weak, scared. 'I can do it all in two weeks.' She glanced over at her daughter. 'Please. For the sake of my children.'

'Not a day over two weeks,' Minette said.

'No,' Freddy said. 'That is too long to have him running freely around England.'

The woman's eyes became crafty, as if she

sensed she could drive a wedge between them and come out a winner. 'The man you seek, he has much to do before he is ready. You will not want him alone. You will want his web.' She nodded. 'Web. That is what Henri called it. Move too soon and you will cut off the head, but you will not have the body.'

'If she's right...' Minette said, looking at him.

He clenched his jaw so hard he felt his back teeth give. 'If she's lying, her children will be orphans.'

A satisfied smile crossed the Frenchwoman's face. Clearly she did not believe the threat any more than Minette did, because she was shaking the woman's hand. 'It is a bargain.'

Freddy reached into the pocket in his coat. 'How much do you need to get you started?'

The woman's eyes gleamed. 'A hundred pounds. It will rent the shop and the accommodation above and buy enough fabric for the first gown.' She narrowed her eyes, her gaze running over Minette. 'A carriage gown like this one,' she said, picking up the doll dressed in green velvet with fancy decoration down the front. 'Are you to attend a ball soon?'

'My engagement ball is in a couple of weeks,' Minette said. 'Many important people will attend. It is to be held at my fiancé's estate in Kent.'

The woman beamed. 'You shall wear my gown.'

'Understand this, *madame*,' Freddy said. 'If this delay causes me to fail in my task to find this man, you will not like the consequences.'

The woman's gaze flew to Minette and back to him. 'I assure you all will be well.' She picked up a small cloth bag at her feet and pulled out a bunch of string. 'I will measure now and send a note to say when I will come to you for a fitting. Then we will choose the fabric for the rest of the gowns. Please, stand and I will help you unclothe.'

Minette rose and turned her back to the woman. 'Freddy, please. Madame Vitesse will help us.'

Madame Vitesse was helping her all right. Helping her to be naked.

Freddy's body tightened at the thought of seeing her wearing nothing but little bits of string. Inwardly cursing, he turned his back. 'Hurry up. I don't want to keep my horses waiting any longer than is needed.'

A low laugh from Minette said she didn't believe his impatience for a moment.

It must have been the hoarseness in his voice.

'That went excellently well,' Freddy said, once they were back on the road. 'The woman gulled you. Gowns.' He snorted.

The derisive edge in his voice brought Minette straighter in her seat. 'It could have been worse.'

'I suppose it could. She could have asked me to dress every lady in the *ton*.'

'You are being a bear. This way you will get both him and his men.'

He grunted. 'If I didn't know better, I might think she knew about this betrothal of ours before we did.'

She winced. 'About that. As soon as we have dealt with Moreau, we will announce our engagement is at an end.'

He sent her a look full of disgust. 'And how do you propose to do that?'

'I'll cry off.'

'Wonderful. Tell me what other schemes there are floating around in that lovely head of yours.'

'There is no need for sarcasm.'

'I'm not being sarcastic. I simply want to know what I am in for next.'

Why was he arguing about this? He had made it quite clear he didn't want to wed her any more than she did him. Contrary man. No matter what she said, he would argue. And yet… She frowned. 'Are you saying you actually want this marriage?'

The glance he gave her was full of exasperation and something else. Bleakness? Loneliness? 'I'm saying we don't have a choice. What about Gabe and your sister? If you don't care about anyone else, what about their sensibilities?'

'I will simply inform them we discovered we did not suit after all.'

His chest rose and fell with a huge sigh. A man tried to the limit of his patience. She braced for his next assault. It wasn't long in coming. 'After what Sparshott and his daughter saw, your reputation will be ruined, Minette. Those things don't go away. There will be no decent men throwing their hats in the ring. Not after that. You need the protection of my name.'

For a man who had been so set against marrying, his insistence was odd. Something inside her twisted painfully. Longing. Surely not. The man was marrying her to preserve his honour. Using her for his own purposes, as Pierre had used her. She wasn't fool enough to think it could possibly be more. 'I don't want to get married. To you or anyone else. You don't even like me.' Dash it, why had she given voice to that little bit of resentment?

'I don't dislike you.' His voice was arctic.

'In truth? When you think I planned to trap you into marrying me?'

He winced. 'I beg your pardon. I am as much to blame as you for what happened.'

She gasped theatrically. 'Are you actually apologising?'

'Now who is being sarcastic?'

She laughed. '*Touché*, Your Grace.'

He smiled, albeit a little unwillingly and fleetingly. Still, it made her heart feel a little lighter to see his expression ease. He looked much younger, more approachable. Perhaps… But no. She was right. When this was over they would part company. Because when this was over, even his honour wouldn't be enough to make him want her as his wife.

A pang twisted in her chest. 'Let us see how we feel about it once Moreau is caught.'

He looked unconvinced but resigned, and that was the best she could hope for.

Chapter Five

The next three days were a whirl of activity for Minette. First Madame Vitesse had involved her and Nicky in the selection of a site for her new shop. Nicky had been more than willing to help the woman after Minette had told her that their countrywoman had provided her with assistance, though she did not correct Nicky's misunderstanding that the help had come while Minette had been alone and struggling to survive in France.

If guilt was a pain in her chest, she consoled herself with the knowledge that the seamstress was helping them both, or she would be, once she retrieved her property from Moreau.

Then there had been the fittings—first the promised carriage dress then this evening gown. Not the one for the engagement ball—that would come later in the week. This one was for a rout they'd been invited to at the last moment. She smoothed her hands down her skirts as she sat at the dressing table while her maid put the final touches to her toilette. Madame Vitesse was undoubtedly talented. The gown was extraordinarily beautiful with a floor-length slip of white satin and a white gauze overdress draped in the style of the ancients. Fastened at the side, the overskirt fell to an inch below the knee and was edged with Greek keys. White satin sandals and gloves finished the ensemble.

No one would doubt it was an original or very French.

Tonight would be her and Freddy's first appearance in public since the betrothal announcement. The *ton* would be watching, waiting to see how he reacted to her. Waiting to condemn if he gave the slightest hint he wasn't pleased with the match. After all, he was a duke and she was nothing but an upstart *émigrée*, even if her sister was married to a nobleman who had the support of the royal family.

More importantly, tonight would give her an opportunity to speak to him alone. Madame Vitesse had been none too happy when she'd arrived with this gown. And with good reason.

Christine settled a tiara of carnations, in a colour Madame Vitesse had called maiden's first blush, low on her brow, careful not to disturb the ringlets framing her face and clustered on her crown. She slipped her hands into the elbow-length gloves her maid held out and stood before the pier glass to judge the effect.

Christine sighed. 'Perfect, *mademoiselle*.'

Yes, Madame Vitesse knew her business. It would not be her appearance that put the Duke of Falconwood to shame this evening. She turned away from her reflection at the same moment Nicky entered.

'Oh, my,' Nicky said, her eyes alight with joy and admiration. 'You will outshine them all.' Her hands went to her stomach.

A self-conscious laugh left her lips when she realised Minette's gaze had followed the movement. 'The baby has quickened,' she said a little breathlessly. 'Little flutters deep inside. The doctor said it is quite normal, but honestly they are quite startling.'

An ache pierced Minette's chest. By falling for the wrong man she had given away the chance to know such joy herself. She shook off the feeling of loss. She would revel in her sister's happiness and be the best aunt any child could have. She crossed the room and hugged Nicky. For several years she had thought she might never see her sister again. The joy of their reunion had been tempered by the knowledge that she had thrown away all that her sister had sacrificed. But she would make amends.

They broke their embrace. 'Turn around,' Nicky said. 'Let me look at you.'

Minette spun around and her skirt gently swayed with her movement.

Christine discreetly withdrew.

'Freddy will be dazzled,' Nicky said. 'I can't believe you two…' Her words trailed off and she cast Minette an enquiring look. A look of concern as well as love.

'I know,' Minette said, putting all the joy and lightness in her words and expression she did not feel deep inside. 'It came as quite a shock to us, too. Who would have guessed that what we thought was dislike was something else entirely?'

She could not bring herself to say the word 'love'. It would be too much of a lie. Even for her. She let her gaze take in her sister, who was dressed in the high fashion of a married woman. The deep turquoise suited her and disguised the coming of a child. 'You look lovely.'

Nicky smiled. 'Gabe loves this colour.' She gave Minette a sly smile. 'And when you are married you won't be stuck with boring old white.' She tipped her head. 'Though I must say you are one of the fortunate few who has the colouring to carry it off.'

They linked arms and headed downstairs.

At the foot of the staircase, two men looked up at the sound of their steps. Both men were dark. Both men were undeniably handsome in their own way. Gabe an absolute charmer with a smile that could melt the hardest of hearts. Naturally he had eyes for no one but Nicky.

Freddy was a very different story. Although his gaze showed approval as he took Minette in from her head to her feet, there was little warmth in him. He used to smile when they had first met years ago. Not at her, but at things Gabe had said. Male humour at things unspoken but understood. He'd even smiled at Nicky from time to time, like a brother at a sister. But where she was concerned, for the most part she'd felt only cool distance.

A layer of ice like a wall to keep her out that seemed to have grown thicker over time.

She wanted to take a hammer to it. Shatter it. Find the man beneath. She'd prefer active dislike to this chilly indifference.

As they reached the bottom step, both men stepped forward, Gabe to take Nicky's arm, his eyes awash with his love as he gazed at his wife, and Freddy to present her with a small posy in a silver holder. The flowers matched those in her hair, but these were real. She took the offering with a curtsey. 'Thank you. How clever of you to find exactly the right shade.'

An expression flashed across his face and if it hadn't been impossible she might have thought he was pleased. 'Lady Mooreshead offered her aid.'

Disappointment flickered to life. No doubt Nicky had arranged the whole thing. 'Thank you, Nicky.'

Her sister gave her an odd look. 'I merely informed His Grace of the colour. No more.'

Gabe was frowning at them as if he sensed something wrong. Minette brought the posy to her nose. 'They are perfect.'

Freddy leaned forward and kissed her cheek, a brief hot brush of his lips across her skin. 'You are welcome,' he said silkily.

As she met his blue-black gaze she had the impression of heat flaring in their depths. An act for the benefit of others? Or something more?

Coolly, deliberately, he set her away. 'I believe it is time we left.'

As the carriage rocked through the night, Freddy relaxed against the squabs and contemplated the woman he was to marry. Lovely. Beautiful. The words didn't do justice to the vision he'd witnessed walking down the stairs of Gabe's townhouse. Freddy didn't have the words to express what he had felt inside him. She was, of course, both of those things, but she was so much more. Warmth. Light. Joy. And there was also darkness. A shadow that lingered around her as if waiting to blanket her inner glow.

If only she would trust him enough to tell him what caused those shadows. To let him help overcome her dragons. But then again, he didn't have the right to her trust. They might be getting married, but they would never be a husband and a wife in the truest sense.

It was his cross to bear.

How he had managed to hide the jolt of lightning that had coursed through his blood the moment his lips had touched her silky skin, he wasn't sure. He was still reeling from the effects of their other physical contacts. His body wanted her. Hungered for her. And now she was his. Or would be soon.

He didn't deserve her. In the years since he had been Gabe's apprentice, he'd washed his hands in so much blood he'd become insensitive to death and destruction. He'd become a tool for the use of his country. Of Sceptre in particular. Weeding out spies and traitors without fear or favour. It was his role. His purpose. He needed it or he'd be nothing.

And now he was to be a husband to a young woman who, while stubborn and reckless, had always seemed to embody what was right and good with the world. The world of youthful hope for the future. A world in which he'd never belonged. She'd always looked at him in a way that made him think she could see right into his darkness. His unworthiness. No wonder she talked of crying off as soon as the dust settled. A kiss in the dark with a dangerous man in the hope of bending him to her will was one thing, but marriage to such a man was a very different matter.

It was too late for second thoughts.

Honour required that he offer marriage. Honour required that he see it through no matter what. At least he had that much honour left.

The glow of the streetlights flickered across her face, her expression changing with each pass of the light so that it was like watching a disjointed progression of thoughts. Thoughts he could only guess at.

His task was clear. He had to make her want to marry him. Use her passionate nature against her reason. Woo her. Blind her to his faults. Once they were wed, she could do as she pleased.

He realised his hands had curled into tight fists. Anger. Frustration. Regret. So much emotion, when he usually experienced none. Minette made him feel too much. And feelings hurt. He relaxed his hands, glad of the deep shadows inside the carriage.

'How on earth did you manage to extract an invitation from Lady Craddock?' Nicky asked her husband. 'I know she didn't plan to invite us, because the invitations went out weeks ago and we didn't receive one.'

'Craddock belongs to my club,' Gabe said. His teeth flashed white with a smile. 'I put him in the way of a good investment.'

'I wager Lady Craddock was none too pleased,' Freddy said. The Craddocks, like Sparshott, were part of his mother's clique. They and their high-

stickler friends saw themselves as the most important in the land because their roots went far
back in the annals of England. Above even the
royal house of Hanover, which had thrown its full
support behind Mooreshead on the occasion of
his marriage to a woman who could have been
considered an enemy.

'Let us hope she is too well bred to show her
displeasure,' Gabe said, and there was something
dangerously protective in his tone. He'd proved
before he wouldn't tolerate any insult to his wife.
A word in the right quarters could be very dam-
aging to even the wealthiest family, when power
was their preferred form of currency.

'Dommage,' Minette said. 'We will dance and
talk with our friends. No one will care what the
stuffy Craddocks think. Indeed, they will wish
they were part of our circle, if they have any sense
at all.'

Nicky laughed.

Amused despite his better judgement, Freddy
mentally shook his head. Spirit. That was the in-
definable quality of Minette. The spirit of a goddess of war.

And that was what made her so damned dangerous.

Freddy didn't dance. Ever. And everyone knew
it.

Minette wasn't sure if he didn't because of his

lameness, or because he didn't want to. His leg, whatever was wrong with it, didn't stop him from doing anything else, even if he did have a bit of a limp. She'd seen him walk across the deck of a pitching ship without losing his balance or stumbling. She'd seen him play cricket on the lawns at Meak the first summer she'd arrived in England. Then he'd stopped visiting.

He worked for Sceptre, a secret organisation that carried on the war with Napoleon in the dark world of espionage. She wasn't supposed to know about it, but she'd been there the day Nicky and Gabe had been carted off to appear before the head of the organisation. To Nicky's everlasting gratitude, Gabe had been relieved from active duty. Freddy continued to serve. No one said he did, but there could be no other explanation for why he had disappeared from their lives.

And neither Nicky nor Gabe had ever commented on his absence. It had been as if they had forgotten he existed. Until she'd gone to find him and they'd ended up engaged to be married. She still didn't quite believe she was betrothed. In some ways it was a dream come true. He was a handsome, if aloof, man to whom she had been instantly attracted. Had he shown interest all those years before, she would have been tempted.

Tonight, he had encouraged her to dance every dance with any young man who asked, including Granby, who seemed to have recovered from his funk. She was dancing with him now, while her gaze sought out a very different man. A man so cold that sometimes she thought he would chill her to the bone with a look.

The music came to a close, and Granby walked her back to Nicky, seated among the matrons and chaperones, no doubt having grown tired of standing.

'May I fetch you some refreshment, Miss Rideau? Or you, Lady Mooreshead?' Granby asked.

'I would love some lemonade,' Minette answered.

'Not for me,' Nicky said.

When the young man was out of hearing, Minette scanned the room. 'Where is Freddy?'

'He and Gabe went to the card room.'

Minette frowned. 'Do you think he gambles as much as everyone says?'

Nicky sighed. 'I don't know. His fortune is vast. I would hate to see him lose at the tables the way so many others have done.' She glance around and lowered her voice. 'It may be a front for other activities.'

Surprise that Nicky would mention such a thing must have shown in her face.

'I don't want you to think the worst of him,' Nicky said.

She didn't know *what* to make of him. So often she had felt as if he didn't like her. At other times she thought he also felt the same wild spark of attraction she did, especially when they kissed. Until he looked at her with that chilly expression. Clearly he was set on this marriage. Except tonight he seemed to be avoiding her. Perhaps he had changed his mind.

The disappointment that hollowed out a painful space in her chest didn't make any sense. His changing his mind would make it so much easier to cry off once they found Moreau.

As if her thoughts had conjured him up, Freddy appeared across the other side of the room, listening to something Gabe was saying, his expression austere, his eyes intense. He looked up and his gaze caught hers. She froze in the intensity of that look, so dark, so cold, until a hint of a smile quirked the corners of his mouth and caused flutters low in her belly.

'There they are,' Nicky said, and the connection was gone as if it had never existed. Remoteness fell over his expression like a shutter as he and Gabe sauntered over.

Gabe smiled down at his wife. 'Are you too tired to dance?'

'Never.'

He walked her into the set.

'I am surprised to find you not up on the dance floor,' Freddy said, clearly not caring one way or the other.

'I sat out because I want to know how Nicky was faring.'

'You care for your sister.'

'Of course. She is my family.'

He looked less than convinced.

'You care for your family, surely?' Wasn't that why he undertook deeds society would frown on? To save his country and his family from being crushed beneath the boot of a tyrant?

'It is my duty to care for them.'

Cold duty. As it was his duty to marry her after they'd been caught in the library. The man seemed to have no heart, no passion. Yet his kisses had been more than passionate. They had been searing.

'Would you care to stroll in the gardens?' he asked. 'I am told they are something to see.'

'Someone mentioned they were lit up like Vauxhall Gardens.'

'Worse.' He gave her an odd sort of look. 'There isn't a shadow or a dark walk to be found and a footman at every corner.'

She chuckled. 'No chance for mischief.' She grinned up at him. 'Probably as well in our case. Who knows where temptation would lead?'

His eyes widened a fraction and again the small flash of the smile she adored made an appearance, much to the consternation of her insides. He held out his arm. 'Shall we go and see? After all, given the purpose of our attendance tonight, it wouldn't do for us not to spend any time together.'

A pang pierced her heart at the coldness in his words. A foolish pang that it wasn't his desire to spend time with her but his need to make it appear as if he did. 'Why not?' She placed her arm on his sleeve and they left the ballroom by way of the French doors.

'Is it too cool out here for you?' he asked, as if he really cared. 'Shall I fetch a shawl?'

It was a beautiful June evening. The scent of lilacs and early roses carried on the warm breeze, the walks sparkling with lights strung from trees.

'No, thank you. It is a relief to get out of the heat.'

They walked in a square around the formal garden. 'I am glad for a private moment,' she said. 'I have been wanting to speak with you alone. I thought you might have had some news of our quarry.'

He gave her a considering look. 'Why would you think that?'

'Because Madame Vitesse says someone has been walking around her neighbourhood, asking questions about her brother. She threatens to refuse to help us.'

He frowned, and she had the feeling he had caught him by surprise. 'Not my men. I am keeping to our agreement and so must she or find herself in dire straits.'

His frown deepened, and he paused to pick a rose. He broke the thorns off the stem and handed it to her in what, under other circumstances, might be seen as a very romantic gesture. She inhaled the delicate fragrance.

Once more he offered his arm, and they continued strolling. 'It is not only us looking for Moreau.'

Her breath caught in her throat. 'Who else?'

'The Home Office boys would very much to get their hands on him.'

She understood from the small things Gabe had let fall from time to time that the Home Office and the organisation Freddy worked for were on the same side, working to save England, they were also in competition and their goals did not always align.

'You think it might be them asking questions?'

'Rumours of our man's imminent arrival in Britain have been circulating for weeks. They might be overly bureaucratic at the Home Office but they are not completely without ability.'

'I should let Madame Vitesse know this. Warn her to be careful.' She clutched at his sleeve. 'What if they find him first?'

'It doesn't matter who finds him as long as he is out of action.'

Not true. Not true. She had to be first. Everything depended on it. 'I will see her tomorrow. I have a fitting for the gown I am to wear for the ball at Falconwood. I will impress on her the urgency.'

He stopped and turned her to face him. 'Why is it so important that you speak to him?'

'There is unfinished business between us.' It was all she dared say.

His mouth tightened. 'Very well. Keep your secrets. For now.'

For now. That sounded very much like a threat.

They had almost arrived back where they had started when he led her down a path leading to a walled garden with a display of fountains, each one in its own pool. He didn't linger, but he opened a gate hidden behind some creeper. The scent of lavender and thyme and other herbs filled her nostrils.

And not a lantern in sight.

'I don't think we are supposed to be in here,' she said.

'No.' He closed the gate and shot the bolt. Light from the moon was enough to see by. The party had been deliberately planned to take advantage of the moon for those travelling back to town. They were in a kitchen garden, the house, ablaze with light, only yards away, its top floors visible above the stretch of the wall. But no one inside the house would be able to see them among the shadows.

Her heart gave a loud thump. Not a warning

exactly but definitely excitement tinged with a touch of wariness.

'Why did you bring me here?' she asked.

He tucked a hand beneath her chin, tipping her face up and looking down at her. One side of his face was in shadow, the other carved by moon-beams into hard, masculine beauty.

'A chance to talk without interruption.' He cast her a wicked glance that made her toes curl. Wicked and charming both. She had never seen him look quite so handsome or so devilish. 'And besides, you look so lovely, so tempting, I couldn't resist a few minutes on our own.'

The lovely words took her breath away.

It would be so easy to let herself believe he'd meant what he'd said. And so utterly foolish.

But that didn't mean she couldn't enjoy him while it lasted.

Chapter Six

'How did you know about this particular garden?' she asked, the hint of breathlessness in her voice calling to his desires.

'I took a walk when I first arrived.' He always made sure he knew the layout of any place he went. A man never knew when he might need to leave in a hurry. It had also seemed like the perfect spot to begin his campaign of seduction. Passion was the one thing that seemed to go well between them, as evidenced by his simmering lust since their kiss.

With any other woman, all he needed to do was wave the dukedom about a bit. Not with Minette. While her physical desire battered at him, she kept herself, who she was, at a distance. Intriguing and worrying. He did not intend to let her end this betrothal. Thus, he must woo her. Ceaselessly. Until she gave up any thought of crying off.

He caged her face within his fingertips, feeling

an overwhelming sense of tenderness. Something that was not part of his plan. The urge to taste her again was like the beat of his heart. Unstoppable.

He lowered his head, slowly, hesitantly, silently asking permission.

Her hands slid up over his shoulders to rest there. She nipped at his lower lip.

A hiss of breath left his lips as lust hardened his body. He took her mouth in a wild and ravening kiss. She responded with a hunger that left him close to mindless.

Her sweet, luscious curves melded with his. A banquet waiting for him to savour it. He couldn't remember the last time he had wanted a woman as badly as he wanted this one. No other woman but she could slake his need. He pressed his thigh between hers, and she gave a sweet little moan of longing. Heat seared his veins as his blood rushed south. He deepened the kiss, tangling his tongue with hers, feeling her lips so soft and sweet moving against his, while her fingers combed the hair at his nape.

Desire shuddered through him.

The urge to lift her skirts and take her against the wall pounded in his blood. She deserved so much more. And, besides, a kiss in the dark between a betrothed couple was acceptable, even expected, but to take her back to the ballroom dishevelled and used hard would be too dishonourable even for him.

He broke their kiss and pulled her close. Breathing rapidly, she rested her cheek on his chest and he bent to kiss her crown, his own breathing none too steady.

'It wouldn't do to be caught out again,' he said gently.

'No,' she agreed, to his body's painful disappointment. She placed a hand on his lapel and stroked the fabric.

Delight with her response to his touch was a wild beat in his blood, despite knowing women were good at pretending things they didn't feel when it suited. This attraction was a positive sign for their marriage. There was much pleasure to be had between them. As long as he made sure not to let things go too far. Not get too out of control.

Hope blossomed in his chest, a strangely warm and painful feeling that they might indeed have a future. He didn't want to leave the shelter of this garden. He wanted to run his fingers through her glorious mane of glossy brown hair, rip her gown from her luscious curves. He could barely keep himself leashed. Which showed just how little honour he had left. There would be plenty of time for exploration and enjoyment when she was his wife.

'We really should go, before someone misses us,' she said, not moving an inch. She sighed. 'We don't want to set tongues wagging again.'

Wagging tongues were the story of his life. He

had told himself a long time ago that he didn't care. But he didn't want her hurt by their vicious gossip. Neither did he want to break his vow by making the mistake of not being fully prepared. 'Yes, we should.' He kissed her forehead and linked his arm through hers, feeling for the first time in a long time a sense of hope.

They strolled back through the moonlight in comfortable silence, until they reached the dazzle of lights strung through trees.

Other couples were also walking around the fountains and along the gravel paths amid the shrubs. The air was redolent with the scent of roses. But all he could smell was her fragrance. Jasmine and summer sun. He wanted to pull her close, press his nose to her skin and inhale.

'Shall we return to the ballroom?' he asked.

'A good idea.' So matter-of-fact. So calm. Certainly she didn't feel as he did. The formal touch of her hand on his sleeve was so light he could barely feel the weight of it, though it burnt him like a brand. Whereas another woman might be blushing and fluttering after that kiss, she seemed unaffected by what had happened between them.

He liked it that she wasn't missish or prone to giggles.

He guided her up the terrace steps and into the ballroom, greeting those they passed. There were no suspicious stares but there was curiosity. It wouldn't take much for the old gossip about him to surface. To send them over the edge of propriety and out onto the fringes of society for evermore. He didn't want that for her, he realised with a protective surge.

He would be more careful in future. More in control. More like himself.

The hope inside him died. He wanted her too much. Once they were married, the wooing would have to come to an end.

A swirl of colour and glitter surrounded them. A girl in white stared at them. A tall girl. Rather thin. Right. Sparshott's daughter, Priscilla. When she realised she'd been seen, she hurried forward and dipped a curtsey.

'Your Grace,' she said, so softly he could barely hear her above the noise of the orchestra and the chatter. She raised her gaze to his and it quickly skittered away. Guilt. She should feel guilty.

He bowed. 'Lady Priscilla.'

She offered Minette a smile. 'I did not get a chance to offer you my congratulations the other night. May I do so now?'

Freddy was surprised when Minette smiled back, a gentle sort of forgiving smile. 'You may.' She glanced up at Freddy. 'Lady Priscilla and I have quite a bit to catch up on. Would you mind fetching me a glass of lemonade?'

The girl looked intensely pleased, and her face turned a bright raspberry shade. Good heavens, the girl was painfully shy. And he'd been sent off on an errand. 'It will be my pleasure.'

Each woman dipped a small curtsey and immediately put their heads together as if trading secrets. Now what was his bride-to-be plotting? He hoped like hell it didn't involve him. He had plots of his own.

'I don't think His Grace likes me very much,' Priscilla said, watching Freddy walk away.

'Don't worry about Falconwood,' Minette said. 'He's like that with everyone.'

'Everyone except you.' Priscilla blushed. 'I am truly am sorry for my gaffe the other evening. I hope I haven't ruined your life. Father says I am the stupidest girl imaginable for always putting my foot in my mouth.'

'Oh, no.' Minette couldn't believe a father would be so cruel. 'If he and I hadn't been so stupid as to meet privately, nothing would have happened.'

'I should not have followed, but you looked so worried I really thought you might need help. It was the worst possible luck, my father coming along right then.'

Priscilla was clearly bent on blaming herself. 'It is water down the river.' Minette patted her arm.

'Under the bridge, I think you mean.'

'Do I? These English sayings are very obscure.'

Priscilla laughed. 'What is done is done, but you know if there is anything I can ever do to make amends, you will let me know, won't you?'

How surprising. It seemed she had indeed made a friend. 'Thank you. I will remember.'

Priscilla cringed a little. 'His Grace is returning. I should go.' The girl pressed her hand and scurried away.

She wasn't surprised at the other woman's cowardice. The expression on Freddy's face wasn't the friendliest. 'Do you have to look quite so, quite so…?'

'Quite so what?' He handed her the lemonade.

'Quite so sternly aristocratic. Looks of that sort would get your head cut off in France.'

He recoiled. Then his mouth quirked in a tiny smile for the second time that evening. Again her heart gave an odd unwelcome lurch. Hopefully he wasn't planning on doing it too often, because she wasn't sure she would be able to resist him.

'Is that what you were plotting?'

'We haven't been plotting anything, either before or now. This is the first time we have really spoken.'

'You seemed on pretty friendly terms.'

He was teasing. She narrowed her eyes at him, but he had already schooled his face into its normal stern aloofness.

He hadn't been aloof outside in the kitchen garden in the dark. Her body heated, as did her face. Blushing. How strange. She hadn't felt the slightest bit embarrassed under the moonlight. What on earth was wrong with her?

Freddy's expression darkened. 'Here comes that idiot Granby.'

Nom d'un nom. If she didn't know better she really might have thought he was jealous. No doubt it was all part of the act to assure the *ton* they were really a couple. She turned in the direction he was looking. It was indeed Granby sidling up to them, his expression hot and bothered. He cleared his throat. 'Good evening, Your Grace, Miss Rideau.'

'Granby,' Freddy said repressively.

'Lieutenant.' Minette gave him a bright smile and dipped her knees.

'I wanted to beg His Grace's pardon. Thought it over. No excuse.'

Freddy's expression didn't ease, but his voice was not unkind when he replied, 'I think the whole incident is better forgotten, don't you?'

More fiery blushes. 'Very good of you, Your Grace.' He tugged at the edge of his jacket. 'Wondered if you'd care to dance this next set, Miss Rideau?'

She glanced up at Freddy. His face remained impassive, no indication that he cared if she danced with Granby.

'Thank you, Lieutenant, I would like that.' She put her hand on his arm.

'I am for the card room,' Freddy said with a slight bow.

It was not disappointment she felt at his display of indifference. Not at all. She had to be glad.

Freddy kept his face expressionless as he left the ballroom. Dancing. She should be dancing with Granby. They were of an age. Whereas he felt ancient. Weighed down by the responsibilities of a dukedom he'd never wanted in the first place and by the mess he now found himself in with regard to Minette. He'd been a fool out there in the garden. Thinking there might be something good in this marriage. He wasn't the right man for her. Never would be.

She'd be better off with a young innocent like Granby. His hands clenched into fists. His inability to retain control had robbed her of choices. When they were married, he would give her all the freedom she needed. The ice inside him grew colder and darker.

He strode into the card room and took an empty seat with men he knew would play hard and drink deep. 'Gentlemen,' he said.

The dealer dealt him his cards.

He didn't emerge from the card room until a footman came to tell him his party was ready to leave. He gathered up his winnings to groans from the other men, who had been hopeful of winning some of their money back.

'Duty calls.' He said the words carefully. It would not do to be seen to have imbibed too much when one was escorting ladies home. Besides, even though he had drunk more than his fair share, he didn't feel more than slightly up in the world. He was accustomed to hours spent quaffing blue ruin in taverns and cognac at his club while keeping his wits about him.

He met Gabe, Nicky and Minette in the foyer.

Gabe frowned at him. 'Ready to leave?'

'Absolutely.'

He held out his arm to Minette, and they walked out the front door and climbed into the carriage. He eyed Gabe warily. 'Something wrong?'

'Tonight was supposed to be damage control,' Gabe said, his tone just a little savage. 'You spent all night in the card room.'

'I did not. Minette and I spent a good long time together.'

'In the gardens, out of sight.'

The implied criticism flicked like a whip across his skin. 'Are you saying you expect us to live in each other's pockets? You know I don't dance. Am I to stand and watch my fiancée flit around the ballroom in the arms of other men, looking sullen? If so, you need Byron, not me.'

'Byron didn't put her reputation at risk.' Gabe's tone was implacable.

'Really, Gabe,' Minette said. 'Am I not supposed to dance at all?'

Freddy clenched his back teeth before he said something stupid like 'No'. And then realised she had actually come to his defence. He frowned at her, puzzled.

'I don't see why you are being so stuffy, Gabe,' she said. 'If we are happy with the way we spent our evening, then you should be, too.'

'They spent enough time together to stem the worst of the gossip,' Nicky said. 'As long as they continue in this way, I think all will be well.'

'Do you? You don't understand our English *ton*, *madame*. They are willing to forgive a romance but they are not willing to forgive indiscretion. You need to give them the romance. Spending half an hour in each other's company doesn't cut it. You might have taken her in for supper at the very least.'

'I am sorry, *mon beau-frère*,' Minette said soothingly. 'I am sure we shall do better next time, *n'est-ce pas*, Freddy?'

There was something in her voice that said she was pleased with the way things had worked out. And that she had not the slightest intention of doing better. No one would be in the least surprised if their passion died a natural death and

the engagement ended. But there would be consequences.

Was that what she had been plotting with her
friend? No wonder she hadn't been concerned
when he'd gone off to pursue his own pleasure
while she'd danced with whomsoever she pleased.

He leaned his head back against the squabs
and watched her face from beneath half lowered
lids. Now he saw the game she played. Well, he
would not be foxed. Not by a chit barely out of
the schoolroom.

'I will call for you at four tomorrow afternoon.
We will drive in Hyde Park.'

'Good,' Gabe said.

Minette looked less than pleased.

Freddy showed his teeth. 'After all, I am
sure you have another new gown from Madame
Vitesse to show off.'

He could almost hear the grinding of her teeth.

Chapter Seven

Minette liked driving with Freddy. His skill meant she could relax and take in all that Hyde Park had to offer on a June late afternoon. Driving was slow at the fashionable hour, but driving wasn't the point. The afternoon was bright and warm. And despite the odd lazily drifting cloud she felt no need for a wrap or shawl. The perfect climate to show off Madame Vitesse's latest creation in a way that would make the seamstress rub her hands together.

They greeted and were acknowledged by gentlemen on horseback and couples in carriages, but not all the nods they received were warm and friendly. One elderly woman turned her head in a manner that made it clear she disapproved of them.

Freddy pretended not to notice.

'What did you do to her?' Minette asked.

His lips tightened a fraction. 'Lady Ransome is my mother's friend.'

She frowned. 'Then why would she cut you? That is what it is called when one presents you with their back, *ne'st-ce pas*?'

'It was more of a cold shoulder.' His face remained expressionless.

'Why, Freddy?'

He shrugged. 'They do not care for my rackety person any more than my mother does. Owning a gambling hell is hardly the thing for a gentleman.'

She was aware that it was considered *de trop* for a gentleman to be engaged in trade of any kind. But the bleakness in his eyes suggested there was more to it.

'It is not unusual for a mother to publicly disapprove of her son and heir?'

He grimaced. 'She sees me as a usurper of my brother's birthright.'

'You had an older brother?'

His jaw flickered, his shoulders tensed. 'I am surprised you haven't heard. He was killed in a driving accident.'

Pain coloured his voice, followed swiftly by such a coldness of expression it discouraged further enquiries. 'I'm sorry. Were you close?'

'Yes.'

She nodded. 'It would be hard for your mother, losing a child, but she cannot blame you because the law requires you to inherit.'

He took a deep breath and let it go. 'I prefer not to discuss my mother's motives.'

The look on his face was so frozen, so icily cold a shiver slid down her spine. Clearly, he did not want her sympathy. She searched her mind for something to say.

A young lady walking with a woman who looked like a governess caught Minette's eye and waved madly. A welcome distraction. She waved back. 'Freddy, stop. It is Lady Priscilla.'

When the young woman realised she'd been seen, she drew closer to the carriage, her face a little pink, no doubt having received a scold for her enthusiastic greeting.

Freddy drew his phaeton onto the verge so others could pass, and bowed. 'Good day, my lady.'

Lady Priscilla gave him a wary glance but beamed at Minette. 'I wasn't sure you'd see me from all the way up there.'

Freddy's phaeton was indeed fashionably high. Minette leaned over. 'How do you do?'

'Oh, very well. This is my companion, Miss Bernice, who used to be my governess. When I left the schoolroom we could not let her go she is so much a part of the family.'

The companion, a short, thin young lady in a drab coloured walking gown and a pair of spectacles on the tip of a pointy nose, dipped a curtsey.

'I am so glad I saw you,' Lady Priscilla said. 'I wanted to ask if you would care to go shopping tomorrow afternoon with Mama and me? We are going to the warehouse in Houndsditch to choose fabric for new curtains.'

Minette glanced at Freddy. 'We don't have any plans for tomorrow afternoon, do we?'

'None. I did have it in mind to ask you to attend an event with me the day after.'

Minette smiled at Priscilla. 'I would love to go.'

'Good. We always go to Gunter's afterwards for ices. We will call for you at two.'

Freddy bowed again and moved back into the traffic on the drive.

'I thought you said you hadn't known Lady Priscilla long?'

She winced at his frigid tone. He was still suspicious. 'Believe it or not, I met her for the very first time at Gosport's ball. It is strange. I feel as if we have known each other for years. It is nice to find a friend.'

'A fortunate first meeting, then.'

'Oh, for goodness' sake, do not tease. You know what happened was an accident.'

His lips twitched a fraction. 'Very well. We will never mention it again.'

'And I will tell Madame Vitesse that whoever was making enquiries about her brother was not you.'

A brow shot up. She'd clearly surprised him. 'You do believe me, then.'

'Gabe wouldn't have you for a friend if you were without honour. And lying is dishonourable, *n'est pas*?'

He bowed. 'You are as intelligent as you are beautiful, sweetheart.'

Sweetheart. A casual endearment that warmed her through and through. She felt the heat of it rise in her cheeks. 'A compliment?' she shot back, with a glance askance to hide her confusion. 'Now, that is something new.'

'Well, you are my fiancée.'

Something inside her delighted at the teasing note in his voice.

She batted her lashes in pretended flirtatiousness. 'So that is the reason. I suppose it makes sense when we have to keep up appearances. What is this invitation you mentioned to Lady Priscilla?'

'A cricket match at Lord's Ground.'

She wrinkled her nose. 'Cricket is a game I do not understand very well.'

'Mr Brummell is to play for Hampshire.'

For a moment she didn't quite believe she'd heard him correctly. 'Beau Brummell?'

'Indeed.' The teasing twinkle was back in the depths of his blue eyes. 'That Mr Brummell.'

She cast him an arch look. 'It would be important to attend, then.'

'Exceedingly.'

'Do you think we could ask Lady Priscilla to go with us?'

He frowned.

'She feels very badly about what happened. It would go some way to relieve her mind that you do not hold her to blame.'

'Not altogether to blame.'

The mock severity in his voice made her chuckle. 'Then you agree. And it would save Nicky the bother of having to act as chaperone. She becomes very tired in the afternoons.'

'Very well. If your friend will bring her antidote of a companion with her to give the whole event a veritable aura of respectability.'

'Then it is settled. I will ask Lady Priscilla tomorrow.'

This new feeling of harmony between them was very welcome. Indeed, the day seemed brighter than it had before. She glanced up. How strange, the sun was covered by cloud, but she was definitely feeling warm. Apparently, it was nothing to do with the sun, it was a glow inside her at their newfound accord.

They reached the end of the carriage road. 'Do you want to take another turn?' he asked.

She cast him a sideways glance. 'Would you let me drive? I hear lots of ladies own their own carriages and drive themselves.'

'They do.'

'And they have races,' she said, recalling a conversation.

'If that is your plan you can ask someone else to teach you.'

She recoiled from the harsh tone in his voice. 'It is all right for a man to race but not for a woman?'

'It is reckless for anyone.'

Her spine stiffened. Always this man had to be in control. 'Then certainly I will ask someone else. If you would be so good as to drive me home? I must dress for a ball this evening. It would not do to rush my toilette.'

He headed out of the gate.

'Are you also going to Lady Cowper's ball tonight?' she asked, breaking the chilly silence.

'I was not invited. She is another of my mother's friends.'

Did his mother really wield so much influence? 'Then I will look forward to seeing you at the cricket match.'

'I'll send a note to Gabe, just to make sure he approves before you invite your friend.'

'Perfect,' she said.

It was anything but perfect. Once more they were at odds. But one thing was certain, she was going to ask Gabe about Freddy's mother and her friends.

After properly messing up their budding friendship during the drive in the park, Freddy hoped today's outing would regain the ground he'd lost. He'd been a fool to react so strongly to her casual remark about racing. Clearly she had not heard the rumours about what had happened to his brother and he should not allow guilt to ride him so hard.

The past was over and done with, and if his mother could not let it go, he could do no more.

She would not be pleased about his engagement. Not one bit. He'd written to her, of course, given her the news and set things in motion for the betrothal ball. The people on the estate would be delighted. An engagement promised a wedding and a bride promised an heir and all the security of a continuing dynasty. Unfortunately, Mother hadn't replied to his missive. Not one word. No surprise there.

She would do her duty to the dukedom, as she always had done her duty. But no force on earth could make her show anything but martyrdom as she did it. A problem looming on the horizon. The woman's negativity would lend the perfect excuse to Minette's diffidence about the wedding. Something he would have to work hard to counter, when he hadn't yet managed to overcome his fiancée's objections.

Meanwhile, he needed to find out who else was clumsily trying to put a hand on Moreau's collar. He didn't want the Home Office or anyone else queering his pitch.

He had been surprised by Minette's acceptance of his word that it was not him or his men stomping around and poking their noses into finding Madame Vitesse's brother. He had discovered the man's last name. Every foreigner who entered the country had to register with the Department of Aliens and one Henri Latour was no different. But that was all they had done or would do—unless Madame Vitesse did not provide the information she'd promised.

To his relief, the ladies were ready and waiting in the drawing room at Gabe's town house.

'You recall Lady Priscilla and Miss Bernice,' Minette said, the light of mischief in her eyes.

'How could I ever forget you, Lady Priscilla?' he said, bowing, 'or you, Miss Bernice.'

'Too kind,' the companion murmured with a quick nervous glance at his face.

'I am grateful you were able to indulge us this afternoon and become one of our party or we would have had to cancel,' Freddy continued. 'Since I understand Lady Mooreshead had another engagement.'

'One of long standing,' Minette said.

Long-standing as of the day before yesterday. It mattered not one whit who accompanied Minette, provided he had an opportunity to spend time in her company and convince her that she desired to be wed. As long as those occasions were in places where he wouldn't be led any further astray by his lust for the woman. Uncontrolled desire came with unfortunate consequences, like children.

'Are we ready?'

'Nicky wondered if we should put up a picnic basket,' Minette said.

'All looked after.'

Minette gave him a brilliant smile, and he found himself wanting to nip at her full bottom lip as a reminder to keep that smile only for him. Damn it all, when had he ever been possessive about a woman?

Not with any other woman. The thought echoed in his mind. He decided to ignore it. Their engagement wasn't about possession or about passion and it would be wrong to let her think it was anything more. It would be not only dishonourable but cruel. He'd been acquainted with the cruelty of false hope all his life.

He helped the ladies into his carriage, seating the Sparshott party facing forward and Minette next to him on the opposite side.

'Oh,' said Miss Bernice, clearly dismayed. 'I should change places with Miss Rideau. It is not right for me to face forward.'

'Nonsense,' Minette said. 'I understand you do not travel well.'

'You are too kind,' the governess said, 'but I feel I really should insist.'

Freddy looked down his nose at the young woman in his best imitation of duke bored to death. 'I can assure you I have no ungentlemanly intentions towards my fiancée, Miss Bernice.'

The poor woman gasped.

'Freddy,' Minette said admonishingly. 'Take no notice, Miss Bernice. He is putting you to the blush because he is trying to be nice to you.' She gazed up at him. 'Isn't that so?'

'When did you become an expert on my intentions?' Then he smiled at the governess. 'Miss Rideau is correct. But you can blame her for my consideration. When she wrote to tell me of your acceptance of my invitation, she mentioned your affliction. And while it may be more proper for you to sit beside me in the polite world, I prefer you not be made unwell, with all its attendant difficulties.'

'Enough, Freddy,' Minette said. She smiled at Miss Bernice. 'Please, make yourself comfortable, ma'am. It is only a very short journey and I will not speak of our unusual arrangement if you will not.'

Lady Priscilla beamed. 'Poor, dear Bernie. She really is the worst of travellers. And she is very grateful for your kindness.'

The woman gave up with good grace. 'You are very kind, Your Grace. Thank you.'

'Have you ever attended a cricket match, Miss Rideau?' Lady Priscilla asked.

'I played once,' Minette said. 'On the lawn at

Meak one summer. I have to admit I had trouble understanding the rules.'

'I expect His Grace will instruct you,' Miss Bernice said.

'Will you, Freddy?' Minette asked, her eyes full of laughter.

'I think between us, Lady Priscilla, who has three brothers, and myself, we should be able to make things clear.'

'Three brothers?' Minette said.

'I know,' Lady Priscilla said with a sigh. 'Such a trial. They are so overprotective.'

'Were they concerned about you coming with me today?' Freddy asked, the darkness inside him rising up.

'Oh, no. They trust Bernie to keep me in line, don't they, dearest?'

The little woman shoved her glasses up her nose, looking terribly unsure.

If they thought a timid companion could handle him, Freddy thought grimly, they were idiots. Which they weren't. He'd met the Sparshott twins and their older brother. He had no doubt at all that he'd find them at Lord's Cricket Ground, glowering at him in case he put a foot wrong with their sister.

The carriage pulled up, and he jumped down. 'This way, ladies. I have bespoken chairs for us.'

Being a duke carried responsibility, but it also had advantages he had, up to now, not utilised.

Partly because the opportunity had not arisen, given his current line of work, and partly because he always felt like an impostor. A fraud. No matter what his mother thought, he hated having inherited his brother's title. He'd been set for a career in the army but once he had become heir to the title, his father had made sure no colonel would accept him. Losing one son was enough. If it had been because he'd been worried about Freddy, it might have mollified him, but it had only been out of concern for the succession. Mother, on the other hand, would have been very happy to send him off to war, never to return.

Knowing that, if not for Gabe's offer of employment he might have enlisted as a common soldier, he'd hated the ducal duties so much. The paperwork. The political manoeuvring. The criticism when he failed to live up to his brother's memory.

He shut the door on those useless thoughts. On the past. As time had progressed he'd come to understand that he would never be forgiven for being the one left alive. He'd learned to enclose his pain and guilt in a layer of ice.

He was Falconwood. For as long as he lived. And awaiting him and his guests were tables and chairs set beneath a shady tree with attendant footmen. 'You should have a good view from here,' he said as he seated the ladies. 'Champagne?'

'Yes, please,' Minette and Lady Priscilla said together.

'Oh, dear,' Miss Bernice said. 'I really don't think—'

'How about tea for you?' He gave her a gentle smile.

Her frown turned into an expression of heartfelt gratitude. 'Thank you.'

He signalled to the footman, who smartly went about the business of catering to the ladies' wishes.

'I don't see The Beau,' Minette said, scanning the field.

'No,' Freddy said. 'Hampshire is at bat.'

She wrinkled her nose, staring at the two men at the crease in what he was becoming to think of as a kittenish expression. It made him want to kiss her every time she did it.

'He is playing for Hampshire county cricket team and he is in the clubhouse,' Lady Priscilla elaborated further. 'Only two people are at bat at any one time.'

Minette seemed satisfied with the explanation and sat back to watch, with the occasional explanation from either Lady Priscilla or himself when terms like 'bowled' and 'stumped' came up.

The buzz of insects, the crack of the bat, the shouts of 'Huzzah' and polite applause of the ladies washed over him in a wave of nostalgia. It was such a familiar scene. He and Reggie had played on the local village team that last year. Happy memories he hadn't recalled for years.

And if it hadn't been for his engagement, he might never have experienced them again, so focussed had he become on the darkness of what he did. He glanced at his betrothed, at her lively, beautiful face as she listened to something Lady Priscilla was explaining, and felt wonder at the feeling of the rightness of the day. Perhaps he could have this for the rest of his life.

Deserved or not.

Once he had served the ladies, the footman handed Freddy a glass of champagne. He lowered himself to the ground, his back to the tree, and settled in to enjoy watching his fiancée try to understand the rules of play.

'Oh, well caught, sir,' he called out, along with several others at a particularly good catch.

Minette glanced over at him with a smile. 'You like this game.'

It wasn't really a question, but he answered anyway. 'I do.'

'Do you also belong to a team?'

It was an innocent enough question, but it meant more than she might have guessed because she didn't see any reason why he might not belong to a team. The villagers hadn't minded his lameness, either. He may not have been a fast runner but he could hit, and had a good eye when it came to catching. He grinned at her. Yes, he was actually grinning. 'Dukes have their dignity to maintain, you know.'

She laughed. 'Lazybones.'

Out of the corner of his eye he noticed the companion twitching anxiously. Looking as if she felt the need to set the record straight, to defend him from the accusation of laziness and attribute it to his lame leg. His grin died.

'Oh, look!' Minette said. 'That is Monsieur Brummell. I really thought it was a tease to get me to come with you today.'

Brummell strode out onto the pitch to a round of applause and a few catcalls. As usual he looked cool and elegant.

'How on earth did they convince him to take part?' Lady Priscilla asked. 'I heard he hates any form of violent exercise.'

They watched in silent awe as the arbiter of fashion made run after run, reaching a grand total of twenty-three before he was finally caught. The man was good. He bowed to the applause that broke out as he left.

During the interval, the servants served delicacies designed to please the ladies—cucumber sandwiches and little cakes, along with more champagne and a fresh pot of tea.

'It is all so very English,' Minette said, glancing over at him with a challenging look.

'Is that good or bad?'

'Très bon,' she said in a decided way that gave

him a sense of great contentment he found unexpected. She frowned. 'There is a man over there, he keeps looking this way.'

He kept his voice low, for her ears only. 'He's probably wishing he was here instead of me, given my lovely companions.'

She sat up a little straighter. 'Are you flirting with me, Freddy?'

'Is it not the duty of a fiancé to flirt with his intended?'

The kittenish look reappeared. 'Now you really are teasing.' She smiled at him, and something inside him contracted.

It wasn't lust, though there was always an undercurrent of that whenever she was nearby, it was about liking. Not something he had ever expected. On a day like today, it was too easy to imagine living this sort of life of easy companionship, mutual respect perhaps even— No. That was too much to ask. This marriage was all about maintaining the proprieties and keeping Gabe's friendship. It would only ever be one small facet of his life, of necessity.

'He's coming over,' Minette said.

Arthur. A cold fist settled in his gut. He rose to his feet. 'Cousin,' he said as the man reached them.

'I hear congratulations are in order,' Arthur said, his expression sour.

'Thank you, cuz. I did not expect to see you here today.'

'Liz's idea,' his cousin said, kicking at a tuft of grass.

Ah, yes. Liz would have been shocked to her toes at the news. Freddy couldn't help feeling a little twinge of satisfaction. Not that his impending marriage would alter the line of inheritance at all, but it might shake Liz out of her complacency.

'May I introduce you to my betrothed, Mademoiselle Rideau, her friend, Lady Priscilla, and her companion, Miss Bernice? Authur Stone. My cousin.'

Arthur bowed low over the two young ladies' hands and gave Miss Bernice a brief nod. It was without question the appropriate greeting, but Minette bristled. Once she knew Arthur, she would understand that his cousin had little or no self-esteem and, therefore, establishing the order of precedence was of prime importance.

'It is delightful to meet a member of Freddy's family,' Minette said, dipping a curtsey. 'You are the first.'

'I was at Gosport's ball,' Arthur said with a disapproving frown, 'though it did not seem quite the right time for introductions.'

Minette raised a questioning brow.

Arthur rocked on his heels, his ears turning pink. 'I had another engagement.'

No doubt he had scuttled off to confer with his wife.

Minette smiled and said nothing.

'Are the boys here?' Freddy asked, looking around. 'And Liz?'

'No. I am here with a friend.' He winced. 'Didn't expect to see you here, old chap, cricket not being your sort of thing.' More foot-shuffling. 'Do you think we can have a word in private?'

'It looks as if the match is about to start again,' Lady Priscilla said.

The players were striding onto the field, talking and laughing, with Beau Brummell in their midst. They separated to take up their various positions. With the attention now focussed on play, Arthur leaned closer. 'About this engagement of yours. Do you think it is such a good idea?'

'I don't think it is any of your business, actually,' Freddy said, smiling.

Arthur flinched. 'There is the business of the *accident*.' He glanced around and lowered his voice still further. 'New information might come to light at any time. No statute of limitations, and that sort of thing.'

Freddy turned to face him square on, his anger icy in his veins. Arthur had always sworn he'd seen nothing of the accident. 'Have you regained your memory, then?'

The other man turned back to the game. 'I was

a boy. I panicked. But in hindsight there are things I remember. Perhaps.'

Freddy's hand curled into fists. This was Liz's work, no doubt. 'Go to hell, Arthur. Whatever scandal arises will taint you, too, you know.'

Arthur shrivelled in on himself. 'You should think about it, though,' he said. 'That's all. Think about it.'

Freddy wanted to strangle him. Or Liz. Or both of them together. But they were his family. And he'd already been the death of one member of it. 'Tell Liz she has nothing to fear with regard to the succession.'

A shout went up and he turned his head to see a ball heading straight at his party. An excellent hit over the boundary. He stretched out a hand and caught it to a burst of applause.

'Well caught, sir,' someone yelled.

He threw it back to the bowler, who bowed his thanks. Meanwhile, the batsman was awarded six runs.

He glanced around. Arthur, the sniveller, had taken the opportunity to scuttle off and was now talking to a group a little distance away, but he must have felt Freddy's gaze on him because he half turned and gave a terse nod of understanding. It seemed he was content to accept Freddy's word, for now.

'Freddy,' Minette said, smiling at him over her

shoulder. 'I cannot believe you caught that ball. They will surely ask you to join their team.'

The bitterness inside him escaped his control. 'No. They won't. I can't run.' And everyone knew it. Half of them had been at school with him.

Her expression of shock at his harsh words followed quickly by the look of pity in her lovely brown eyes only made him feel worse.

Damn it all. He never whined about his foot. 'And as I told you, dukes are far too important to be playing silly games. I invited you because you need to know about one of England's most important institutions.'

The ice coating his voice must have reached her as her back straightened. The smile disappeared. 'You are right.' She turned away from him and addressed a remark to Lady Priscilla.

He didn't hear what she said for the angry rush of blood in his ears.

Curse Arthur. If he really knew something, why had he never mentioned it before? He was bluffing. Applying pressure.

And with that sort of thing in the wind, the thought of Minette meeting Mother made him feel physically ill.

Chapter Eight

While Freddy had maintained an outward calm and the rest of the afternoon had been enjoyable, it was perfectly clear to Minette he had withdrawn inside himself. Leaving only a walking, talking, icy shell.

The guilt of her careless words weighed her down, but it wasn't until after they had deposited Priscilla and her companion on the Sparshott doorstep and the carriage had moved off again that she dared to broach the subject. 'I beg your pardon. When I said about you joining the team, I forgot about your leg. I did not mean to cause you embarrassment.'

'You didn't.' His voice was shards of ice grating down her spine.

Oh, the man was too infuriating. 'Then why are you being so distant?'

He blinked. And something more humane appeared in his dark blue gaze. 'I apologise. I was thinking about something someone said.'

A flash of light went off in her brain. 'Your cousin. He said something that upset you, didn't he?' She pressed a hand to her stomach to still the sense of unease she felt.

His expression shuttered.

'I see.' She folded her hands in her lap. 'You do not trust me.'

'It isn't that.'

'Then what?'

'It is old family business. I'm sorry, I should not have let it affect me that way. But there is something else I need to tell you. We have the name of Madame Vitesse's *brother*. He is Henri Latour and he has black hair and brown eyes and a scar at the base of his right thumb.'

She gasped at the detail. 'How do you know this?'

'If I know it, the Home Office knows it, too. You need to trust me in this, Minette. Convince Madame Vitesse to put us in touch with the man right away and give me the information, or they will make a mess of the whole business.'

He had not answered her question, but it was no longer of importance.

'I apologise for not trusting you, Freddy. And I will persuade her to tell us everything. If you will promise to trust me.'

If he didn't Nicky's life would be ruined.

He regarded her for a long moment. 'I trust you.'

Her foolish heart gave a little skip. But her foolish heart did not always listen to reason. She only dared trust Freddy in this. After that she was on her own, as she had always been.

Minette called on Madame Vitesse the next morning. The interview proved uncomfortable, to say the least, once the woman realised what she was asking.

The woman folded her arms across her chest. 'You have not yet kept your side of our bargain.'

Minette lifted her chin. 'Why should I, if someone else obtains the information before I do?'

Madame Vitesse blinked. 'No one but me knows where my brother is.'

'You know that is not true. Someone knows. A street sweeper. An innkeeper. A landlady. There is always someone. And those seeking him are not all as honourable as Falconwood. He *will* keep his word to you. I *will* wear your gowns.' She reached out and grasped the other woman's hand in her own. 'Why would I not? They are beautiful. Unique. I have had more compliments this past week than ever before.' She gestured around the upstairs workshop at the women plying their needles. 'You already have more work than you can handle alone.'

Madame Vitesse swallowed. 'He is the only family I have left, apart from the children.'

'We both know what it is to try to protect our families,' she said softly. 'If I don't find this man we seek, if others reach him before me, those I care about will be in danger.'

The woman took a deep breath and leaned close. 'You will find Henri in the evenings at the The Town of Ramsgate in Wapping. He has work at the docks. There he goes by the name Henry Tower. It is what the English call him.'

Minette squeezed her hand. 'Thank you. I promise you will not regret it. Now, let me try on the ballgown.' She had to hurry. Freddy would want to hear this news.

'*Merci, Mademoiselle*. You are very kind.'

'Not at all. We Frenchwomen must stick together.'

Freddy left his phaeton with his tiger. She had apologised for not trusting him. Twice. Freddy didn't believe it. The lady doth protest too much. Shakespeare might be every schoolboy's worst nightmare, but he was also an insightful man. If Freddy had to make a wager on it, he'd bet his estate that Minette didn't trust him one little bit. And he couldn't help but wonder who had abused the trust of such a very young woman.

He glanced down at the note he had received at his lodgings.

I have what we need. Call for me in your phaeton. I will tell Nicky we have arranged to go for a drive, but come late, after six.

Given his visceral understanding, how was he to convince her to trust him to visit the seamstress's brother without her? Appeal to her sense? The risk? Danger came in a variety of guises. If the Home Office boys followed them, who the hell knew what they would do with the information that his French fiancée was involved in Sceptre business?

The butler bowed him into the Mooreshead town house. 'The ladies are in the drawing room, Your Grace.'

'Thank you. No need to show me up, I am expected.' He climbed the stairs to the first floor and found Nicky working on some embroidery while Minette read aloud. A picture of domesticity that tugged at a chord in his chest. Longing. Good God, since when had he found such dullness appealing? He didn't.

Minette put the book down the moment he entered. 'Freddy, what took you so long? I thought you were to come earlier.'

'One of my horses threw a shoe.' He bowed

to Nicky. 'Good day, Lady Mooreshead. I hope I find you well?'

'Very well indeed,' Nicky said with a warm smile. She looked radiant. 'I am glad you are finally here to take this fidget out for a drive.'

Minette laughed. 'She made me read to stop me from pacing. It won't take me a minute or two to get my hat.'

She dashed from the room.

Nicky shook her head. 'So much vivacity. I am glad you are able to take her out. Gabe is so busy with the estate and Parliament he scarcely has a moment to spare.' She touched a hand to her stomach then blushed. 'The very thought of getting into a carriage makes me feel unwell at the moment.'

A child. What would it be like to bring another being into the world? One to care for and who would follow in your footsteps? Bile rose in his throat. Not his footsteps. He forced a smile. 'Then I am glad to relieve you of the duty and make it my pleasure. It is the only chance we have to converse alone.'

Nicky's eyes shadowed. 'You are sure about this, Freddy? I would hate her to marry for such a reason and be made unhappy.'

Frank words indeed. His shoulders tensed. The ice inside him spread outwards. 'I will do nothing to make her regret our union.' She would be a duchess, and have everything any woman could ever want. As long as she didn't want children. Thankfully she need never know it was by design rather than accident.

Minette appeared in the doorway, bonnet on her head and sunshade in hand.

'We are lucky it is not raining,' she said, once they were settled in his phaeton.

'Don't count your chickens,' he said, looking up at the fluffy clouds floating above their heads. Some of them had the darkness of rain in their hearts.

'Your tiger doesn't come with us?'

'He will wait for our return. I assumed we needed a bit of privacy. What did Madame Vitesse have to say?'

'I know where to find her brother. He is using the name Henry Tower and working at the docks. We can find him at an inn, The Town of Ramsgate, in Wapping, at the end of the workday.'

'The reason you asked me to delay our drive until later.'

She nodded. 'I am hoping we will find him there this evening.'

'Devil take it, Minette, gently bred girls do not visit dockyard taverns. I will tell you everything when I return.'

She folded her arms across her chest and glared at him. 'Nonsense. It's an inn. A public place.' She leaned closer. 'What could happen with you there to protect me?' She glared when she realised he was not going to change his mind. 'Now I wish I had kept this information to myself.'

'Wasn't it bad enough that you came to the Paradise, without exposing yourself to the sort of men who frequent a place like the Ramsgate?'

'There you go again, treating me like a child. Well, I'm not a child. And the taverns in France are far more dangerous than anything here England.'

She'd been a child when Nicky had left. He could well imagine what a girl left to fend for herself might have encountered. Or seen. The idea of it made his hands curl into fists. He forced himself to ease off on the ribbons before his horses did more than toss their heads in objection. 'You are not in France now. I will meet Henry and relay what he says upon my return.'

'Then I won't know anything for two days. We are invited to visit some friends of Gabe's and will leave early in the morning. We won't be back until the day after tomorrow.'

'It can wait a day or two.'

She huffed out a breath. 'I hate waiting.'

The urge to laugh surprised him. In some ways she was older than her years and in others she seemed so much younger than him. Not that he would dare show his amusement. He could certainly see from the determined look on her face that she wouldn't accept not knowing what he learned right away, and that was something he could arrange.

'I'll report back the moment I have spoken to him.'

Suspicion filled her gaze. 'You promise?'

'I swear it. Where will you be this evening?'

'At home. Because we leave Town tomorrow, we dine there with friends.'

'I will come when they have left.'

She frowned. 'I don't think Gabe will be pleased.'

'He isn't going to know. Leave your window open when you retire for the night.'

Her eyes sparkled. 'You are going to enter my room through the window?'

'Try not to give me away, would you? I don't want Gabe calling me out.'

She shuddered. 'Neither do I.'

He breathed a sigh of relief. Then why did the back of his nape prickle? Damn it all, why did he have the sense her capitulation had been far too easy?

Crammed between Oliver's Warf and the alley leading to Wapping Old Stairs, the Town of Ramsgate was indeed not the sort of place a young woman of good breeding should think about entering. On the opposite side of Wapping High Street, Minette hugged the shadows of St John's Church. Freddy was going to be furious.

And not just because she had gone against his express wishes that she wait for him at home.

She'd meant to, she really had. She'd been truly charmed by the idea that he intended to protect her, until her doubts had bubbled up. Hadn't she also been charmed by the way Pierre had sought to keep her safe? Hadn't she adored him and his protectiveness? Until she'd discovered it had all been a front. Freddy had never even pretended he wanted her participation in his plans. Once he had the information she had discovered, what was to stop him going off to find Moreau without her?

He could tell her anything when he visited her after his meeting.

No, she had been finely tricked by Pierre. She wouldn't give Freddy the chance to do the same.

Two men in rough clothing wandered down the street, shoulders slumped, feet dragging. They stopped at the door of the tavern, where the light over the door lit the profile of the taller man. Her heart picked up speed. Freddy. And from his brawny build, the other man was Barker from the Fools' Paradise. Their disguises were perfect. What would they think of hers?

They disappeared inside.

Squaring her shoulders, she pulled her ragged shawl up over her head and around her shoulders. She and Pierre had played this game often enough to make it second nature, but as always her heart beat faster and her breathing quickened, bringing to her nostrils the stink of the clothes she'd acquired, along with the dank smell of river, fish and the smoke from river coal. She forced herself to take ten deep, slow breaths to let the air become part of who she was, let poverty and hunger wash over her and then she shuffled across the street.

Inside, the Ramsgate smelled and tasted like so many other taverns she had lingered in, listening for information. For Pierre. Never guessing the use to which he had put it. The noise of men's voices, the acrid smoke of pipes, the stench of beer and unwashed bodies were the same. Only the language was different.

Behind the bar, a grubby innkeeper thumped a pair of pewter pots in front of his most recent customers. The men took their ales to a table in the corner, Barker lighting a pipe, Freddy burying his nose in his tankard while he discreetly scanned the room.

Keeping her shoulders hunched and her face lowered, she shuffled around the room. 'Spare a copper for a poor auld wider lady?' she begged in quavering tones, and leaning heavily on her cane so people would see little but the top of her head. She had been practising her accent on the street sweeper on the corner since her arrival in London. A game she'd played for entertainment mostly. She had an ear for accents and she had amused Nicky and Gabe with her imitations, and shocked them, too.

One docker shoved her away fiercely. Another pressed a ha'penny in her mittened hand.

'She'll only spend it on gin,' his companion observed, and turned his back.

A glance from Freddy, who sported a scar on his cheek and nose reddened by drink, flickered over her. Without recognition.

Hah! She'd spotted him right away. To be fair, she had known to expect him. Still…

She sidled up to their table, clawed hand shoved under his nose. 'Spare a copper.'

'Clear off.' Barker tossed her a coin. It glinted silver as it spun on its edge on the scarred and stained tabletop. A 'thruppny bit', as the street sweeper called it. Threepence. She reached for it.

Strong fingers clenched around her wrist as she caught up the coin.

'What in hell's name are you doing here?' Freddy rasped in her ear.

She tittered. Let the shawl slip down to her shoulders, revealing the tangle of her hair and red-painted lips, changing from hunched old crone to ravaged prostitute. 'Want company out in the alley?' She danced the coin between her fingers. 'Sailor's choice.'

Freddy cursed.

Barker buried his face in his tankard, his shoulders shaking. Was he laughing?

The man who had given her the coin started towards them. 'You cheating baggage.'

Freddy's lowered brows halted him in midstride. He took the coin and tossed it back to the man. 'Sit.' He jerked down by her arm to perch on his knee.

She batted her eyelashes. 'Changed yer mind, guv? Wot's yer fancy?'

Barker choked back laughter. 'Does yer want me to leave yer to it?'

Freddy grinned. An evil leer. 'You can leave us to it, mate, when we get outside.' His accent was also of the lower orders and spoken with the ease of long practice.

A shiver went down her spine at the lecherous promise. Not fear. Anticipation. Damn him. Because she had no doubt he intended it as a threat of retribution, not a promise.

Freddy gestured to a waiter passing with a tray. 'Gin.'

Barker nudged Freddy with his elbow, and Minette caught the jerk of the innkeeper's unshaven chin at a man entering the taproom.

Minette gave Freddy a winsome smile, careful not to reveal her teeth. 'That our mark?'

Freddy lifted his pot of ale to his lip. 'It is.'

He nodded, and the innkeeper handed the new customer a bumper of gin and gestured in their direction.

The man, Henri, narrowed his eyes at her and then at Freddy, then shouldered his way to their table. 'You ask for me?'

''Ave a seat, mate,' Freddy said, lifting his tankard in salute.

The man glanced around him, grabbed a stool and subsided with a sigh. He took a long pull at his gin. 'So, *messieurs*?'

Freddy lowered his voice. 'You sister says you have news of a certain party.'

'Name begins with M,' Barker added.

'This man, he arrives six week ago. Here.' He made a vague gesture, encompassing them, the river, London.

'Where does he stay?' Freddy leaned back and swigged at his beer.

Henri shook his head and leaned forward, his voice little more than a whisper. 'He recently travels north. Urgent business.'

How vague could the man get? 'Not helpful, *mon ami*,' Minette muttered under her breath.

He looked startled.

'Ignore her,' Freddy ground out. 'Tell us what you do know.'

Minette bristled but contented herself with a scrape of her nail across the table, knowing it would irritate Freddy and, more importantly, not allow him to forget her presence.

'*Un homme.*' Henri grimaced. 'My friend. He says he returns.'

'He's coming back to London,' Freddy rephrased.

Henri nodded. 'He is expected. Soon.'

'What is he doing in the north?' Barker asked.

Henri shrugged. 'Gathering information?'

'Is there anything else you can tell us?' Minette asked, ignoring Freddy's glare. 'His appearance. The name he is using?'

Freddy kicked her under the table.

'Beard. Spectacles.' He touched his cheek. 'Dark of skin. He goes by Smith.'

Smith sounded nothing like Moreau. But, then, none of them looked like themselves to-night. Moreau was a master of disguises. He'd certainly fooled her for years.

'You will let your sister know the moment he returns,' Barker said. 'Warn him and you are a dead man.' He issued his threat in a dangerously conversational tone of voice.

Henri ignored him and kept his gaze fixed on Freddy's face. ''E is a bad man. I speak truth.'

Freddy nodded. 'Then we will get along famously.'

The Frenchman got up and went back to the bar. Minette leaned against Freddy's shoulder and started playing with his hair and stroking his cheek. He looked at her. She raised a brow in the age-old question.

'I'll see you back at the club,' Freddy said to Barker, and drew her closer to his side, bit the point of her shoulder, hard enough to make her twitch away. 'This mort owes me thruppence-worth.'

Barker stretched, got up and left. When he was clear, Freddy grabbed her arm and staggered out into the night air. While his steps were sloppy, his eyes slightly unfocussed, his grip was steely. He didn't lighten it until they were well clear of the inn and he was sure, as she was, that they had not been followed.

He put his arm around her shoulders. Slowly, inexorably, he backed her into the shadows of the nearest alley. He took her chin between her fingers and tipped her face up so she was forced to meet a gaze glinting from a nearby streetlight. Oh, my, he was angry.

'So, tell me, my dear Minette, what the hell did you think you were doing?' He spoke in a voice so calm as to be terrifying.

Intimidation. Her own anger rose. 'I wanted to hear what he had to say for myself and well you know it.'

His gaze dropped to her bosom. 'Dressed like that, you could have got a lot more than information.'

She pulled her knife from the pocket hidden in her ragged skirts, the pocket she'd sewn into the seam when Christine had come back with the dress, and held it to his Adam's apple. 'I think not.'

He cursed softly and fluently. At least she guessed he was cursing. They were English words and not familiar.

'Now, do you want the value of your thruppence,' she said softly, 'or do you take me home?'

He took her wrist and forced the blade away, taking it from her now nerveless fingers and stuffing it into a pocket. 'A man can get a lot for three pennies, my dear.'

He meant to frighten her. She knew those tactics.

He bent his head and took her mouth in a scalding kiss. Well-remembered sensations struck her low in her belly. She found she could not recall why they were standing in an alley late at night. She was too busy returning his kiss, tangling her tongue with his, plastering herself tight to his body while his fingers cradled her head and held her still to receive his punishing kiss.

Punishing, ravishing and utterly delicious.

Enough to make a girl lose her mind for want of more. Especially a girl who'd been celibate for years and had been tempted for days and days by this virile man.

As if he sensed her thoughts, he backed her up against the wall, while he kept her head angled just right. She felt his lovely weight all down her length and the ridge of his arousal against her belly. Her hands explored the musculature of his shoulders and the bones of his spine. She burrowed beneath his coat to feel the warmth of him, to shape the narrowing of his waist and the firmness of his buttocks.

A lean, beautiful male body she wanted on top of her, all around her, inside her.

He tasted of ale and smoke and of Freddy in the faint whiff of his soap.

He groaned softly and dragged his mouth away. 'Where on God's sweet earth did you learn to kiss like that?'

The words were like a dash of cold water. Like a wanton, he'd meant. A woman no better than she should be. As he'd soon find out, if they didn't stop now.

She pushed him away, breathing hard. 'You kiss pretty well yourself.' She flicked her skirts straight. 'For an Englishman.' Let him make of that what he would.

He gave a shake of his head as if to clear it. Then struck the wall behind her with the side of his fist. 'There is no need for you to take such risks. You are not in France any longer. You are not friendless and alone. When will you learn I am not your enemy?'

'Never.'

'Then we have a problem.'

'We have a worse one. We have lost Moreau.'

'We know he will return to London in due course. In the meantime, I will have men searching the north for him.' He took her arm. 'Come, time to see you home. We will be able to pick up a hackney in the next street.' He glanced down at her. 'I presume you left the garden gate open?'

'*Naturellement.*' She kept her voice calm. It wouldn't do to let him see how much Moreau's disappearance had her worried.

Chapter Nine

Minette climbed down from Gabe's carriage at Falconwood Hall. Dear man that he was, he'd insisted that his coachman drive her, along with a footman and her maid, while Freddy went on ahead, to be there to greet her along with his mother. Gabe was still angry at the incident that had brought them to this pass and hadn't been about to trust her to Freddy's tender care when he'd realised that he and Nicky would not be able to accompany her to Kent. Gabe's parliamentary business could not be abandoned on a whim.

She stared up at the house while she waited for her maid to gather up their belongings and alight. She had expected something on a grand scale—after all, Freddy was a Duke—but she had not expected anything quite so old and rambling. Freddy had called it a pile. It was a sprawling, warm red-brick place with stone towers above the arched front entrance.

The drive from the gatehouse, where she was sure there had been a portcullis at some point in time, had been extraordinarily beautiful, spreading oaks scattered across a rolling green park filled with deer. She could almost imagine Freddy riding hell for leather around the grounds as a boy. It would have been a wonderful place to bring up children.

A pang caused a hitch in her breathing. A sense of loss. The knowledge that it would not be her children who would grow up in this lovely old house. The footman climbed down from the box and hurried to ring the doorbell, but a butler with a prim mouth and small stature was already walking sedately down the steps. A groom appeared around the side of the house and led the carriage away, along with her maid and luggage.

'If you would care to follow me, miss, Their Graces are waiting in the drawing room.'

At that moment Freddy stepped out onto the drive. 'It is all right, Patterson,' he said. 'I will show Miss Rideau the way.'

The tension in her shoulders flowed away, though she hadn't realised quite how nervous she'd been about this meeting until it dissipated. After their last encounter, when it had been obvious she didn't trust him, she hadn't been sure he wouldn't withdraw from her completely. Every time she thought of the way she'd dressed and played her part, she flushed hot then went cold.

If he didn't know the extent of her carnal knowledge, he must now guess she knew far more than a gently bred girl ought.

Pierre had been bad for her in so many ways, and not just because of his betrayal.

With the utmost courtesy, Freddy held out his arm and walked her beneath the stone arch, through an ancient door and into a rectangular medieval great hall. A beautifully carved screen occupied one end and a huge fireplace dominated the centre of one long wall. Faded banners and painted shields hung on stone above the dark panelling, along with ancient weaponry. The only items of furniture were an enormously long trestle table and some horribly uncomfortable-looking carved wooden armchairs.

'Mon Dieu,' she said in a low voice. 'It is positively antiquated.'

Freddy patted her hand. 'Don't worry, most of the house is quite modern. We only use the Great Hall for large events and when the Duke needs to make an impression.'

She breathed a sigh of relief. 'I can just imagine the three of us dining here in state, you at one end and your mother at the other and me in the middle, unable to speak without shouting.'

'If Mother had her way, your imagination might not be far from the truth.'

Another wry remark about his mother. The

woman must be a veritable dragon. But then, she was a duchess.

He led them through yet another arch into a paved corridor and from there into an elegantly appointed room full of light, with pale green walls and cornices of white and gilt. It was, she realised, a perfect cube in the Palladian style.

The woman seated where the light from the window fell on her embroidery looked up at their entry. She was lovely. Dainty, with gold-blonde hair shot through with threads of silver and skin that made one think of peaches and cream. She was dressed in lavender. Half-mourning? Blue eyes arctic enough to freeze one's blood remained fixed on Minette's face while Freddy made the introductions. Now she knew from where Freddy inherited his cold expression.

Minette dipped a curtsey.

The eyes assessed her performance with chilly intensity, while the face showed no expression at all. The perfect aristocrat.

'Miss Rideau.' The duchess gestured for her to take a seat. 'Welcome to Falconwood. My son has told me much about you.' There was a fragility to her air, in the lightness of her voice. As if it was almost too great an effort for her to speak.

Oh, dear. This was likely to be a lot worse than she had hoped. She sat down in the seat set at a right angle to the Duchess.

'Was your journey bearable?' the dowager

asked. '*I* would have sent our carriage for you. It was built for me by my husband, who took every care of my person, but Freddy said it was not necessary.' The blue eyes turned to her son. 'Not worth the bother of getting it cleaned and polished, I think you said.'

The barb apparently sailed over Freddy's head. 'Lord, no. You haven't had it on the road in years. The last time you went in it to Town you said it was the most dreadfully uncomfortable trip you had ever undertaken.'

'You misremember,' his mother said. 'It certainly was not the fault of the carriage. The roads are much improved since then.'

The atmosphere in the room was frosty. Minette smiled. 'It was a very pleasant journey, thank you. Mooreshead made sure I had all the necessary comforts.'

The duchess frowned. 'You accent is quite noticeable.'

'Miss Rideau is half-French, Mother, and lived in France until quite recently. I informed you of that fact both in my letter and when I arrived yesterday.'

Defending her, when he had not defended himself. Warmth spread in her chest.

His mother's shoulders stiffened. 'You said nothing about her speech. I am sure I had no intention to criticise, I just didn't expect…' Her voice trailed off in a weak gesture of her hand.

Freddy's lips flattened to a thin straight line as if he was doing all in his power not to say something harsh.

Minette kept her expression pleasant. 'My mother was English, but she died when I was very young. I am sure, in time, I will become less noticeably French.'

'I like the way you speak,' Freddy said stiffly.

She gave him a grateful smile.

His mother gazed at him thoughtfully, her glance holding such coldness Minette stifled the urge to shiver. 'Ring for tea, Falconwood. Miss Rideau must be parched after her journey.'

Stone-faced, he strode across to the bell-pull beside a hearth of brilliant white plaster carved with vegetation and ferocious-looking animals.

'Your leg is dragging more than usual,' his mother said with a grimace. 'I told you not to hack out on that animal of yours this morning. It tires you.'

Freddy glared at her as he returned to his seat. 'What would you have me do, take up embroidery?'

His mother laughed, a tinkle of sound laced with malice. 'Do not tease so, Freddy. No, you would be better off spending time with the accounts, seeing to the business of running the estate. A gentle walk in the park...'

Fury heated Minette's blood. How could the woman be so stupid as to treat Freddy with so little regard for his pride? She wanted to take the woman by the shoulders and give her a good shake.

Fortunately for them all the butler entered at that moment, followed by a line of footmen carrying ludicrously enormous silver trays. The butler set a side table in front of the Duchess, and the footmen carefully set out a tea urn, sandwiches cut so fine it looked as if they would blow away if one breathed too hard, and small fancy cakes along with sweetmeats.

'Will there be anything else, Your Grace?'

'No, thank you,' Freddy said.

His mother stiffened as if he'd offered her some insult.

Freddy winced. 'Mother, did you require anything?'

'No, thank you, Patterson,' the Duchess said, her face a frozen mask. 'I will ring if I need you.'

What was going on here? It was horrid. Mother and son were at loggerheads in the politest of ways. Minette felt as if there were sharp daggers flying about her head. If she moved incautiously she might lose an arm, or worse.

The duchess commenced the ritual of tea.

'I assume you drink tea, Miss Rideau?' The Dowager Duchess's mouth turned down. 'I have heard the French prefer coffee.'

'I like tea,' Minette said, wishing her smile didn't feel so stiff and awkward.

Were mother and son always so tense? Was it the presence of a stranger in their midst making them so uncomfortable with each other? Hopefully, when they were used to her company, things would become more relaxed. She had a feeling she might be wishing for the moon.

Freddy glowered across the tea tray. If Mother made one more unpleasant remark to or about Minette, he would take her to task and to hell with propriety. She could carp at him all she liked. He didn't care. Neither did he any longer give a fig that the sight of him walking across the room made her queasy. He was hardened to her verbal attacks.

It did matter if she hurt Minette's feelings, though he couldn't help the surge of pride at the way Minette had stood up for herself against Mother's claws. Perfectly polite and yet showing the steel in her spine.

'From which part of France does your family come?' Mother asked, after a silence that had lasted a fraction too long. Deliberately so.

'The Vendée.' Minette smiled. 'Our château was like your house, very old. Dating to the fourteenth century in parts.'

'Older than Falconwood, then,' Freddy said, glancing at his mother, who always bragged about the antiquity of their line.

'Our ancestors came over with William, Duke

of Normandy,' Mother said. 'It was later in the family history that we settled here at Falconwood.'

Minette sipped at her tea. 'Perhaps we have some ancestors in common. I know that at least one chevalier from my father's family joined the Duke.' She put down her cup and saucer. 'I always feel sorry for the Saxon King, Harold. William's was the flimsiest excuse on which to base a claim to the throne.'

Mother pursed her lips. 'I am sure I have no idea what you are talking about. I am no bluestocking, Miss Rideau. Such topics are best left in the schoolroom.'

Freddy felt a growl form in his throat.

'Mais oui,' Minette said calmly, agreeably. 'I notice Englishwomen have a horror of being thought educated. In France the gentlemen admire a woman with whom they can converse.' She lowered her lashes a fraction. 'Among other things.'

An incautious mouthful of tea caused Freddy to choke. He carefully set his cup down on the table at his elbow. 'If you have finished your tea, Miss Rideau, perhaps I may give you a tour of the house before you retire to change for dinner?'

His mother gave him an assessing glance. A small smile touched her lips, and he steeled himself to parry her next thrust. 'Make sure you show Miss Rideau the Long Gallery, Falconwood.'

Oh, very clever, Mother dear. The last place he would want to take his intended.

She continued without pause. 'Our most recent addition is a wonderful portrait by Lawrence. A fine example of his work, I am told.' The smile disappeared. 'Dinner is at six. I like to keep country hours when we are dining *en famille*.'

'Naturally,' Minette said, rising to her feet and dipping a respectful curtsey. 'We always do so at Meak, my brother-in-law's estate.'

Freddy held out his arm, and they strolled from the room.

The fingers on his sleeve trembled. Damn Mother's mean-spirited innuendoes. Only when they were a good distance from the drawing room did he let himself speak. 'I apologise for my mother's sharp tongue. I hope she did not give offence.'

Her short, sharp exhalation spoke of impatience. 'Why is she so awful to you?'

Cross. Not hurt. Good lord, was she angry on his behalf? 'I was more concerned for you.'

'She looks at you so coldly, as if...' She breathed in and when he glanced down at her face he was surprised to see twin spots of anger on her cheeks. 'It is as if she has not a scrap of maternal feeling towards you.'

'She doesn't. Her firstborn was the sun, moon and stars in her eyes. I am a poor replacement.' The moment he'd spoken he regretted the bitterness in his words, but it was the truth. Some of it.

The concern remained on her face. 'I thought your older brother died years ago.'

'Yes. But as yet she is not reconciled to her loss.' It was one way to couch his mother's antipathy.

'It is almost as if she blames you for his death.'

He was to blame. He'd tormented Reggie into taking up his challenge. Freddy had always known how to make his older brother rise to the bait. And then he'd watched him die. Something burned at the back of his throat. He stiffened against the surge of emotion. Took a deep, slow breath. Damn it all, he never talked about the accident. Surely reliving that day over and over in his dreams was punishment enough? He let the ice inside him surround his unwanted emotions and took a deep breath. 'She is angry.' Angry that he had been the one to survive.

'She hurts you.'

How could she imagine she knew what he felt, when he felt nothing? His back teeth ground against each other. Forcibly, he relaxed his jaw. 'I don't let it trouble me, but I will speak to her.' He would not have Mother making Minette's life miserable. 'Would you like to see his portrait?'

She looked sad. 'Only if you would like to show me.'

For some reason he couldn't fathom, he did want her to see Reggie and he didn't. His brother would have liked her. They would have competed for her attention. And Reggie's innate easy charm would no doubt have won the day. It was a hard truth to swallow.

He walked her up to the second floor and along to the east wing. The long gallery was one of the most beautiful parts of the house and also one of the most ancient. He and Reggie had spent endless hours here on rainy days when not tied to their books. As they had grown older, Reggie had spent more time with their father, learning the duties he would one day inherit, spending less and less time with Freddy. He'd been envious of his father's attention to his older brother. Of his father's pride in his elder son. It was partly why he'd tempted Reggie into playing truant on the day of the accident.

They walked past the family portraits, some large by famous artists of the time and some little more than miniatures, until they came to the portrait of his immediate family done by a local artist. They stood together in front of a view of one of the most beautiful parts of Falconwood's park. Dogs gambolled at his father's feet, his mother a radiant beauty, not the pinched, pale creature she was today. Reggie stood beside his father, so like his mother with his golden hair and bright blue eyes, already showing signs of the man. Both parents were looking with pride at their elder son. On the other side of his seated mother stood Freddy. The ugly duckling, dark-complexioned with a beak of a nose and overly large hands and feet for the size of his frame. At twelve, he'd been embarrassingly short and skinny. He certainly didn't look like the rest of his family, though his father's hair was brown, not golden.

Minette viewed the portrait, tilting her head first to one side then the other. 'He looks like your mother and you look more like your father.'

'My colouring mostly comes from my mother's grandmother, I'm told.' Along with other less desirable traits.

'It is easy to see they loved your brother.'

His throat closed, but he forced himself to speak. 'As did I. He was one of the best brothers a fellow could wish for.'

He moved on to the next portrait. This one was of his brother alone, a few years older than in the previous one, a shotgun over his shoulder, a brace of partridge at his feet and a look of pure mischief in his bright blue eyes. 'This is the Lawrence Mother spoke of. Reggie was going to be eighteen later that summer.' He'd never reached his eighteenth birthday. Freddy had been sixteen.

'He makes one think of an English Apollo. Where is your portrait by Lawrence?'

The question jolted his gut. His hands clenched. His shoulders tightened. He turned from the picture and went to look out of the window, coward that he was. 'There was no need of a portrait of the spare at that time.'

He'd been so damnably jealous.

'His loss must have been a dreadful shock to you, as well as your parents.'

Worse than she could possibly imagine. 'I was devastated. And then, God help me, I was expected to step into his shoes. It was years before I could bear to think about it, let alone apply myself to the matter.'

'The reason you do not come to Falconwood very often.'

That and the bitter recriminations from his mother. Recriminations that echoed loud and clear in his conscience. 'I hate coming here.'

Chapter Ten

His words were cold. Perhaps even calculated to shock. He stood looking out of the window, so alone, so remote. And beneath the coldness Minette sensed the pain of an old wound. Something he was not talking about. She strolled to stand beside him at the window, looking out at the view. 'Thank you for bringing me to see your brother's likeness,' she said softly. 'I am sure he would be proud of you.'

He looked startled then turned away as if he did not want her to see his reaction. Sadness filled her that he would not share his thoughts with her, but it was only to be expected. Theirs was a betrothal of convenience and they barely knew each other and trusted each other even less.

Giving him time to collect himself, she gazed silently at the vista, from the formal gardens near the house across the ha-ha and out over the large expanse of treed park. A gleam of white beside a lake caught her eye. 'Oh, what is that?' She pointed. 'At the edge of the lake.'

'The Pantheon. My family's version of a folly from the early part of the last century. There's a hermit's cave in the woods nearby, too. And a grotto. Would you like to see it?'

'As long as we are back in time for dinner,' she said, smiling at the eagerness in his voice. Clearly this was something he would enjoy showing her.

With the day warm and sunny it was not a hardship to take the path that led from the house down to the lake and meander across the grassy arched bridge to arrive at the folly she had seen from the upstairs window. The view of the house was lovely from this vantage point, the red-brick fiery in the afternoon sun. But it was the folly that held her attention. A fully realised Roman temple of glowing white marble. 'It looks so real,' she said. 'As if we have stepped back in time and been transported to Rome itself.'

'One of my ancestors had it build after the Restoration. They were all the rage.'

'Can we go inside?'

'Of course.' He took her arm and walked her up the steps and through an enormous set of oak doors. Inside there were marble statues and reliefs around the circular chamber.

'Oh, my goodness,' she said. 'It is astonishing. One almost expects to meet Caesar in his toga.'

'My mother used to hold picnics here when my

father was alive. Before…' He pressed his lips together. 'Their summer parties were famous. No one ever turned down an invitation. Come, let me show you the grotto and the hermit's cave.'

'Was there really a hermit?'

'Oh, yes. There were three of them over the years, when they were fashionable. Before my time. They were paid a handsome sum to stay in the cave all summer. When the last one retired, the duke at the time gave him and his wife a cottage on the estate. Reggie and I used the place as a fort when we were young.'

They strolled back out into the sunshine and wandered to the other end of the lake. There, rocks had been placed artfully to form a tunnel that led to a grotto complete with natural spring. A shaft in the roof brought in light from outside, but the effect was cool and damp and unpleasantly gloomy. The white marble statue of a water nymph tucked against the wall behind the bubbling spring gazed at them soulfully.

Minette shivered.

Freddy took her hand. 'You are cold. Let us go back outside.'

The sunshine was a welcome relief. They turned the end of the lake, and he showed her the ruined walls of the hermit's dwelling. 'A great place for boys to play,' she said.

His eyes seemed to look inside himself, and then he smiled. 'It was.'

They strolled arm in arm back to the house. The coldness that had settled over Freddy in the portrait gallery had thawed and there was a pleasant easiness between them. It was as if they were becoming friends.

'Your home is beautiful,' Minette said, standing in the dappled shade of a tree at the edge of the lawn leading up to the house. 'This tree is huge. Oak, *n'est pas*?'

'It is supposed to be three hundred years old. It is on one of the earliest drawings of the house.' He looked up into the branches. 'It is amazing to think this tree was right here at the time of Henry the Eighth.'

She stroked the bark. 'If trees could only talk, they would whisper a great many secrets.'

His hand came down beside hers. Large. Encased in black gloves as hers were in tan. He didn't move. Slowly she turned to face him, and he brought his other hand up to cage her against the tree.

The heat of his body washed up against her like a wave. She raised her face to meet his intent gaze. While she could make out nothing from his expression, the heat in his eyes said exactly where his thoughts had gone. Her body flushed with answering heat, as it always did when he looked at her that way.

What was it about this man that brought forth longings she'd thought she had long ago repressed? She knew too well the heartbreak of giving a man what he wanted. The pain of betrayal. Yet inside she trembled with familiar sensations. The bloom of desire.

'We shouldn't be doing this,' she whispered.

'No.'

'Someone might see us.'

'No one can see us here.'

He would know all the secret places where a man could be alone with a woman.

When his eyes searched her face and his head dipped slowly, giving her every chance to reject his advance, she rose up on her toes and claimed his lips with her own.

His sigh of satisfaction made her breasts tingle and long for his touch. She arched into him, pressing her body against the hard wall of his chest.

One strong arm pulled her into him, the other caressed the curve of her spine, and he nudged her backwards until she was supported by the tree. His thigh pressed into her and she widened her stance to accommodate the sweet pressure against her lower body, rocking against him, purring deep in her throat, the sweet ache throbbing low in her core. Slowly one hand skimmed her bottom, then up her side until it rested heavy on her breast. She pushed into his palm, longing to feel his touch against the aching fullness.

He broke the kiss. 'Every time. You drive me beyond reason,' he said, his voice harsh. 'Have you any idea of the consequences of this game you are playing with me?'

'I think you are the cat and I am the mouse,' she whispered. Of course he was. He tempted her unbearably. Made her want things she should not want. And if she let him have his way, he thought she would have no choice but to marry him, when in truth it might cause him to send her away. Something she could not allow until the threat of Moreau was vanquished.

She pushed at his shoulder.

He lifted his head, gazed around and groaned. 'You are right. This is not the right place.'

'Or the right time,' she said as calmly as her frustration would allow.

'We should not anticipate our vows.'

She gave him a tight smile. 'Precisely.'

He glanced at the ground and then at her face with a wicked smile she'd never seen before, wicked and boyish. 'If it hadn't rained yesterday, I might think about trying to change your mind.'

Loverlike teasing. Such a shock from this emotionless man. 'Thank heavens for the rain, then.'

The smile remained.

She wagged a finger at him. 'A kiss between those newly betrothed is perfectly acceptable. It fits with our story. But anything more is not a good idea.' Oh, what a dissembler she was. She would like nothing more than to romp with him in the grass, but she didn't dare give him a glimpse of how she was tempted. She had no doubt he would take advantage of any sign of her weakening under the onslaught of his charm.

'You are right,' he said, though he sounded grudging.

A tone that made her foolish heart lift.

Dinner over, Freddy forwent the glass of port in solitary state after the ladies withdrew. Instead, he took it with him to the drawing room. He would not leave Minette to the tender mercies of Mother, despite the fact that over dinner she had more than held her own.

Once the tea was poured, he leaned back in his chair and sipped his port. 'Thank you for attending to the arrangements for the ball, Mother.'

'Given how the little time I have been given to prepare, I hope you are not expecting anything extraordinary,' his mother said stiffly.

'It was too bad of us,' Minette said, clearly trying to soothe the other woman's ruffled feathers. Given Mother's penchant for slicing into one with her tongue while looking as if butter wouldn't melt in her mouth, he could only feel admiration. Minette was kind as well as lovely, no matter how much she tried to hide it. But kindness would not help her with Mother.

'Perhaps we should scale back on the guest list. Keep it to family only,' he said, stretching out his legs.

Mother pursed her lips. 'The betrothal of a duke is a matter of great importance. It cannot be skimped.'

As usual she took the contrary position to anything he suggested. Just as he'd hoped. He shrugged. 'The wedding celebration is usually the main event.'

'You would put us to shame?'

Minette winced. 'If it would not be too bold an offer, I would love to help.'

Mother stiffened. 'I am perfectly capable of arranging for the entertainment of a hundred people, Miss Rideau.'

'A hundred?' Minette put down her teacup with a shaking hand. Her gaze flew to Freddy's face. 'I had no idea so many had been invited.'

Freddy winced at the sight of her consternation. 'A hundred is small for us.'

'Oh, Your Grace,' she said to his mother, 'you must allow me to be of assistance.'

Not unexpectedly, Mother turned frosty. 'My steward, Carter, and Mr Patterson are all the help I require, thank you. However, I did not receive instructions with regard to those to be invited from your family, Miss Rideau. How many people am I to expect from that quarter?'

Clearly she did not like it that he had asked Nicky to send out invitations to her and Gabe's friends. 'I gave the list to Patterson when I spoke to him before dinner.'

'Should I not know who is invited to my house?' Mother said.

'My house,' he said with lethal quiet.

The frost turned to a wall of solid ice. 'I might have known you would have no notion of what it is to take responsibility.' She sniffed. 'I trust you found your accommodations suitable, Miss Rideau?'

'Thank you, they are lovely.'

A scratch at the door, and Patterson entered. 'A message for you, Your Grace,' the butler said with a stiff bow, and held out a salver.

Freddy reached out to take it at the same moment as his mother.

'It is addressed to Falconwood,' the butler said with an apologetic glance towards Mother.

Freddy took the note, and as the butler left the room he slit the seal with a thumbnail. The shock of the words he read held him rigid for a second. He tucked the note in his pocket.

'Who is it from?' his mother asked. 'One of the neighbours thinking to ingratiate themselves now that you have finally decided to come home?'

Freddy looked up. 'No. It is business. Mother, why not let Miss Rideau plan the supper menu?'

Mother looked horrified, but he could see the calculation going on in her mind, the realisation that if she wasn't careful he might wrest all control from her hands. 'I suppose someone needs to plan the arrangement of flowers for the ball-room,' she offered.

'I would love to help with that,' Minette said. 'I will begin first thing in the morning.'

'Don't forget our plan to drive out in the morning,' he said, 'so I can show you more of the estate and some of the surrounding countryside.' Show her the note.

Her eyes widened. 'Oh, yes. I had forgotten.'

He nodded his acknowledgement of her quick wit.

Minette turned to his mother. 'I can work on the floral arrangements after lunch, if that is all right with you. Is there a budget?'

'You can spend whatever you think is necessary,' Freddy said.

His mother let out a small sound of protest.

'You have some ideas, Your Grace?' Minette said, as if she had no idea that Mother wasn't happy. 'Shall I come to you for direction first? Before Freddy and I leave for our drive. Say around ten?'

Mother never left her chamber before noon.

'Certainly not, my dear,' Her Grace said with sugary sweetness. 'I will leave it all up to you. I will have one of the gardeners put at your disposal.'

'The head gardener, Mr Jevens,' Freddy said, knowing the way his mother's mind worked. 'Since Minette will shortly be taking over the running of the household, I think that is a very good idea, Mother. She should also be present when you speak to Chef.'

The longing to object writ large on his mother's face was a painful thing to observe. She had prided herself on the running of the household since her marriage and Freddy had done nothing to alter her role since his father had died. Now was the right time to make changes. The servants, all loyal to his mother, had served him some unpleasant meals when she had been annoyed with him, and once his bed linen had been damp. Punishment for arriving at his home unannounced. There would be none of that unpleasantness for Minette. He was determined.

'Of course, dear,' his mother replied, and he heard the little break in her voice without a shred of emotion. It was all an act designed to make Minette feel uncomfortable.

'I shall look forward to it,' Minette said with forced brightness.

'Then I suggest you speak to Jevens first thing, before we drive out,' he said. 'Mother will make herself available after lunch.'

Ready for bed, Minette had never felt less like sleeping in her life. What on earth had made Freddy so anxious to take her driving in the morning? She'd seen insistence in those dark eyes that could be so expressive—when they weren't keeping her at a distance.

She still couldn't believe his mother's coldness towards him. It was horrible to be in the same room with them. Couldn't the dowager duchess see how much she was hurting her son? Or how much she lost by keeping him at a distance? She had barely stopped herself from taking the woman to task. She picked up the book Nicky had given her to read on the journey and flicked through the pages to find her place. She stared at the words. Clearly there had been something important in the note Freddy had received. Although he'd hidden it quickly, he had been surprised by its contents. And then he'd talked about arrangements they hadn't made.

The door to her chamber opened. Expecting to see Christine returning on some forgotten errand, she gaped at the sight of Freddy in a silk dressing gown closing the door behind him.

His hot, dark gaze swept over her. Answering heat raced across her skin. 'Freddy?'

He inhaled a breath and his expression shuttered.

Control. The man had icy control.

Something inside her wanted to smash down the walls. Only if she did, her own walls might come tumbling down, too. Not a good thing. 'Why are you here?'

'The note. It is from Vitesse. Things have changed.'

Her heart stilled at the seriousness in his voice. 'What is it?'

'Moreau is not returning to London.'

'We have lost him?' Damnation. She should not have left Town.

'According to Latour, Maidstone is his destination.'

Her heart lurched as if the ground beneath her feet had shifted. 'Maidstone? Is it not nearby?'

'It is.'

'Why does he go there?'

'There are only two reasons I can think of. The first is the barracks located in the town. Information about troop movements and so forth.'

'The second?'

'The news of our sudden engagement was in all the papers, and the ball was announced at the same time.' His mouth flattened. 'As a sop to the sensibilities of those that care about such things. He would no doubt have seen the London papers, wherever he was. He might see it as a chance to get to Nicky. Or he could be plotting yet another assassination. Someone attending our ball.'

She hadn't yet seen the guest list. 'People of importance will attend?'

'I'm a duke. Invitations went out to the Prince Regent, half the cabinet and a couple of royal princes.' He sounded defensive.

'Will they come?'

A shadow passed across his expression. 'They might. For Gabe's sake.'

'What on earth made you invite—? Oh.' Furious, she strode across the room, glaring up into his face. 'You think I won't cry off if doing so would be utterly embarrassing for Gabe later.'

A slow smile dawned on his face, his eyes gleamed. 'I have always liked that about you, Minette. Your mind is as quick as a whip.'

'Not quick enough, since I did not realise what was in your devious mind.'

He leaned forward, kissed the tip of her nose, then shrugged apologetically. 'A man has to do what he must to achieve the outcome he wants.'

His eyes gleamed. Mischievous. Wicked. And, oh, yes, with a hint of triumph. Not since they'd played and cheated each other at cards all those years ago had she seen that look on his face. Her heart tumbled over. The sensation stole her breath. Blinded and robbed of speech by his pure male appeal, she could only stare. Why had he become so bleak and cold in the intervening years? And what was thawing the ice?

If it wasn't impossible, she could almost—almost—believe he really wanted this marriage. As if honour and duty had not forced him into offering for her hand. Something inside her unfurled. A sweet kind of longing. A flicker of hope. She doused the flame with a cold dash of reality. He

was a duke. A man who should expect his wife
to come to him pure, unsullied. He would not be
looking so pleased with himself if he knew the
full extent of her past, though he might guess at
some of it.

An Englishman of principle, of honour, could
not possibly marry a woman who had done what
she had done. Using their betrothal to get to
Moreau was one thing. She didn't care what she
had to do in that regard. But marriage was out of
the question. And not at all necessary. Moreau
must be caught and be behind bars before the
banns were called.

She spun away. Went to the table beside the
bed and poured a glass of water. Anything to
keep her hands busy, to resist the temptation he
presented. 'So the purpose for our drive tomorrow is to seek him out?'

'He could be anywhere in the district. We need
to net him before he gets close to Falconwood.'

She turned back to face him and was glad to
see the man of ice had returned. He was handsome, no matter what he did, but when the ice
cracked, when he smiled, he was overwhelming.

'It is good of Madame Vitesse to warn us, and
I am grateful you told me. You could have said
nothing.'

'We have an agreement.' He leaned against
the door frame. 'And, besides, she could have

sent a similar note to you.' His gaze narrowed. 'Did she?'

'No.'

'Would you have told me if she had?'

Heat crept into her cheeks. 'I don't know.'

He cursed under his breath and moved slowly towards her, like a panther stalking prey. A dark creature of the night who would stop at nothing to get what he wanted. 'Not good enough.'

A shiver rippled through her body, heating places she should not be aware of. The man was positively dangerous.

The closer he got the stiffer her spine became. Every nerve in her body urged her to run. She refused to back away. Would not give him the satisfaction.

He caught her upper arms in a firm but pain-less grip, looking down into her eyes with such intensity, she wanted to look away, but knew she must not or he'd know how weak she was when it came to him.

'Don't think I will give you a chance to act alone,' he ground out. 'I am not going to let you out of my sight. And you will tell me the truth of this overwhelming need to speak to Moreau before I even consider allowing you near him.'

She swallowed the dryness in her throat. 'I shall do what I think best.' Her voice was far hus-kier than she thought possible. Her heart pound-ing hard behind her ribs. Her body tingling as if the air was caressing her skin. She could not stop looking at his mouth, so close to hers, so very beautiful, so very good at kissing.

It descended on hers, gentle, soft, sweet.

She sank into its tenderness with a moan of surrender. Sensations swept her away, the feel of his mouth, the liquid heat in her core, the ache in her breasts.

When he finally broke the kiss she shook her head at him. 'You should go.'

'A man can kiss his betrothed once in a while.' The wicked gleam was back in those dark blue eyes. His hand curved over her breast, firm, hot, gentle. His thumb brushed across the beaded tip of her nipple. 'I won't tell anyone. Will you?'

She couldn't think for the distraction of his touch.

Chapter Eleven

She looked like a goddess in her snowy gown with her chocolate-brown hair in a tumble down her back and over her breasts. Irresistible. Temptation incarnate. All soft curves and pillowy swells. He wanted to take her onto that bed and lick and bite and suck.

The heat of her desire shimmered on her skin. Glowed in her slumberous eyes. Echoed in the catch of her breath. She wanted him, too.

Now. At this moment. And if it was wrong, dishonourable to use it to force her to keep her promise to wed him, he did not care. He would not let her walk away once their quest was over. His pride would not allow it. She was his. His? Where had that come from? This was not about possession, it was about protecting her reputation.

He curled his fingers and tipped her chin with a knuckle. 'Will you?' he asked again.

'No.'

The word was a low, husky murmur that sent his blood careening through his veins, heightening his lust and piercing him with other sweeter emotions. He pulled her tight against his body, taking her mouth with his, plundering the sweet depths, sliding his tongue against the silk heat of hers. He pressed against her hip, thickened and hardened. Ached.

She tilted her pelvis, and he swore he could feel the heat of her centre through the fabric of his trousers. Her hands roamed his shoulders. One stroked down his spine and skimmed his buttocks.

He left the tender softness of her lips to kiss her jaw, the sensitive place beneath her right ear. The clean, fresh smell of her, the scent of jasmine and warm feminine flesh filled his nostrils and his lungs. He opened his mouth and took a bite. Not hard enough to leave a mark but enough to make her shudder.

She gasped. Not a sound of shock or outrage but a sigh of pleasure. Her long black lashes swept up. The gold in her eyes sparkled like treasure as she met his gaze with a sinful abandon he hadn't expected.

The sensual pout of her mouth drove any thoughts of honourable behaviour from his mind, sending pounding heat to his groin. Only an opportunist, a man who lived by his wits would take her momentary weakness to tie her to him irrevocably. He was such a man and the chance was too good to pass up. He gazed down into her face, running his hands through the silken mass of her hair, feeling it slide over his skin like a lover's touch. 'You are so beautiful to look at it hurts.'

Her eyes widened. Surprise. He liked it that he'd surprised her. Something bubbled up in his chest. An odd feeling that made him want to laugh. As if he were young and carefree. As if the lives of thousands did not rest in his hands, and there was only this moment, this woman. Joy. It was joy. He stared at her in wonder. Was it possible that this woman could bring him out of the dark?

A twinge of conscience. A knifing pain deep in his chest. She couldn't. No one could. He was a man who had killed his brother.

Accident. His voice. *Jealousy.* His mother's.

How could he be sure he was right when he didn't remember? A clawing doubt he'd lived with for years. But there was no doubt in his mind that he wanted Minette as his wife. And, ruthless bastard that he was, he would make sure she had no way out.

He pulled her close. Their mouths melded. A perfect fit.

His eyes held the intensity of a predatory male, Minette thought, dizzy with sensation as he ran his fingers through her hair, watching his hand stroke and pet. The expression on his face curled her toes inside her slippers and caused her inner muscles to clench in sweet, painful little pulses. Shivers ran down her spine. Her breasts felt tight and needful of touch.

Her fingers fumbled at the tie of his robe. She wanted to feel the heat of his skin beneath her fingers. With a low murmur, he let the heavy silk fall from his shoulders to puddle on the floor in a whisper. She smoothed her palms over the fine linen of his shirt and felt the thud of his heart against her fingertips. A heart beating as hard as her own.

He was built on the lines of a stallion. Sleek and elegant yet powerfully male. The skin exposed at his throat was more Mediterranean in tone than that of most of his countrymen. Darkly exotic. She breathed him in, the scent of his cologne, bergamot and lemon and the musky scent of him, like dark spices in mulled wine on cold nights.

More. She wanted more. There was no need to deny herself the pleasure he could bring. Marriage was not required for that.

Breathless with desire, she rose on tiptoe and pressed her mouth to his, wooing, seducing, teasing his tongue with hers, arching into his hard wall of chest. A satisfying rumble of pleasure rolled in his throat. A hot wildness inside her held her in thrall as their lower bodies came into con-

tact and she rocked her hips, feeling the pleasure
of his hard-muscled thigh against her pelvis, separated from her only by the thinnest of garments.

Delicious. Tempting. Not nearly enough to satisfy feminine needs driven wild by his kisses. In
a swift movement that had her gasping, he swept
her up in his arms and dropped her in the centre
of the bed. He leaned over her, a lock of black hair
falling onto his forehead. Unable to resist, she
brushed it back and he smiled down at her with
low-lidded sensual pleasure on his face.

A starkly beautiful man. And not the least bit
cold.

She reached up for him and he lowered his
head, brushing his mouth across hers, his tongue
tracing the seam with delicious little flicks. In return, she nipped at his lower lip. His hiss of indrawn breath, a sound of pleasure-pain, jolted to
her core. Her insides felt liquid, her breasts tingling in anticipation of the touch of a man who
was clever with his lips and tongue.

He raised his head, looking down at her as if
considering the effect of his actions, like a master craftsman checking his work.

'Freddy,' she demanded, pulling at his shoulders, wanting the weight of him against her hot,
demanding skin.

His gaze searched her face as if seeking an answer to a question he had not posed.

Had she been too bold? Too demanding? Was he a man who preferred to take control?

Right at this moment she didn't care. She wanted, no, she needed, what his kisses promised. She raised herself up on her elbows, pressing small kisses to the line of his lightly stubbled jaw, the rasp against her lips an erotic reminder of his masculinity. Heat bloomed upwards from her belly. Her core ached.

She grazed her teeth against his throat.

One lithe spring and he landed on the mattress beside her, his weight rolling her towards him as he cupped her face in his large, warm hands, his gaze fixed on her face. 'There is no chance of going back after this. No possibility of crying off.'

Dark warning filled his voice. And triumph.

Her mind cleared of the sensual haze that had held her in thrall. The realisation that once again he was using the attraction between them, her weakness, to control her, as Pierre had. Using her for his own purposes. And when he had what he wanted, what then? Would he leave her in this house with his mother and continue with his life, honour and duty satisfied?

The very idea was a betrayal, yet without question all a convenient wife could hope for.

'That was not our agreement.' She pushed at his shoulder. 'I believe it is time you returned to your own chamber.'

Bleakness filled his eyes. 'Your idea of our agreement, you mean.'

'The betrothal lasts only until Moreau is in custody.'

In one swift move he left the bed and picked up his robe. 'Then you need to stop playing with fire.'

He unlocked the door and left her with her body humming with desire and her heart feeling as if it had been ripped in two.

Because what she had seen in his eyes had been frustration, but also, she thought, hurt. Was it possible, when all that was between them was the need to bring down a traitorous spy? It hardly seemed likely. And that meant she was allowing her own emotions to colour her judgement.

The next morning, Minette wasn't sure whether to expect Freddy to take her driving or not. She'd met with the gardener, discussed what was available from the flowerbeds and greenhouses and prepared a list of what would have to be ordered from the nurseryman he had recommended. Then she'd gone upstairs and dressed for riding. Now ready and waiting in the drawing room, she could not help wondering if Freddy would, after her rejection of his advances, set out alone. Or she might have if she hadn't known deep in her heart that he was a man to whom his honour meant a great deal. He would keep his word.

When he entered the drawing room in breeches and top boots that set off his muscular legs, and a coat that skimmed wide shoulders she knew intimately, she was both relieved and saddened. Relieved that he had kept his promise and saddened that they could never be more than friends. If that. Likely he would want nothing at all to do with her after this was over.

A cool gaze swept her person. A nod of approval. 'The horses are saddled.'

So they were back to chilly distance. She felt the loss but had to be glad. It would be easier to keep her own longings in check. And yet from the way her pulse fluttered she was no closer to keeping her longings under control this morning than she had been the previous night.

He escorted her out to the stableyard, where the horses stood ready. A small chestnut mare with a white blaze on her forehead and three white stockings carried the lady's saddle. The mare tossed her head and sidled, pleasing Minette no end. She'd half expected him to order her a quiet horse. The other animal was a beautiful bay gelding with black points.

They mounted up and set off down the drive. Both horses were fresh and ready to run, but well behaved enough to hold steady in the trot.

'What is your plan for this morning? Go to Maidstone and see if he is there?' she asked.

'Too obvious. I wrote to the commanding officer and warned him to keep an eye out for unusual activity. He's a man I knew at university.'

'And us?'

'We protect Falconwood. I thought about it last night. If the occupants of the house are his target, he will need a base of operations.'

The frost in his matter-of-fact tone, the lack of the warmth she'd begun to enjoy in his company was a painful reminder of her rejection of him the previous evening. It was exactly what she had wanted. Then why did it hurt?

'A local inn, perhaps? We could ask at those close by.'

He nodded. 'We could but I have a better idea. The vicar's wife, Mrs Farmer, knows everything and everyone in the district. She will know if any strangers have moved into the parish.' He shot her a hard look. 'She would also expect a visit from the future Duchess of Falconwood, given that it is a family tradition to be wed in the parish church.'

Minette tried not to wince. It was terrible how many people they were involving in their lie. Yet it made perfect sense. No one would question their reason for visiting this Mrs Farmer, thus they would not alert Moreau should he be nearby.

'Will she not be offended by my arriving in such a fashion?' Ladies did not call in their riding habits as a general rule.

'We will make a formal visit later in the week,' he said. 'Mrs Farmer is an old friend. She will be delighted to see us. News travels fast in the country and she would be disappointed if I did not land on her doorstep my first morning home.'

'Mrs Farmer holds a special place in your life?'

'The Reverend Farmer was tutor to me and my brother. He used to bring us home with him sometimes for tea and scones. They were kind.' His dark eyes shuttered. 'Especially kind during my convalescence.'

Minette could remember what it was like to have neighbours who cared for one. Without them she would have perished on the day of the fire. They had hidden her away from the soldiers for days, before they had passed her on to a group of nuns who were escaping the area.

In the end, it hadn't done her a bit of good because she had ended up in Moreau's hands. But they had tried to help and if she ever saw them again she would want to express her gratitude.

It was another perfect June day and the ride to the village church took a scant twenty minutes. A man working in the small front garden of the stone house beside the church came and took their horses. By the time they had walked up the path to the front door a maid was waiting to greet them. She showed them into a comfortably furnished parlour. A plump grey-haired woman in a lace cap and a plain chintz gown rose as they entered.

'Your Grace,' the woman said, dipping a curtsey. 'How good of you to call so soon after arrival at Falconwood.'

'I am glad we found you home, since we sent no warning. Is your husband around?'

'Called out to visit a parishioner, I'm afraid. The Widow Redfurn. She's been ill in her bed for days.' Her glance went to Minette, her grey eyes twinkling.

'May I introduce you to my betrothed, Miss Minette Rideau,' Freddy said.

The woman curtseyed again. If she had notice the strain in Freddy's voice she didn't show it. But Minette had noticed. Clearly he did not like deceiving this woman. She held out a hand. 'I am very glad to meet you, *madame*. His Grace has informed me of your past kindness.'

Mrs Farmer blushed and beamed with pleasure. 'My husband and I have always been fond of Freddy, him and his brother. Pair of mischievous lads. Always up to something they were.'

Freddy's expression softened. 'And we knew where to come when we were in a scrape.'

Mrs Farmer smiled at Minette. 'My husband had a soft spot for those two lads. Not an ounce of malice in either of them, he always says. It was the worst of bad luck, that accident. And so I'll say to anyone who asks.'

Her voice held a bit of a challenge, for which Minette felt grateful on Freddy's behalf. Before she could ask about this rush to defend him,

Mrs Farmer gestured for them to sit. 'You will take tea?'

'Absolutely.' Freddy deposited his hat on a side table and helped Minette to sit, before sprawling beside her on the sofa. 'Tell us all the news. It is an age since I was here. How fares everyone?'

Having rung the bell for tea, Mrs Farmer sat down and began to talk about what seemed like an endless list of people. The tea tray arrived. The tea was drunk and still the gossip continued. Minette did her best to look interested when she was dying for Freddy to ask the all-important question.

'Mrs Pearson's husband died last year, you know,' the woman said, leaning forward with a sad expression. 'She moved to Yorkshire to live with her daughter.'

'Did she sell the house?' Freddy asked.

Mrs Farmer shook her head. 'Leasing. She was at her wits' end, with no one local interested. She had to leave a solicitor to handle the matter.'

'Really?' Freddy said.

'It will be a blessing if she can find a tenant. If not she'll have to let it go and her Sammy always swore it would go to his grandson. It would be a real blow if she can't honour his wishes.'

'Have her to send word to me,' Freddy said. 'I could likely make use of the land, if not the house.'

'Oh.' Mrs Farmer looked surprised.

'What is it?' Freddy asked.

She shook her head.

'You asked Mother,' Freddy said in a flat tone.

Her face coloured. 'I mentioned it, but she said that while she could see you purchasing the land, Mrs Pearson's pure foolishness in wanting to keep it was not to be encouraged.'

Freddy got to his feet. 'As I said, if she doesn't find a tenant have her write to me.' He turned to Minette. 'It is time we were going if I am to show you more of the estate, my dear.'

They made their farewells, and Minette promised she would call with Freddy later in the week and discuss arrangements for the wedding with the Reverend.

'You didn't ask her about strangers.'

She sounded worried, as if she feared he could not protect her from this Moreau. A stinging blow to his ego indeed. Or perhaps it was simply part of the game she was playing with him. A way to lull him into a false sense of security. 'Asking would only make her curious. She would have told me if anyone new had moved in or been asking questions.'

The furrow in her brow said she was not entirely satisfied. 'So what do we do now? Seek him in Maidstone?'

'Hardly. Not with the ball in the offing.'

'You would let Moreau go free for the sake of a stupid ball?'

He decided to be honest. Up to a point. 'It is not stupid. The coincidence of the ball and Moreau travelling to this district at the same time is too much to discount.'

'You think to let him come to you. It is a very dangerous ploy.'

So intelligent. Whatever she had been doing in France she had not been sitting in a nunnery, saying prayers. Her appearance at the Ramsgate and her responses to his far-from-respectable kisses meant she had been involved in something far less innocent, something dangerous. And Moreau was at the heart of it. And was she warning him? Or pushing him one way so he would go in the direction she preferred?

The way he did with Mother.

He would have to tread very carefully if he was going to find out exactly where she stood in regard to this Frenchman. He'd hoped to gain her trust, but since he hadn't he would have to treat her as an enemy, until proved otherwise. 'Do you have a better idea?'

'How can you stop him, if someone at the ball is his ultimate goal?'

'We will watch. I would like to take a look at this farm that is up for lease. If I recall it correctly, it is quite isolated.'

'Oh.' She nodded and brightened considerably.

'Yes. It is the sort of thing that would be very useful. A place to hide. Do we go there now?'

'That is where we are headed.'

'You don't think we will scare him off?'

'If a tenant had taken up residence, Mrs Farmer would have told us. There isn't an ant that moves in this parish without her knowing.'

To his surprise, Minette blushed. The realisation why hit him a second later. 'The servants at the manor are completely trustworthy. Mother wouldn't allow anything else. One word of gossip about the doings of Falconwood and they would be tossed out onto the street.'

'Your mother is a formidable woman.'

'True.' He grinned. Couldn't help it. 'Not looking forward to your interview later?'

'I think it is going to be difficult. The head gardener was astonished that I was meeting with him and kept saying he would have to check with the "missus".'

Anger scored his insides, which were already raw enough. 'I'll have a word with him.'

'I really don't think we should be upsetting your mother to no purpose.'

He repressed the urge to tell her that he didn't care what she thought was going to happen after they caught Moreau, they would be wed. One battle at a time. It was wisdom he'd learned early. And this particular battle wasn't going to be easily won.

Beyond the village he turned off the main road and up one of the lanes that wound its way from farm to farm. The Pearson place was one of the most remote. They rode side by side at an easy walk, each apparently busy with their own thoughts. A rabbit darted out in front of them. Her mare startled and tossed its head but she quickly brought it under control. Whereas with another woman he might have moved closer ready to grab the reins, he merely gave her room to manoeuvre. She gave him a small smile of triumph as the horse quickly settled.

He'd already seen that she had an excellent seat and managed the spirited mare with ease. It pleased him to watch her lithe body sink into her saddle, her competent hands guiding the mare. He pictured them riding around the estate together, visiting tenants, discussing plans. He stilled. He was thinking like the Duke of Falconwood. Not like the second son. It was a bit of a shock to re-alise he was coming to accept his role in life. Because she would be part of it.

This would be his last job for Sceptre.

It would have to be. A man with a wife, with the kind of responsibilities that went with the dukedom, could not continue to play ducks and drakes with the estate's future by letting Mother have a free hand as he had been doing these past several years. It needed a different hand on the reins, according to his steward. Mother had too many old-fashioned notions. He'd seen the evidence of that on their ride this morning. The idea of serving the place where he grew up no longer felt like a penance. Not if he had the help of a woman he cared about. Liked. Lusted after. None of those words seemed to cover exactly what he felt for Minette, although he certainly felt all of them. And he still wasn't sure she'd have him, not in the way he wanted, on terms he would have to make clear before the wedding, if he was going to be fair.

The hedgerows were full of dog roses and the air redolent with their scent. The likelihood of meeting traffic on such a remote lane was slight, but it would be better to be sure. At the first gate they came upon, he called a halt. 'We'll cut across country.' He lifted the latch with his crop and ushered her through.

The mare rolled her eyes but trotted through as nice as you please. Minette held her at a stand while he closed the gate behind them.

'Which way?' she asked.

'Straight across.'

She eyed the distance with a look of mischief. 'I wager I can be over the wall before you. I dare you.'

'No,' he said.

The mare needed little encouragement. *'En avant, Freddy,'* she cried over her shoulder over the thud of hoofbeats.

Freddy urged his horse to follow. Damnation, she was a fine horsewoman. There was no doubt he would win but… His heart rose in his throat as he recalled the nasty drop on the other side of the wall.

'Minette. Stop,' he yelled, encouraging his gelding to greater effort when she didn't appear to hear him.

His heart pounded in his chest. His vision narrowed to one horse, one rider and the looming wall. The image of a twisted, broken body careened through his mind. Not his brother's this time but hers. And then they were neck and neck. He threw himself off his mount and grabbed at her horse's headstall, using his weight to bring the animal to a bone-wrenching halt. The mare stood, chest heaving, three short yards from the low stone wall, while his own mount swerved, slowed and started cropping at the grass a short distance away.

Fury in her eyes, she raised her crop. *'Idiot. Qu'est-ce tu fais?'*

He grabbed the whip from her hand and threw it down. 'You are the idiot. Do you know what is on the other side of that wall? No. Of course you don't. You'd sooner get yourself killed than lose a race.' Nausea rolled through his gut as he heard his voice speak the words that had resided so long deep in his soul. He took a step back. Pain shot up his leg. Damn it. He'd twisted his ankle. Furious, he let go of the bridle and hobbled across the grass to collect his mount.

When he had himself mounted and his horse turned around she was at the wall, looking over. She glanced over at him with an expression of chagrin.

'*Mon Dieu*. One would never guess the ditch was there.' She gave a little shudder. 'I beg your pardon.'

His heart refused to settle. His blood was surging hot in his veins. His throat was still dry. 'Even a schoolboy knows better than to go at a hedge he has never seen before.'

A red flush spread upwards over her face. 'Perhaps an English schoolboy,' she shot back. 'In France our boys have more courage.'

A red haze blurred his vision. The picture of her broken and bleeding on the ground slithered across his mind. 'Courage? Crass stupidity, more like. Perhaps you need to be led.'

She glared at him. 'Try it, if you are in the mood to lose a hand.'

Dammit, she'd apologised. What that hell was wrong with him that he couldn't let it go when she'd come to no harm? But he couldn't. The past remained too close to the surface. An unhealed wound. 'The gate is over there.' He pointed with his whip.

They once more moved off in silence, but it was no longer friendly and comfortable.

'You were limping. Are you injured?' she asked stiffly.

'No.'

Her lovely mouth twisted. 'Perhaps I should look to make sure.'

His blood turned to ice. Just the thought of her seeing… 'I did no more than wrench my ankle.' An ankle that did not like rough treatment at the best of times.

She looked away but not before he caught the tremble of her lower lip. A sniff. Was she crying?

'Minette?' Something inside him twisted painfully.

She turned back to face him, her eyes suspiciously moist. 'Why does it seem that you bring out only the worst in me?'

It was like a blow to his gut, those words. His mother had always said he brought out the worst in his brother, too. He closed himself off from the stab of pain. 'I beg your pardon if my presence troubles you. I shall be more than happy to return you to Falconwood.'

She stared at him. 'You will not be rid of me so easily, Your Grace.' She lifted her chin. 'Are we near the farm we seek?'

Damn it all, she was back to Your Gracing him. 'Beyond the next field.'

'Are their further dangers I should be aware of?'

A curse caught in his throat. Pain pierced his

chest. She was making it sound as if her near accident had been his fault. His gut fell away. She was right. It would have been. He should have warned her about the lie of the land. Had he been with another male, he would have done so the moment they entered the field. 'Nothing I am aware of.' He sounded as stiff and cold as she did, when he should be feeling glad no mishap had occurred. After a small pause, as if she expected him to say more, she turned her horse and set off at a brisk trot.

It seemed their brief hours of truce were over.

Chapter Twelve

Why could he not have simply accepted her apology instead of scowling and looking grim?

Did he think she did not care that she could have badly injured his horse?

The blood in her veins seethed with her anger at his injustice, as well as her embarrassment at her temper.

When they reached the gate she waited in frigid silence while he let them both through and closed it behind them.

He came up alongside her. 'I apologise for my rudeness. I feared for your safety.'

While his face remained grim, his tone was sincere. The hurt inside her subsided. 'Apology accepted. I had no wish to cause you concern, but I can assure you I have survived more than one tumble.'

The muscle in his jaw flexed. 'Not every fall is survivable.'

It was then that she remembered his brother. The reason for his unreasonable fury was suddenly clear. Not that she was about to let him wrap her in cotton wool but she should not have been quite so angry.

'I beg your pardon for striking out at you.'

His lips twitched at the corners. 'Likely I would have done the same if someone took control of my horse.'

She smiled at him. 'It seems we are both endlessly sorry. Shall we put it out of our minds?'

He nodded. 'The Pearson farmhouse is over that hill. We will enter the lane up ahead and come at it from the road.'

'In case anyone is lurking about.'

A small smile curved his lips. 'Exactly.'

The distance to the farmhouse took no more than a few minutes to cover. It was a thatched house washed white and gleaming in the sun. Several outbuildings ranged behind the house. No animals. No sign of inhabitation.

And yet…the place did not feel deserted. 'Someone is here.'

A surprised glance shot her way. 'I was thinking the same thing.'

'*D'accord.* What do we do? Pretend to notice nothing amiss and knock on the door?'

'I'm not out to invite trouble.' He raised his arm and pointed to the buildings and the house as if telling her something about them. 'I wish we could get closer.'

'Moreau would know me in an instant.'

'And you could tell me if he actually had chosen this place in which to hide.'

'Damned if we do—'

'And if we don't,' he finished. At that moment the door to the house opened and a grey-haired man stepped out.

'Hello?' he called out. 'Can I help you?'

'Not Moreau,' Minette confirmed over the pounding of her heart. It was already slowing now that she knew he was not the man they sought.'

'Will you please leave the talking to me?' Freddy asked as they started closer.

How could she say no when he asked so nicely? 'As you wish.'

He cocked a brow, but there was definitely a hint of a smile curving his lovely mouth. Perhaps she was truly forgiven.

The man strode into the courtyard and they brought their horses to a halt beside him.

'Good day,' Freddy said. 'Falconwood.'

He didn't introduce Minette. The man looked like some sort of well-to-do tradesman.

'Pocock,' he said.

'Ah,' Freddy replied. 'The solicitor.' He looked about him. 'I didn't realise you were here, since there is no visible transport. I heard the place was available for lease.'

'Yes,' Pocock said, squinting against the sun as he looked up. 'My man went off to the village in the gig to arrange for a cleaning woman to go in once a week, to make sure the place is clean and to check on the place.'

'No tenant in the offing?' Freddy said.

Pocock shook his head.

Minette wasn't sure whether to be pleased or sorry. The thought of Moreau taking residence so close to where she was living was nerve-racking, but it would have meant they knew where he was.

'I'm surprised you didn't take up the lease, Your Grace, it butting up on your land,' Pocock said. 'The house is barely habitable, but it might do for a labourer.'

Freddy looked thoughtful. 'I'll do it. Send the papers to my steward.'

Pocock's jaw dropped. 'I was told Falconwood didn't need more land.'

'I've changed my mind.' He touched his crop to his hat. 'Send the papers along to my steward at your earliest convenience.' He turned back. 'Oh, and if anyone else enquires about leasing the property, anyone at all, would you let me know?'

'Certainly, Your Grace.'

Freddy said nothing until they were well out of earshot. 'Old Pearson would have been pleased.'

'It is kind of you,' she said. 'But do you really need more land?'

'Need, no. But having a legitimate interest

in the place will make it easier to make sure no one moves in that I haven't vetted personally.' He pointed to a nearby copse. 'From just beyond those trees there is a good view of Falconwood's park. I will have Barker set up a command post there so we are not taken by surprise.'

He was actually telling her his plan. She couldn't help it, she smiled at him and, while he didn't blink the way Granby did, his eyes widened a fraction, a response that warmed her in ways it should not. 'Unfortunately it brings us no closer to finding where Moreau is at this moment.'

His expression darkened. 'No. It seems we are going to have to let him come to us. But with my men here we should have advance notice of any strangers in the vicinity.'

'And there's always Mrs Farmer.'

A smile appeared on his face and he looked like the mischievous boy Mrs Farmer had spoken of. It was enchanting. It touched a place inside her that was far too vulnerable for her liking. But it did seem as if they were on friendly terms again and for that she could only be glad.

And that feeling of gladness was a worry.

Because, in the end, she was going to disappoint him terribly.

While Minette discussed flower arrangements with his mother, Freddy closeted himself in his steward's office. The man seemed overly grate-

ful and a little fearful. It didn't take Freddy long
to understand why. His mother had been assidu-
ous in her duties. Running the estate the way his
father had. Everything done logically but without
an iota of humanity. An unpaid lease resulted in
an immediate eviction. An innovation resulted
in a reduction of farm labourers. The pattern that
emerged was troubling. All of those gone from
his land were people he'd thought of as friends.
People who'd believed him when he'd said the
death of his brother had been a terrible accident.

In particular, his old friend Jake, the under-
gamekeeper's son, who had started them off. He
looked up from the ledgers. 'Where did Jake's
family go?'

The man looked uncomfortable. 'North. To
look for work. The factories are always hiring.'

'Jake was in line for the position of head
groom.' No one knew horses like Jake. Nausea
pushed up into his throat. He should have known
about this. Stopped it. 'Do you have a forward-
ing address?'

'No, Your Grace.'

'And the Biggses?'

Bill Biggs had been at the bridge, cheering
them on like a madman. His father had been a
labourer on Falconwood lands, as had his father
before him.

'Her Grace decided to pull their cottage down.

It was in sight of the folly. A bit of an eyesore, you understand.'

That was what had been missing from the view when he and Minette had walked around the lake. 'Locate them.'

'Yes, Your Grace.'

He leaned back in his chair with a sigh. 'How many more?'

'The Clappers and the Webbs. They missed a payment on their leases because of a bad harvest.'

'Try to find them also. Webb had a widowed sister.'

The steward shook his head. 'She died two years ago.'

He cursed softly. 'Not because of us?'

'No.' The man's tone of voice dismissed any such notion, to Freddy's relief. 'A bad cold. Went to her lungs. Your mother did all that was proper. Fuel for her fire. The doctor.'

Thank God she'd had that much heart. Clearly, he could no longer leave the management of the estate to Mother. He hadn't worried about it because the income was always as expected. But money wasn't everything. A landowner looked after his people. And a man took care of his friends.

The butler rapped on the door and came in. 'Her Grace sends her compliments. The ladies are taking tea in the green drawing room.'

The drawing room wasn't the place to discuss these particular issues with his mother, so he would still his tongue for now and enjoy Minette's company. He looked at his steward. 'Let me know as soon as you have located any of our people.' He gave the man a sharp stare. 'Me, you understand. No one else.'

The steward touched his forelock. 'It will be my pleasure.'

The sincerity in the man's eyes was genuine. The steward was clearly glad Freddy was taking up his affairs in person. No doubt he thought he'd left it a bit late.

Damn him. He was right.

When he wandered into the green drawing room, one of the least friendly rooms in the house, he found the two ladies sitting in what he could only describe as a strained silence. If Mother would only unbend to Minette a little, make her feel welcome, he would be able to forgive her anything. The realisation came as a surprise he did not want to examine too closely.

'How are the plans for the ball coming along?' he asked, sitting beside Minette on the sofa opposite his mother, who was presiding over the most formal tea set they owned. Likely using it as a means of intimidation. Something she had off to a fine art.

'I had a long discussion with Mr Jevens.' Minette picked up a portfolio bound with a green ribbon and opened it. 'I made some sketches of the ballroom and the terrace with some ideas for how we might utilise the flowers from the greenhouses.'

His mother looked down her nose. 'As I said earlier, Miss Rideau, I will look at your proposals and discuss them with the staff when I have a moment.'

In other words, Minette's ideas were not worth her time. Freddy looked through the drawings. The sketches of the rooms were excellent, giving the proportions and proper perspectives, but the ideas for the arrangement of the vegetation was extraordinary. 'You have brought the outdoors inside.' He looked closer. 'These are orange trees.'

'Jevens said that if he is careful he can have them all in full bloom. The room will be filled with their perfume. He believes the trellises will not be too difficult to construct with some help from some of the men from the estate, and they will be perfect for the roses.'

'What of the flower beds?' Mother said. 'They will take years to recover if you strip them of blooms.'

'Jevens assured me that would not be the case,' Minette said. 'Indeed, he was saying that so few of the roses have been picked these past many years that they will benefit from a little thinning.'

'The Duke did not like flowers inside the house,' Her Grace said. 'He said they made him sneeze. I do not want my guests walking about sniffling. And this idea of yours of setting up the dancing on the terrace will not work. What if it rains?'

'Then we will move the dancing indoors,' Freddy said.

'Why have it outdoors at all?'

'It will be a full moon,' Minette said. 'It will be romantic. According to my sister, our mother often arranged *al fresco* parties.'

'That is France,' Mother said in a quelling tone. 'This is England.'

He could see that Minette was frustrated by his mother's intractability, but he was proud of the way she had made her case so reasonably. She would make a good Duchess.

And he was going to make sure she did not slip through his fingers, even if he did have to play dirty to do it. Last night he'd let his honour get in the way of accomplishing his goal. It would not happen again.

'I think it is a fine idea,' Freddy said.

Mother's spine stiffened. 'Well, if you do not mind your guests going home chilled to the bone and blaming us for their subsequent illness, I shall have nothing more to say on the matter.'

'Good. Then the matter is settled.'

'I would still appreciate your views on the detail,' Minette said to Mother, attempting to act as peacemaker.

As if she had not heard, Mother poured the tea

and handed each of them a cup. 'I understand you spent the past hour or so with Carter, Frederick.'

That was one way to change the subject.

'I did.'

'You should have come to me if you have questions. Carter is all very well in his way, but he has not had the benefit of working under your father. He has no concept of our history. Of what is important.'

The man had been his choice after their old steward had begged to be permitted to retire. He forced himself to remain outwardly calm. 'He understands modern farming methods.'

'Modern.' She tutted. 'What was good enough for your father and for his father should be good enough for you.'

For the son who had stolen the true heir's birthright. He could hear the meaning in the inflection in her voice. He quelled his anger. Swallowed the bitterness. 'If the estate doesn't change with the times, our fortunes will suffer.'

Her mouth tightened. Then she trilled a brittle laugh. 'The man is impossible. He actually suggested ploughing up the five-acre meadow and planting some sort of disgusting vegetable. And then he wanted to buy some infernal machine to sow seeds.'

'I know. I told him to do so.'

Her back stiffened. 'You overruled my decision?' She stirred her tea.

'Because it was wrong.'

She fairly vibrated with indignation. 'My decisions are those your father would have made.' The tea in her cup became a veritable storm. 'He must be turning in his grave. If your brother had lived, he would know the right way to go about things.'

Back to that. Of course. 'I am sure he would.'

Minette took his mother's cup and set it on the table. 'Please, Your Grace. Do not upset yourself.'

'I know what I am doing,' Freddy said. 'I have been reading up on modern methods.'

Mother gazed at him sorrowfully. 'I might be less concerned had you applied yourself while your father was alive. Night after night he bemoaned your lack of application. Your disinterest. All you thought about was raking around Town. You were a constant source of disappointment.'

Minette gasped.

Freddy closed his eyes briefly. The silent accusation in his father's eyes and the bitter condemnation of his mother out of his father's hearing, along with his own guilt, had driven him to the worst kind of excesses, until Gabe had come along and given him a purpose. And then his father had died and left him with the blasted dukedom.

'It is all water under the bridge. You have been carping at me for years to take up my responsibilities, so here I am.'

Mother bristled. 'You should have discussed

these decisions with me before countermanding my instructions.'

His hand clenched on his saucer. A taut silence fell.

'Mr Jevens thinks the weather will be fine for the ball,' Minette said. 'Something to do with his rheumatism.'

The look of appeal for support she sent Freddy made him take a deep breath. He had fallen into Mother's trap of trading barbs. As usual she had goaded and goaded until he could stand it no longer.

'If you ladies will excuse me, I am going to visit the home farm this afternoon.' What he really needed to do was get away from his mother before he tossed her out on her ear.

Chapter Thirteen

'I suppose it is time I went down,' Minette said to Christine.

'Yes, *mademoiselle*.'

The thought of another meal caught between Freddy and his mother made Minette shiver. The way his mother battered him with her disdain explained a great deal about the man. Particularly his chilly distance.

Clearly, his mother held him responsible for her elder son's death. Shouldn't she be happy that one of her sons had survived?

Poor Freddy. She had no trouble imagining his feelings, the guilt laid on him by his mother. Every time she thought about Moreau and the damage he could do to her family, she felt ill. It was why she had to make sure he was stopped.

Christine placed a sprig of silk flowers in her hair. *'Tout finis.'*

'Thank you.' She moved away from the mirror

and picked up her shawl. Her gown was modest enough but somehow the chilly gaze of the Duchess always made her feel as if she was flaunting her wares.

When Christine opened the door, Minette was surprised to see a young footman loitering outside. He bowed. 'His Grace's compliments, Miss Rideau. Dinner will be served in the dining room in the ducal apartments this evening.'

She had never heard of the ducal apartments. There was something about the footman's expression, the twinkle in his eye perhaps that seemed a little conspiratorial. As if he was privy to some interesting information. Or was it just the novelty of dining *en famille*? She couldn't help but be glad if the Duchess had decided to be a little less formal. Or perhaps not. Perhaps the Duchess would give even more free rein to her sharp tongue. She winced.

'If you would follow me, miss,' he continued, 'His Grace asked me to show you the way.'

He led her down the stairs and along a corridor on the ground floor past the library and along a passage that ran at a right angle. This was one of the wings of the house she hadn't yet seen.

He opened a door and stood back to let her into a room that was very different from anything she had seen in the rest of the house. Not a dining room but a sort of parlour. A room with overstuffed chairs, dark-panelled walls and several rather battered tables. It looked comfortable. Welcoming. And very male.

Freddy strode towards her. 'I hope you don't mind. Mother decided not to join us this evening. She is taking dinner on a tray in her room. I thought we might allow ourselves to be a little more comfortable.'

'Where is here?'

'This is my suite of rooms. Where I entertain friends without disturbing Mother.'

'When the footman mentioned the ducal suite I envisaged something different. I like it.'

'May I offer you a glass of wine? Or sherry? Dinner will be in the room next door. Patterson will let us know when they are ready for us.'

'Sherry, please.'

While he went to the sideboard against one wall, containing several decanters and glasses, she walked over to the window, which, as she approached, she realised was, in fact, a door out into a shrubbery with a path leading through it to the stables.

'Have all the Dukes used these apartments?'

He came back with her glass. 'No. These were the rooms assigned to me once I left the schoolroom.'

The heir at the time no doubt had something far grander in the main part of the house. 'It all seems very comfortable.' Unlike the rest of the house, which seemed cold and oppressive.

His shoulders eased and she realised he'd been expecting some sort of criticism with regard to his choice. 'It is. I spend little time at Falconwood as a rule and these rooms suit me very well.' He flashed a grin. 'I like being able to come and go as I please.'

She sipped at her sherry. It was of the finest quality. 'Something a young man might see as an advantage.'

A smile curved his lips and mischief flashed in his eyes. She had never seen him look quite so approachable. 'Mmm…'

She laughed at the noncommittal sound.

'Dinner is served, Your Grace,' the footman said, entering through the internal door to the room next door.

Freddy held out his arm and led her into the small dining room, panelled to match the previous room with a dining table large enough to seat six comfortably but set for two, the places adjacent to each other and facing yet another French window overlooking the shrubbery. An array of dishes was set out on the table—a duck, asparagus, a meat pie of some sort and a fish in white sauce.

The butler pulled out a chair for her, while Freddy seated himself.

Patterson poured red wine into their glasses and stepped back. 'Will there be anything else, Your Grace?'

An enquiring glance from Freddy had her shaking her head. 'No, thank you,' he said.

He gestured for the man to leave and they were alone. Surprising. Unusual.

Freddy must have seen something in her face because he smiled all too fleetingly. 'I thought we would be better off serving ourselves, if you don't mind. There are things we need to discuss that I would prefer to keep between us, and opportunities for private conversation are rare in this house.'

True enough. There seemed to be a footman in every room and at every corner. They were unobtrusive and no doubt carefully screened for discretion, but there were some things to which no one should be privy. Conversations and other things. She felt her face warm. Blushing. At the thought of his visit to her last evening. Had any of those footmen seen him enter her room in *dishabille*? Would they report him to his mother? The morals of the *ton,* or rather their lack of them, created little stir, as long as those involved were not innocent misses with impeccable virtue. As she'd discovered at first hand.

'What is on your mind?'

'Barker will be *in situ* at the farm tonight and will scour the neighbourhood for any sign of our quarry.'

The thought of Moreau stole her appetite. She watched without pleasure while he carved the duck and put portions of some of the other dishes on a plate and passed it across. 'Is it your belief that it is Moreau's intention to target someone at our ball?'

He stared at the slice of duck on his fork. 'Our enquiries have not located him in the north, though we know he took a post chaise to York. After that, he disappeared. I honestly don't see the connection but I believe we would be taking a risk not to assume he will arrive here in Kent during our celebration. If I am wrong and the garrison is his goal, then they have been warned.'

'And if he does not show up at all?'

'Then we will know we have been gulled by your Frenchman.'

Her stomach dipped and then she realised the Frenchman he referred to was not Moreau but Latour. 'I hope he is wrong. The house is vulnerable to attack when we have no idea what he wants.'

'Barker's men will set up observation posts around the house and watch for anyone coming or going. My tiger will liaise between Barker and me two or three times a day.'

'It sounds as if you have done this before.'

He met her gaze. His face was serious. He was worried and trying to hide it. 'More than once.' He addressed himself to his dinner as if what they were discussing was the most commonplace thing, like the weather or a horse race.

She took a sip of her wine. The knowledge

that Moreau might be trapped before she had a chance to speak to him was troubling. She needed to recover her property without anyone knowing. And she couldn't do that unless they discovered where he was staying. It seemed Freddy and his men were focussing all their attention on catching him on the move.

Nom d'un nom, could nothing go smoothly?

His betrothed looked enchanting tonight. Her glossy brown hair, caught high on her head and falling in ringlets on one side, made his fingers itch to pull out the pins. The secrets in her eyes were a constant source of temptation to a mind as curious as his. While she did her best to hide her thoughts, it was clear to Freddy from the way she picked at the food on her plate that she was worried. The exact cause of her concern he had not as yet divined. And clearly she wasn't going to tell him.

The imparting of confidences required a high level of trust, and he didn't have hers. He hadn't even been able to convince her to marry him to save her reputation. A pretend betrothal was as far as she would go. While he didn't blame her for her lack of trust, since he didn't trust himself all that much, he was not going to let her escape her vows.

He was a patient man. If being shut up indoors

for weeks on end because of his foot had taught him one thing, it had taught him endless patience.

'Is the duck not to your taste?' he asked. 'Shall I ask for something else to be sent?'

She startled. 'Oh, no. The duck is delicious. You must excuse me, my mind was wandering.'

'Wool-gathering.'

'Pardon?'

'When someone's mind is engaged elsewhere it is called wool-gathering.'

She laughed. A delightful sound. Full of merriment. 'I beg your pardon. It is rude to gather the wool, I think.'

'No. I like watching your face. You give little away, but you were clearly not pleased by the direction of your thoughts.'

'I was thinking about our plans, what we will do if things go awry.'

She pushed a carrot from one side of her plate to the other. The urge to take her on his lap and feed her one mouthful at a time until he was sure she was suitably nourished had him putting his hands flat on the table in preparation. He forced himself to remain seated. She was a woman of spirit and pride. She would not welcome him ordering her about. Yet.

'Moreau is a clever and devious man,' she mused, sending a potato to join the carrot. 'He might sense a trap.'

The pain in her voice, the way she hid her gaze

made him look forward more than ever to catching up with the man. He wasn't sure what he had done to Minette but apparently it had affected her deeply. 'We will catch him, no doubt about it. Sooner or later he will make a mistake.' He took a swallow of wine. 'Eat. There is no sense in worrying about the future. Plan, yes, but worry, there's no sense to it. We can never know what is to come.' Like becoming a duke because of one stupid bragging statement he'd do anything to retract.

'You advocate patience.' She cast him a brief and considering glance before returning to the rearrangement of her vegetables. Peas were now making the journey, one at a time.

'Eat. If we are to chase French spies around the countryside you will need your strength.'

A small smile appeared and this time her glance did not flitter away. 'You are right. And, besides, I gather your fancy French chef is likely to take a pet if the dishes are sent back untasted.'

'He's as French as my elbow.'

She grinned. 'I know. I met him on my tour with the housekeeper. He was clearly terrified I would ferret out his secret.' She forked up some fish in white sauce. 'I pretended not to notice. French or not, his food is excellent.'

'I will be sure to pass along your approbation.'

For the next few minutes they applied themselves to the meal in front of them in silence, and it wasn't long before they were finished. He rang for the footman to clear away and bring the dessert course. He would have preferred to have done away with the servant's services, but even a duke could only go so far down the road of informality before his servants began to regard him with disfavour. These were things he'd assimilated without realising as a child. Other things he'd had to work harder to learn, like when his father had finally accepted he had a new successor to train.

'What is this?' Minette stared at one of the desserts after the footman had left the room.

'Bread and butter pudding.'

'Pudding.' She made a face. 'It is a very English thing, this pudding.'

'I suppose it is. I hadn't thought about it. However, it was one of my Reggie's favourites. Mother has it served at every meal.' He never touched it, though he had liked it as a boy.

'Another slap across the cheek?' she said.

He frowned. 'I do not understand.'

'Always, she throws the death of your brother in your face. It almost seems that it pleases her to hurt you.'

He stiffened. He wasn't surprised that she had picked up on the relationship between him and his mother—they were, after all, at war, but it was hardly her place to have an opinion. He gave her a quelling look and hoped she would drop the subject.

She raised a brow. 'One feels the chill in the room when you are together.'

'You don't really expect me to respond to that, do you?'

She sighed. '*Tiens.* I will say no more.' She stared at the pudding on her plate and put down her fork. '*Je suis finis.*'

'Hopefully with dessert and not with me. I beg your pardon. Things have been less than pleasant with my mother for a very long time. I have given up caring. Come, let us retire to the sitting room. They will bring tea there while they clear away the dishes.'

They strolled back into the other room. 'You call this a sitting room?'

'It seems more apropos than drawing room. It really isn't elegant enough for such a distinguished term.'

He guided her to the chair by the hearth.

She glanced around, her face carefully blank. A chilly distance had opened up between them, no doubt because he'd refused to let her commiserate with him over his mother's behaviour. He couldn't do it. It would open wounds older than his brother's death.

'I feel as if I should have brought some needlework or some sheets to hem,' she said brightly. Too brightly. 'It is the kind of room where a *maman* plies her needle while *papa* reads aloud.'

A crack of light appeared somewhere in the

darkness inside him. The idea of something as warm as domestic bliss. A far-off dream now dangling before him like a bauble he had only to reach out to grasp. A lie, though. Even when they married, it would never be true for them.

The footman arrived with the tea tray and put it in front of her.

'Everything like clockwork,' she commented.

Glad of a neutral topic to redirect the darkness of his thoughts, he took the seat opposite her and stretched out his legs. 'An establishment of this size cannot run on a whim.'

'But it could be less regimented.'

The implied criticism made him bristle. He wanted to defend, but forced himself to be more rational. 'You see improvements that are needed?'

She pursed her lips. 'The grandeur is impressive.' She gave a sad smile. 'But I would not be the right person to uphold such consequence, I fear. It is a house, not a home. It is cold.'

Like its occupants. The thought lingered, silent, accusing.

He left his chair and sat beside her on the sofa. Her perfume drifted into his lungs with each breath of air. 'You are too modest. You underestimate your abilities.' He took her hand and raised it to his lips, inhaling the scent of her skin to the sound of a soft gasp. 'As my duchess, you would be welcome to make whatever changes you wished. I think we would deal well together as husband and wife.'

'You didn't think so when we met first,' she said, sounding a little bit breathless. 'On board ship.'

That husky sound gave him something he hadn't felt in a long time. Hope. She was attracted to him, and he intended using his every advantage, though it seemed he had some lost ground to make up.

'You mistake the matter,' he said, stroking his thumb over her palm and smiling at the way the small hairs on her wrist stood to attention. 'There is this unwritten gentlemanly code of conduct. A man who is not in the market for a wife does not flirt or in any way show an interest in his friend's little sister-in-law. You were barely eighteen when we met. Gabe knew I had no thoughts of marriage. He would have put a bullet in my brain if I had so much as hinted I found you interesting.'

'Did you?'

'Find you interesting? *Bien sûr.*' He kissed the inside of her wrist and inhaled her delicious scent. 'Do you doubt it?'

'You called me a brat.'

'A smokescreen. As I said, there is a rule. I think you might have been throwing off a little smoke yourself at that time.'

She averted her gaze, and he knew he was right. 'What were you hiding?'

She stilled, but the pulse beat in her wrist picked up speed.

'Very well,' he said. 'It is not important. But, Minette, do not hold my past behaviour towards you against me. It will make for an uncomfortable marriage if you do. And we will be married. Make no mistake.'

'Because of your honour. Because of Gabe.' Her words were calm, accepting, but he wasn't idiot enough to step into that sort of trap.

'Because I want you for my wife.'

Her head whipped around. There was disbelief on her face, but was there hope there also? God, he hoped so. Another woman in his life who couldn't abide him was going to make life hell on earth. Not that he deserved anything much better. To be contemplating marriage when he had sworn he would take no benefit from his brother's death and serve simply as custodian. The only defence he'd had to the accusation in his parents' eyes. But he did not expect his Duchess to live on the proceeds of Fools' Paradise, as he had done these past several years. When he married he would have to keep her in proper style. She'd be entitled to wear the family jewels, too. And she ought to have some of her own. Personal items.

He looked at her left hand. Ringless. He should have bought her a ring, a token, something to mark their engagement. To mark her as his.

Hell's bells, where had this feeling of possession come from?

He tipped her chin with a fingertip and gazed down into those fascinating eyes. 'Well, brat,' he said softly, 'shall we make the best of it?'

And would she let him seduce her this time?

The heat in his gaze made Minette feel giddy with longing. He almost had her believing he wanted this marriage. Almost. The recollection of his face when he'd realised they'd been caught in a compromising position had faded but not completely disappeared.

'I did not arrange for us to be found in the library,' she said. 'The last thing I wanted was to ruin my reputation.' For Nicky's sake.

'I believe you.'

'You do?' She could not keep the surprise from her voice. It was rare for any man to admit he was wrong.

'I do,' he said firmly. 'While you were reckless in coming to my club to find me, foolhardy in the extreme, you were open and honest about your intentions. At Gosport's ball I let past experiences colour my judgement. I should not have said what I did to you that night. But we can't keep apologising for something that has happened. We have to move on.'

Guilt washed over her. 'To be truthful, I wasn't displeased that it happened. It suited my plans.'

He went to speak, and she touched a finger to his lips. 'You must understand.' She stared into her teacup as if it would give her the words she so desperately needed. 'If all else failed, I might have thought trapping you a perfectly acceptable strategy.'

He chuckled softly. 'Honest to a fault. I think my rush to judgement that evening was coloured by your previous partiality for cheating.'

'That I did to annoy you,' she admitted ruefully. 'You seemed so irritated by your role as bear leader. As if you would sooner be anywhere else than playing cards with me.'

'Irritated? So much so I couldn't make out one card from another. All I could think about was kissing you.'

His eyelids dipped a fraction, his gaze dropping to her lips, his mouth softening.

Her breath caught in her throat. The man was positively seductive when he set his mind to it. And his kisses were deliciously tempting, especially as there had been no kissing in her life after coming to England, except for his. There had been no one else she'd wanted to kiss, if she was truthful. Not after Pierre. But there was something else playing on her mind. He was a duke. He had to marry and produce an heir. How would she feel once Moreau was caught and she cried off and he married another?

She would be lying if she said she wouldn't

care. She wouldn't like it one little bit. Not now that they had become co-conspirators, friends and perhaps something more.

Yet what right did she have to hold him to his promise of a marriage of convenience, forced upon him by circumstances in which she had played an active part, even if it had been unintentional?

How could she marry him when she'd given away her virtue to a man he considered an enemy of his country? It didn't matter how honourable Freddy was, or how kind; once Moreau was dealt with in a way so that he could never harm Nicky, she must cry off. For his sake. Whether or not the miniature came to light.

Letting him make love to her, as he so obviously wanted to do, might be one way to make sure he didn't object to her ending their betrothal. He'd know for certain she was no innocent miss.

'So you want to kiss me now?' she asked.

'Can't you tell?'

Eyes hot, he lowered his head, and she lifted hers to meet him halfway.

This she would have. This would be accomplished between them, or she would regret it for ever. She wound her arms around his neck and parted her lips to welcome the most sensual of kisses. The strokes of his tongue against hers. The taste of him. The feel of his heart beating against her breasts. Their loud, frenzied breathing.

His hands were large and warm, one on her spine, the other cradling her nape. She felt cherished. Wanted. She stroked his cheek with her fingertips and slowly they broke apart. His eyes were heavy-lidded, his lips curved in a smile, his chest rising and falling in ragged breaths.

Passion personified. Her blood heated, her core fluttered pleasurably, her nipples felt uncomfortable in the confines of her gown. All that with a kiss and a glance. Dark and delicious passion. The man was a wonder.

In a swift, almost negligent move he lifted her onto his lap, one hand casually stroking her shin while the other toyed with a curl that had slipped from its pins. He had a lithe strength that appealed to her femininity in blood-stirring ways. Made her limbs feel languid.

'What if someone comes in?' she said.

A small smile curved his lips. 'One advantage of being a duke. No one enters unless sent for.' He ducked beneath her chin and first kissed and then licked the base of her throat with the sounds of a connoisseur enjoying a fine wine. 'You smell and taste of my favourite things.'

'And what would they be?'

'Aroused woman and jasmine.'

She couldn't help a smile at the sheer devilment in his voice as he drawled the shocking words. She put a hand to her knee to stop his hand wandering above her garter. 'What about your mother?'

'Believe me, that would never happen.'

Utter confidence. And why not? His mother would never arrive unannounced. Not because she was discreet or understanding, she realised with sadness, but because it would never occur to the woman to visit her son.

'Why the worried face?' he murmured, twirling that unruly curl around his finger. He cast her a sidelong glance that glittered in the light of the candles. 'Are you hoping for rescue?'

'Quite the opposite.'

He cracked a short laugh of genuine amusement. 'You are so hard to read. I never have a clue what you are thinking.'

'That is a good thing. A man needs to be kept off kilter.'

'Who told you that?' he asked as he raised his head to look at where his mouth had been. 'Your sister?'

'Something I overheard once.' Minette should not have been listening. But it was how she had learned just what Nicky had endured to keep her safe. She had learned other things, too. Things that had made her feel oddly breathless and hot. Later, she'd understood. She'd also realised what sort of man Nicky's husband had been. His death had not been much of a loss.

He must have heard a note of bitterness in her

voice because he gave up teasing her breast to look at her face. 'Unhappy memories?'

'Things best forgotten.' She smiled and pushed up to kiss his cheek, knowing full well the effect of the added pressure on his groin.

He ran his fingers in a light caress down her shin. 'Do you know what attracted me to you the first time I saw you?'

'No.'

His hand closed lightly around her ankle. A gesture of possession that she found very much to her liking. 'This. The prettiest ankles I have ever seen stepped on board that ship. And then, when I looked up at your face, I was done for.'

'I don't believe you.'

'Do you know what the next thing I saw was?' He nipped at her ear lobe, and a shiver shot through her body. 'Gabe's face. Giving me the fish eye.'

'Fish… What?'

'Glaring murder. Warning me off.'

'And so you were following orders when you were so rude.'

'Mmm.' He dipped his head. Hot lips seared the rise of her breast, his hand curving beneath the swell to plump it up for better access. 'Delicious.'

Delicious indeed. His mouth hot and wet and his tongue teasing at her flesh.

He groaned softly and caught her around the

shoulders so he could kiss her with open-mouthed ardour. A kiss of skill and temptation that set her body on fire. She turned into him, her breasts, heavy and sensitive, pressed against his hard chest. He cupped her buttocks and lifted her, adjusting her position on his lap, and she felt the hard ridge of his arousal against her hip.

Once she was settled to his satisfaction, he skimmed a hand up her thigh beneath her skirts and a low sound of approval rumbled through his chest.

Chapter Fourteen

When she'd arrived at his club, he'd done his absolute best to remember she was his best friend's sister-in-law. The woman he'd held in his arms was a passionate, sensual female who appealed to his most primitive of male instincts. Warm and delicious in every way.

An unexpected gift in his life he had no intention of refusing. Not when it would ensure she became his wife. And perhaps, since she wasn't objecting, she wanted the decision taken out of her hands. Please, all the saints above, she didn't say no this time.

The rest of it he'd deal with later. Find a way for them to be together. There were ways a man could make love to his wife and ensure no children resulted. If he was careful.

Her tongue tangled with his, her body melted into him. Her sweet, lush bottom rocked against his rock-hard arousal. Lust clawed at the cage of civility. It was all he could do not to lower her to the floor and take her on the carpet. She deserved more. Better than him, better than this. But it was too late for her to have choices.

She may not have intended their discovery in the library at Gosport's ball, but from that moment on it had been too late to turn back. From that second she'd become his responsibility, no matter what she thought. His to protect.

He stood with her in his arms, found his centre of balance and headed for his bedroom, where he'd closed the curtains and lit the candles after dressing for dinner.

A pang of regret twisted in his chest. Tonight his aim was to make her admit the inevitability of their marriage.

'Oh,' she said softly, as he pushed open his chamber door. 'How unexpected.'

He looked around. Tried to see what she saw. The pile of books on the nightstand. His cricket bat, unused for years in the corner. A bow and arrow next to his shotgun on the wall. The rapiers with which he and Reggie had practised swordplay in the Long Gallery above the mantel. The things he and his brother had collected—birds' eggs, rocks, an old flint arrowhead on the desk in front of the window. It was the bedroom that belonged to the boy, not the man. 'I don't spend much time here to be bothered to change it.' In truth, he had never found the heart.

He lowered her feet to the floor, enjoying the friction of her soft body down the length of his, and nuzzled at her throat, licking and nipping until she turned her head and bit him hard on the jaw and lifted her face, offering her lips.

His body hardened to granite.

He took her mouth softly, wooing her with lips and tongue, nudging her backwards in the direction of his bed. She broke free with an awkward laugh. Had he read her wrong? Had the promise of passion he'd sensed in her, the blatant sensuality of a woman ready for more than play, been driven by hope?

The hunger raking at his body did not want to be denied, but forcing her was not an option.

She turned in a slow circle, her face full of puzzlement. 'You aren't the person I thought.'

A cold hand fisted in his gut. It was the sort of thing Mother would say. 'Your meaning?'

'There is a lot of affection in this room, when you often seem so cold and withdrawn. I like it.'

Not quite the comment he'd expected. Mother always complained about the clutter. He was certainly far from cold at the moment.

She opened her arms.

He stepped into them, gazing into her smiling, welcoming face, and felt something shift deep inside him. A change that was both tender and painful, as if something had broken and been formed anew from the pieces, yet they didn't fit perfectly.

Odd thoughts. Why question what was being offered with such generosity of spirit?

He glanced down at the rise of her breasts, slowly caressed the curve beneath with one hand while the other explored the dip of her waist. The full swell filled his palm and rose in creamy magnificence above the neckline of her gown. Such exquisitely generous flesh and so bounteously exposed to his feasting gaze. So temptingly displayed, yet their full glory hidden from his view. Leisurely, despite the urgings pounding in his veins, he paid them homage with his hands and then his lips and then his tongue. They tasted of honey and cream and delicious woman.

Her fingers threaded through his hair, and his skin sprang to life beneath her touch. His own body ached for the same gentle exploration.

He slid one hand down her leg and drew her skirt upwards, stroking the underside of her knee and the soft silken skin above her garter, sensing her shivers of pleasure in the little catches in her breathing.

She cupped the sides of his face in her small hands and rose up on tiptoe to brush her lips against his, pressing up against him, her hips arching into him. 'Freddy,' she murmured, her hands wandering down to clutch at his shoulders, her breathing increasing until she was panting, her hands fumbling at the buttons of his coat.

The longing in her voice required no explanation.

His heartbeat quickened. Naked. He wanted her naked.

He tore off both his jacket and waistcoat. Spun her round. Her head fell forward. Vulnerable. He pressed a hot open-mouthed kiss to her nape, inhaling the scent of jasmine and summer, then made short work of her fastenings, pressing small kisses to each inch of her back as he worked the gown down her hips until it slid to the floor. The corset went next, leaving her in nothing but her sheer chemise and stockings, the swell of her hips and buttocks so tempting beneath the filmy veil as she lifted one foot, using the bedpost for balance.

He prowled around her, admiring every inch of that sweetly tempting female body, high, full breasts, long, slender legs with the dark triangle at the apex of her thighs.

He went down on one knee, removing first one slipper then the other, the scent of her arousal making him so hard it hurt. Lifting the hem of her slip, he untied a garter, peeling her stockings down over her calf and off before massaging her small, perfectly formed ankle and foot. He kissed her knee and the inside of her thigh above the remaining garter. She gave a soft moan. Pleasure. Longing. Want.

His hands shook as he removed her other stocking while she balanced with her hands on his shoulders. He pressed a quick kiss between her thighs, feeling the heat and the dampness against his lips and shuddering at her gasp of shock.

Slowly. He had to go slowly.

He lurched to his feet, relieved when she didn't react to his clumsiness.

To his surprise and delight, she hopped up the steps, arms held out like a tightrope walker, and leaped into the middle of the bed. The bed creaked as it accommodated her weight. She cast him a look from beneath her lashes that was pure wickedness. 'Care to join me?'

With an answering growl, he leaped from the floor to the bed, kneeling beside her, taking her tempting mouth in a searing kiss.

Her hands fluttered over his chest and shoulders, sending delicious hot chills down his spine.

Slowly, she yielded to his weight and sank back against the pillows. Their lips clung in a long, lingering moment then he lifted his head and looked down at her, so lovely, flushed with desire, lips full and rosy from their kisses, eyes dreamy with sensual longing.

He had never desired a woman as much as he did Minette. The knowledge she also desired him and yet insisted that she would leave him once their quest was over drove him to the edge of madness. Instead of the respect she deserved, he was going to engage in seduction.

A pang of guilt. Easily vanquished.

It was for her own good after all.

Taking his weight on his knees, he gazed down at her and removed his shirt.

Her gaze roamed his upper body then lifted to his face. *'Magnifique.'*

She had always thought of him as lean. Elegant. She hadn't expected his musculature to be so well defined. His lithe figure and grace belied his now clearly revealed strength. The masculinity of the dark patch of crisp hair on his chest, the ridges of muscle across his abdomen awoke her darkest desires, the longing to taste, to bite. She raised herself up on her elbows and licked at the closest nipple. Rough hair rasped across her tongue.

His hiss of indrawn breath tightened a chord deep inside her with a pleasurable pulse.

She suckled at the beaded nub.

A groan vibrated through his chest.

She released the suction and blew across the damp peak.

His hips involuntarily rocked against her core.

Cold on the outside, this man was molten heat within.

Surprise bloomed in his eyes, warning her she'd been too forward, shown too much knowledge for the innocent he'd no doubt expected. She had no wish to scare him away quite yet. He'd discover the truth soon enough.

Next time, if there was one, she would use her powers of seduction to make him writhe and moan and perhaps even beg. She sank back against the pillow and languidly raised her hands above her head, offering him access to her body, handing over the reins, at least this time.

Eyes hooded, his lips curved in a sensual smile, his hot gaze roved the length of her with hunger. The heat of him washed over her body in waves. He pushed up the hem of her chemise until all but the apex of her thighs were exposed to his gaze. 'Lovely.' He stroked her inner thigh with unbearable tenderness, sending sparks of heat all the way to her core. Of their own accord her thighs parted and he shifted one knee between her legs, looking down at her, raking every inch of her with his gaze, his hands following the path in slow, gentle strokes, down her side, over her breasts, traversing the plain of her belly.

He cupped his hand over her mound and pressed its heel against her sensitive bud. So sweetly painful. She arched into his hand, seeking more of the pleasure just out of reach.

He groaned softly and took her mouth, stretching out beside her, one thigh encased in fine wool over hers. The fabric was silky smooth against her skin and his thighs pressed against the juncture of her thigh, while his hand moved to her breast, gently weighing and softly squeezing, his thumb teasing at her nipple. Heat darted along her veins, the muscles in her core tightened until they hurt.

She moaned into his mouth. Writhed beneath his weight, seeking more of the pleasure he gave. He kissed his way from her mouth to her chin to the pulse at the base of her throat. Hot kisses, his tongue laving, his mouth sucking, promising... Ah, yes. He took her nipple in his mouth, toyed with it with his tongue and then suckled.

The arrow of pleasure streaking to her core almost undid her. She arched her back, rocked her hips against his thigh. He broke away, kneeling over her, his breathing ragged.

'I need this off,' he said roughly. He tugged at the hem of her chemise. 'I need to feel every inch of your luscious skin against me.'

She lifted her bottom so he could push it up over her hips, then sat up to help him take it off over her head. 'And these,' she said, pulling at the waistband of his pantaloons.

Never taking his gaze from her face, he leaped down from the bed and snuffed the candles.

The light of a not-quite-full moon filled the room with shadows and patches of soft light. She sensed, rather than saw, him remove his shoes, strip his nether garment down his legs and step out of them. A glimpse of his arousal. The flash of bare flanks as he climbed onto the bed again and his face caught in a stray moonbeam as he leaned over her once more. The shadows sculpted the muscles of his chest into gleaming planes and shadowed curves. He looked otherworldly, dark as sin, handsome as the devil, and unbelievably sensual.

But she had wanted to see him. All of him.

He had quite deliberately made sure she could not. Was it so bad, then? His leg? That he must hide it in the shadows? She wanted to ask but did not quite have the courage. 'Why leave us in the dark?' she said instead.

He stilled. Stroked her hair back from her face in so tender a motion her heart gave a painful twinge. 'I thought you might be more comfortable.'

Protecting her maidenly fears? Or worried about his appearance? She reached up and pulled his head down for a kiss. No sense in hurting his manly pride. The little she had seen of his body had not disappointed, and there would be other occasions on which to see and explore before they finally parted. Hopefully.

He kissed her back, first palming her breasts and then dipping down to kiss and lick and suckle until she thought she might go mad with wanting—no, needing—fulfilment. The evidence of his own arousal pressed against her hip, so hard and so hot she wanted to take him in her hand, but she had already surprised him with her boldness once so she wasn't going to risk shocking him again and having him stop to question what it meant. Instead, she satisfied her need for touch by caressing the solid muscle across his back and the curve of his buttocks, trying not to score his back with her nails as he drove the pitch of her wanting ever higher with his mouth at her breasts.

Unable to bear it any longer, she could not stop from saying his name. 'Freddy,' she pleaded. It had been so long since she'd had a man inside her.

He lifted his head, his gaze searching her face, but she could not make out his expression. Shock? Surprise?

'Impatient, are we?' he said, his voice teasing, his eyes gleaming with amusement.

He was pleased.

He petted her breast, her stomach, and then moved lower, his fingers stroking through her curls. One finger slipped into her. He made a sound of pleasure. 'You are wet for me.'

Her insides were molten heat. 'Freddy, please.'

He worked one finger inside her, gently stroking. Intrusion. Pleasurable friction. But not nearly enough.

'So tight,' he murmured. 'So ready.'

Another finger parted her folds and slowly pushed deeper, while his thumb pressed against her *perle*. She fell apart, shattered into bliss.

He pressed the blunt head of his shaft against her entrance as the sensations rippled through her body.

Mon Dieu, the man knew his way around a woman's body.

'This will hurt,' he murmured, 'but not for long.'

She winced, not in pain but chagrin in anticipation of his disappointment.

He pushed into her swiftly and stilled, staring down at her, and despite the shadows she saw him realise the truth. And then he was moving. Slowly at first, but as she found the counterpoint to his thrust by lifting her hips, he increased the tempo and the depth. He drove into her hard, building the tension, pushing her back up to the crest of desire, watching her face, easing back when she was sure she was going to shatter, holding her there, punishing her with intense, unfulfilled pleasure and need until she clawed at his back to raise herself up, bit his earlobe and thrust her tongue in his ear. He shuddered and rotated his hips to bring pressure to bear against her *perle*. So wickedly sensitive. She toppled over the edge, her vision turned black, pinpricks of light dancing across the dark.

He rode the wave and gave one last powerful thrust, withdrawing from her body at the moment before he, too, reached his climax. A needless protection but a gesture so heartbreakingly sweet it made her want to cry.

Bones melting, limbs useless, heart pounding at the surge of bliss, she lay beneath his hot, heavy weight. Her hard breathing melded with his so precisely she was not sure that he wasn't breathing for her and her heart wasn't beating for his.

Never had *la petite mort* taken her so completely. It really had felt like a moment of death.

With a groan, he rolled off her and pulled her tight to his side, one hand resting on her breast, one thigh pinning her to the bed.

His warmth, his weight made her feel safe. Treasured.

Since when had she started dreaming of such foolishness?

She couldn't hold the thought and drifted into darkness.

Not a virgin. He wasn't surprised. His body was lax, sated, immovable, but his mind, no longer enslaved by lust, calculated and reasoned with swift efficiency. It made perfect sense. Her boldness. Her comfort with her own sensuality. Her lovely kisses. Somewhere in her past there was a lover. And he found he didn't mind. Much. It had made for a very pleasurable, intimate encounter, one that might not have gone so well if she was inexperienced.

Only one question caused him concern. Why would such an intelligent woman allow him to make the discovery prior to their marriage?

Because she didn't still want to marry him. His gut dipped. With the ease of long practice he quelled the pain of loss. There was no emotion in their bargain. It had always been a convenient arrangement, to save her reputation and keep his honour intact. Keep his friend Gabe from repudiating their friendship.

She might well be surprised to discover it changed nothing. They would still marry. And one thing he knew without a doubt, they were compatible where it counted most.

A quiet sense of joy filled him at the thought of a future of such pleasurable intimate encounters. After the knot was tied. Hopefully it would be enough for her, because they would not be having children.

The small fingers, flat on his chest, flexed briefly. A telltale sign she was awake, along with the slight change in her breathing. Awake and pretending.

'Who was he?' he asked.

The fingers tightened into a fist. She pushed away. He refused to let her go, held her firmly, but not to cause hurt. After a second or two she gave up the struggle.

'It is a fair question,' he said.

'*Tiens.* Wasn't it enough that I tell you I do not wish to marry?'

Upset. She sounded upset when he'd expected defiance. Or wheedling. Or excuses. But, no, she was upset, as if it was somehow his fault. Mentally, he sighed. When it came to women, it was always his fault.

'Fine. I don't need to know,' he said evenly. He hoped he didn't. He hoped like hell the man was in her past and not her present.

This time when she pushed away he released his hold.

She sat up and wrapped her arms around her knees beneath the sheets, giving him a glorious view of her delicate back, the dip of her waist, the dimple above each rounded swell of her buttocks. He rolled onto his side and bit lightly on that firm, silky flesh. More to bring her attention back to him than as punishment, though there was an element of that, too, a primal need to mark her as his.

'Ouch.' She turned and gazed down at him, a crease in her brow.

He hoisted himself up, lit the candle on the nightstand and rested his back against the pillows and headboard. He pulled her back to rest against his shoulder. Her body remained rigid, unyielding, but she did not pull away. He nuzzled her neck. 'Does your sister know?'

'No.'

He waited. Sometimes it was better to say nothing.

'He was a mistake. A very stupid mistake.'

The pain in her voice tore at his heart like a serrated blade. Whoever this man was, he had hurt her badly. And was likely the reason she found it difficult to trust. He wanted to call the man out. 'You met him here or in France?'

'France. In Challans.' She sounded ashamed.

His heart wrenched for how young she must have been. Alone, without family. It was hardly surprising she'd sought protection. 'I'm sorry.'

The words sounded trite, and yet she relaxed against him, giving him her full weight.

Trust. More than any she'd given him before. He kissed the point of her shoulder.

'After you escaped the fire the soldiers set at your house,' he murmured. He knew the story of her escape from the house burned to the ground by Napoleon's troops in an attempt to root out loyalists. He knew that the sisters had been separated by the event, Nicky making her way to England and in the process meeting Gabe. Minette had been taken by a group of nuns. She had been little more than a child. He could only imagine how fearful she must have been. How brave.

'A few months later. The nuns were hidden in the house of a merchant. It was dreadful. Locked up day after day in the cellar. Prayers every few hours. I took over obtaining supplies for the kitchen. It got me out of the house. I met Pierre at the market. He was charming, interesting, alive. I left with him.'

His blood chilled at the thought of a gently bred girl alone in a country in the throes of unrest. He threaded his fingers through hers. 'You took a huge risk.'

'It was an adventure. We would join a group harrying the soldiers. When things got too dangerous we would move on, find another group by listening to conversations in the taverns. Quite often they would find me.' She shuddered. 'Such young men. So full of fire and hope.' She shook her head, her face filling with sorrow, and...guilt? 'They didn't stand a chance.'

He put an arm around her shoulders and gave her a small squeeze. 'I am glad you found people who cared for you.' Much as he wanted to hate this Pierre. 'Where did you come across Moreau?'

'He was...' Her expression shuttered. Clearly her trust only went so far. 'He infiltrated the royalists.' Her voice lowered to a whisper. 'He killed them one by one by one.'

'Pierre?'

Bleakness filled her gaze before she buried her face in her hands. 'Moreau fooled us all. He was so very clever.' Anger and desolation rang in her voice. 'Then he used me to get to Nicky.' She lifted her head. Her gaze was bright with unshed tears and the glitter of anger.

'And now you will have your revenge on him.'

'Nicky gave up everything for me. She married to keep me safe. I want to make sure he can never harm her.'

There was something she was not telling him.

A part of him wanted to press the issue, the other part wanted only to offer comfort. He decided on comfort.

He put an arm around her shoulders 'We will catch him. Believe me.'

He held his breath, waiting for her answer, hoping that after tonight she would at least trust him that far.

She said nothing.

As he had taught himself so long ago, he absorbed the blow in silence.

But there was more pain in it than he had expected.

The silence stretched and Minette knew he was disappointed with her responses to his questions, though not angry as far as she could tell. Which in itself was a surprise. She wished to tell him all the rest. Desperately. But then he'd no doubt be disgusted. And she didn't want that, not now, when there was a chance to destroy the evidence of her foolishness.

She needed a change of subject before she confessed everything. 'Why do you blame yourself for your brother's death?'

He turned his head sharply, looking at her in surprise and as if trying to decide what to tell her. She kept her expression neutral. If he did not care to talk about it, she was not going to press him. They were both entitled to their secrets.

He stared upwards at the canopy for a long time. He wasn't going to tell her. She startled when he finally spoke.

'My brother and I had been arguing for weeks about who was the better whip. We argued a great deal. Mostly about foolish things. He was two years older and liked to lord it over me. He was, after all, bigger and stronger. But when it came to book learning and logic he didn't stand a chance.'

He smiled softly, his gaze becoming unfocussed as if he saw the past played out before him. 'One thing we were matched in was riding and driving. Our styles were very different. I like precision in a horse. He preferred brute strength. We both had a penchant for speed. I told him I planned to beat his time from the house to the village on a route that involved a couple of turns and one tricky narrow bridge. Naturally, he challenged me to a race. We set it for the following day.

'On the straight his horses pulled ahead, but he took the second turn too wide. He always did. I was expecting it. I feathered by him.' A sad smile curved his lips. 'I can still see the shock on his face as I pulled ahead. He was catching me up as we approached the bridge, though. The rule is that whoever is behind, even by a nose, must drop back to cross that bridge.'

He shook his head slowly and closed his eyes as if in pain. 'Being ahead there was my strategy. But his team was a whole lot faster than I had anticipated.'

He reached for a glass of water beside the bed and offered her a sip. When she declined, he drank. She watched his throat move as he swallowed. This was hard for him. She felt honoured by his confidence and saddened at her own lack of honesty.

He pulled her closer and twined his fingers in a lock of her hair, brought it to his nose and inhaled. 'The last thing I remember was heading for the bridge a nose in front. Then I was on the ground, the carriage on top of me. I was dizzy. Sick from a blow to the head. And then I saw him a short distance off. Watched the light go out of his eyes.'

'Who was ahead at the bridge?'

His fist clenched, bunching up the sheets at his hip. 'I was so sure I could beat him. I had it all mapped out in my mind. All I can recall is the roar of blood in my ears and the sight of the bridge coming closer. My blood was running so hot I felt invincible. I so wanted to beat him, just once.' He closed his eyes. 'And then nothing. I can't remember if he pulled ahead or not. Damn it,' he whispered. 'Why can't I remember?'

The agony in his face caused her chest to squeeze. 'You fear you didn't follow the rules. That the accident was your fault.' She frowned. 'You are not that sort of person.'

She wanted to bite her tongue when his body

stiffened. When she glanced up at his face his eyes had gone as dark as midnight, his expression stark. He took a deep, shuddering breath. 'It was my fault. I should never have challenged him. Not when I knew I had a chance to win.'

'And that is why you let your mother treat you so badly. You think she is right to blame you.'

'Yes.'

Chapter Fifteen

God. Had he really said all that? Spoken about that day for the first time since his father had listened to his version of the event? It was certainly the first time he'd expressed his deepest fear.

The possibility that beneath the civilised veneer of a gentleman lay a cold-blooded killer. *A fratricide.* The *ton* whispered it behind his back. His throat dried and he took another swallow of water before putting the glass down. In his heart he was sure he hadn't cheated. In his mind he wasn't certain. He had been so very determined to win.

What the hell had he hoped to gain by talking about those things? Was he really so devious, so deeply committed to his work that he had bared his soul to encourage her to reveal what she was so obviously intent on concealing? Or had he been hoping for sympathy? Neither felt particularly good.

'Was that how your leg was injured?'

Shocked, he could only stare at her. Of course she was likely to think that was the cause. It would be so easy to make it seem as if he, too, had suffered the consequences of that stupid race without exactly lying.

'My foot, not my leg.' He shook his head. 'It's been that way since birth.' The reason his mother had barely been able to look at him without flinching. And the cause of his vow to never have children. No child of his would suffer the shame of being a cripple.

She cocked her head on one side. 'May I see?'

Bile rose in his throat. There had been others who had wanted to see, when he had been young and had not realised their interest had been ghoulish rather than the concern of friendship. Until they'd grimaced and called him a freak. Schoolboys, so very cruel. And honest. He'd been lucky Gabe and Bane had not been similarly disposed. 'Why would you want to?'

'You saw all of me before you blew out the candles.'

'You are worth looking at.' No, that was not self-pity he heard in his voice. It was a statement of fact, nothing more. 'It is not a pretty sight.' And a woman's sensibilities were delicate.

'Shouldn't I be the judge?' The determined set of her chin said she would not be denied. And, besides, having revealed the worst of it, she may as well satisfy her curiosity now as later. If she found it disconcerting, he could as easily keep it from her sight in future, as he had this evening.

He flung back the sheet. 'Look your fill.' He leaned back against the headboard so he wouldn't have to see her face. He'd seen both pity and disgust, depending on the woman. He didn't need to see either in her face.

When a warm hand skimmed down his calf, his leg jerked with the shock of her touch. He glared down, seeing the ugliness of his foot and ankle next to the white perfection of her hand. He jerked away. 'What are you doing?'

Hand in hovering in mid-air, she looked at him, puzzled. 'Does it hurt?'

'It aches a bit in cold or damp weather.'

A finger traced the place where his foot went awry, turned inwards. 'What did the doctors say?'

'Doctors can do nothing.'

'Are you saying your parents did not have it looked at by a surgeon?'

Anger. On his behalf. Surprising. And very dear. Something inside him warmed. 'If they did, I do not recall. We never speak of it.' They had done nothing, because they had known the outcome. One of his mother's uncles had undergone surgery and had been worse after than before.

A palm smoothed over the crooked bone. The touch a shocking pleasure. His body reacted. He made a grab for the sheet but she was kneeling on it.

'This leg is shorter than the other, yet it barely hinders you.'

Admiration, yes, but also strangely an admonition.

'My boots are specially made. It doesn't hamper me at all.'

'You don't dance or play cricket.'

'I am a duke,' he said. 'I have my dignity.'

She gazed at him aslant, across her lovely shoulder. 'How is that relevant?'

'It would not suit me to go capering and hopping about, though others might find it amusing.'

'Have you ever danced?

'No.'

'Too bad.' Her gaze dropped to his pelvis. A brow arched. 'It is one of life's pleasures.'

His relief at her common-sense practical acceptance, Heaven help him, her touch where he didn't recall anyone ever touching him before was almost more than he could stand. 'Enough about my foot's shortcomings.' He grinned when she got the joke and wasn't the least bit embarrassed. To distract her, he slid his palm over his own arousal and watched her gaze follow the up and down motion of his hand. 'There are many pleasures where it makes no difference at all.'

She smiled brightly. 'So I see, but it is not better alone, surely?'

The purr in her voice, the wicked gleam in her eyes, the flush across her skin caused his body to further harden. She eyed him and licked her lips.

'Tease,' he growled, entranced by her unself-consciousness and obviously rising passion. What man would want an innocent when he could have this?

She knelt up, straddling his calves, gazing down at him stroking himself.

He let his hands fall away, leaving himself open, wanting her to come to him, to prove that she was not horrified by what she had seen. Not disgusted. Or fearful. Or, worst of all, prurient. All these reactions he had seen from one woman or another. She circled her fingers about him, taking over where he had left off. Without his volition, his hips pushed up, welcoming the heat, the tightness, the sensuality of her touch. He swallowed the urge to plead for more, fisting his hands in the rumpled bedclothes each side of his hips. Gently, she cupped him. He groaned. Eyes alight with mischief, she gazed down at him. 'Too much?'

'Never,' he ground out. He pushed himself up on his elbows, kissed his way across each breast, teasing her nipples with teeth and tongue until she moaned and arched against him. He flipped her over onto her back. The gold in her eyes sparkled. Her lips curved in a welcoming smile. Never had he felt so comfortable with a woman.

'What now?' she asked, her voice teasing.

What came now was pure pleasure. Hers. If she'd allow it. He made his way down her belly to the nest of black curls. He sat back on his heels and parted her delicate rosy pink folds. So achingly beautiful and pearly with her moisture, and perfumed by her arousal.

He licked.

She moaned.

He found her tiny bud already knotted and ready, and licked and flicked with his tongue, learning what had her writhing and what made her so weak she couldn't do any more than cry out her pleasure, and he tormented and teased until he could no longer see for wanting to be inside her.

He lifted her legs over his shoulders, leaving her deliciously open to his gaze. So beautiful. So enticing. He rose up on his knees, pulling her onto him. Pushing into her hard, burying himself deep.

'Yes,' she cried. 'Harder.'

Hard and fast, he pounded into her, their bodies coming together in hard slapping sounds, his grunts of pleasure-pain mingling with her softer cries of approval. Her inner muscles tightened around him, milking him in steady pulls. Seared by flame, he lost control. He heard his name on her lips, felt the flutters of her orgasm around

him and pulled out, spilling his seed on the plain
of her belly.

In time. Heaven help him, had he been in time?

He collapsed to one side, grabbing for the
sheet to wipe her belly and his, and rolled on his
side. She rolled to face him, kissed the tip of his
nose. 'Next,' she said, breathing hard, 'we will
try dancing. At our ball.'

Did that mean she intended to honour their engagement? If so, it was a battle won. Or did she
only mean what she had said? If so, it was a battle
lost. For he would not dance.

Above all else, right at this moment he needed
what was left of his brain to get her back to her
room and quickly, before the house began stirring.

Stiff and sore in a very satisfying way, Minette wended her way down the grand staircase
to breakfast. Freddy rose to his feet as she entered and greeted her with a smile, but there was
fatigue in his eyes.

The butler hovered over the sideboard. 'Tea,
miss?'

'Coffee, please.'

While he poured her a cup and set it on the
table, she helped herself to rashers of bacon and
a scoop of fluffy scrambled eggs, along with a
couple of slices of toast.

She took the seat to Freddy's right, added
cream and sugar to her coffee. Her first sip was

delicious. Hunger gnawed at her belly, and she attacked her food.

'That will be all, thank you, Patterson,' Freddy said.

The man looked down his nose, but left swiftly.

Minette spread butter on her toast and looked at Freddy in enquiry.

'Barker arrived early this morning.'

'You have seen him already?' No wonder he looked tired.

Freddy gave a terse nod, his face thoughtful. 'Yes. He's setting up camp.'

Minette glanced out of the rain-streaked window at the scudding clouds. 'Poor man. Could he and his men not stay at the farm?'

He shook his head. 'He'll keep an eye on it as well as Falconwood.'

'You think Moreau might take advantage of its vacancy?'

'It would be wonderful if he did. But the man is as slippery as an eel.'

He was right about that. Moreau was also devious, self-serving and conscienceless.

'I'm going to ride out shortly to confer with Barker.'

'I will come with you.'

He raised a brow, looking grave.

She opened her mouth to object to what was clearly going to be a refusal.

He grinned at her. 'I've asked for your horse to be saddled for ten.'

Teasing. He was teasing her. Astonished, she gazed at him and grinned back. *'Très drôle.'*

'I'm glad you are amused.'

There was a softness in his voice. Affection. Did he think last night had changed things between them? While he hadn't said much about her lack of virtue, surely he wouldn't want to marry her now? How did one approach such a question? Inwardly, she winced. One didn't. Besides, there was no need. In this matter she was the one in control. He could not stop her from crying off. Could not force her to the altar.

The regret causing her stomach to squeeze uncomfortably was foolish in the extreme. Appetite gone, she put down her knife and fork. 'I will be ready.'

His expression changed to one of concern. 'Are you well?'

'Of course,' she said lightly, rising to her feet, forcing him to rise also, noticing the way he adjusted his stance for balance. She'd never really noticed that little adjustment before, and now it made her heart ache sweetly. She forced a smile. 'If I am to go riding in the rain, I must change. Please, excuse me.' She left without a backward glance, but she had the very real sense his gaze never left her until she disappeared through the door.

He'd taken them across country, but with the ground wet and heavy their progress was slow.

Freddy glanced over at the lady riding beside him, rain dripping from drooping feathers, face set in a determined but cool expression. She wasn't going to make his wooing easy. Rain hadn't brought on her dark mood. So busy was she with her own thoughts, she barely seemed to notice her surroundings, or him. Whereas last night she had seemed so full of joy.

Perhaps it was the thought of Moreau holding her attention. Or memories of the man he had betrayed. Pierre. Did she still love him? Her first love? And if she did, why would he care? He took a deep breath and enclosed himself within the familiar chill of feeling nothing. It didn't work. Too many fissures ran through his defences, old hurts and new leaking through him like acid.

He glanced up at the sky. 'It's raining harder. Do you want to turn back?' He leaned closer so he did not have to raise his voice and so he could bring the scent of her deep into his lungs. The smell of jasmine and wet summer mornings.

She shot him a brief glance. 'No. Who can tell when it will end?' She lifted her face to look at the sky and lowered it swiftly, using the wide brim of her hat to shield her from the slash of rain.

'Let us hope it lets up before the night of the ball,' he said for something to say, some way to keep the conversation going. Clouds and rain would mean only those who had been invited to stay overnight would attend. 'The locals will be disappointed.'

When Mother had observed the weather this morning, she'd suggested a postponement. He'd vetoed the idea immediately, despite his betrothed's hopeful expression. Something he hadn't anticipated after their intimate relations. Clearly they had not meant as much to her as they had to him. A bitter thought.

'I would have thought you would have preferred a postponement,' she said, as if she had read his thoughts.

The words were delivered in a light tone but they were edged with wariness. He bared his teeth in a predatory smile. 'Certainly not. The sooner we celebrate our engagement, the sooner we can be married.'

She leaned forward to pat the dripping-wet neck of her mount, hiding her expression. 'Are you sure you want a wedding?'

So they were going to have this conversation now. He stared at the track ahead, taking account of the deeper ruts and higher spots, while he formulated words little more civilised than *You're mine*, which had risen instantly to his tongue. 'There is no reason I know of why I should not.'

Her head whipped around, her eyes wide. 'You don't care, then, that I do not come to you *intacta*?'

He gave her a hard look, because she was

right. Under society's rules, lack of virginity was grounds for a man to walk away, and no doubt that had been her plan in giving in to his importunity. He, however, wasn't going to let her use it as a weapon or an excuse. 'Do you care that *I* do not come to you that way?'

'A different thing for a man,' she muttered. Then smiled a little ruefully. 'Though I cannot help feeling it is unfair.'

A chuckle pushed past his reservations. Her ability to surprise him shook him free of dark thoughts. 'It seems we are well matched in our experience. And given a choice between the pleasure of last night and the task of teaching an innocent, I would take last night every time.'

Her eyes showed relief, quickly hidden by a brittle smile. 'All you care about, sir, is winning.' Her expression froze as she realised the import of her words. She winced and gave him a worried look that told him she believed he could well have deliberately forced his brother off the road.

The joy went out of the day. It was back to rainy and chilly and dark and the dull ache deep in his ankle. He held her gaze. 'Never forget it.'

They reached the entrance to the woods and he urged his horse into a trot that made further talk impossible.

Nom d'un nom. She had not intended to imply that she thought he was responsible for his brother's death. She didn't believe it for a moment. Her ill-thought-out words had sounded too much like the doubts he had expressed the previous evening and he had jumped to the conclusion she had doubts, too.

It would be so easy to use his guilt against him. His mother did it all the time. A horrid female trick she would not resort to in order to get her way. It was too cruel. Too destructive.

No. When she cried off, the flaw would be hers. He had never been anything but a gentleman. Even last night, when he had learned she was not pure, he had treated her with respect. As well as given her more pleasure than she had ever experienced in her life.

Pierre had been an expert lover, astonishingly so, and had taught her much. How to be wanton. How to be bold. How to use her femininity to achieve goals she had never dreamed of. His ultimate betrayal. Because she'd thought him her knight in shining armour. Her saviour. When, in truth, he had been the apple in the Garden of Eden.

Freddy led them between large oaks and beech, the ground carpeted with loam and old leaves that muffled the sound of their horses' hooves. When they slowed and entered a clearing, a man appeared from behind a tree, pistol at the ready, an alert expression on his face.

His eyes widened a fraction at the sight of her then twinkled. He bowed. 'Miss Rideau. A pleasure to meet you again.'

'Mr Barker,' she said, inclining her head. 'Good day.'

'Hardly,' he growled, passing a hand down his face as if to sweep the raindrops away. Then he beamed at her. 'But it does seem brighter for your presence.'

Freddy dismounted, pulled at the strap fastening a saddlebag and a rolled bundle behind his saddle. He tossed them to Barker. 'Do you have all you need?' Freddy said, chill in his voice.

The man opened the packs, sorting quickly through the contents. 'This is everything I asked for.'

'Good. Any sign of anything untoward?'

'Nothing so far.' Barker's gaze returned to Freddy. 'I'll send the lad to you if we see anything out of place.'

'You are letting a small boy sleep out in this weather?' Minette was scandalised. She knew what it was to be cold and wet for hours at a time. She'd seen children die of chills.

Freddy stiffened.

'Now, then, missy,' Barker said, his face glowering. 'Think I don't know how to build a bivouac? Nice and snug we'll be. And the best of oilskins money can buy, too, thanks to His Grace.'

Oh, dear. It seemed she'd insulted their competence. Both of them. 'I should have known the two of you would be prepared for rain,' she said by way of apology. 'It always rains in England.'

Barker bristled. 'We get our share of good days.'

Hopeless.

'Watch your step,' Freddy warned his man. 'When they come, they will no doubt scout the area. They won't want anyone straying onto them by mistake. I'll ride out again after dark to inspect the perimeter around Falconwood that you'll spend today setting up.'

A small figure entered the clearing with a couple of rabbits strung on a stick over his shoulder. 'Guv'nor.' He strode over to his employer with a flash of crooked teeth and displayed his catch.

Barker rolled his eyes. 'I told you no hunting. We can't light a fire. The coves we're after will spot the smoke as quick as a wink. It's cold beef and beer for us for the next couple of days.'

The boy grimaced and held out his catch to Freddy. 'You want them?'

'I can see you want me hanged for poaching,' Freddy said, taking the offering.

'Nah,' the lad said. 'They'll be your rabbits, I'm thinking.'

'Yes. And don't let my gamekeeper catch you snaring them, or you'll find yourself in the local lock-up and that won't suit my purposes at all.'

'Sorry, Guv.'

Freddy whipped off the lad's cap, ruffled his hair. The boy backed up and smoothed his neatly cut hair, looking indignant but secretly pleased.

Freddy tossed him his hat. 'You'll have your chance to catch rabbits when we are done here.'

A grin split the lad's face. 'You mean it?'

'Yes. If you manage to stay out of trouble and do exactly as Barker says for the next day or so.'

'Agreed,' the boy said, and stuck out a grubby paw.

Freddy shook it without a flinch.

He was good with the child. Kind. He would make an excellent father. Surprising when one considered his mother's coldness. He was also an honourable man. A woman would be lucky have his love and his children. Little black-haired imps of Satan if they were anything like their father—or her, if she was honest. A pain speared her heart. They couldn't be hers. Must not be. He would stick to his word and marry her, if she let him. But it wouldn't be right.

She'd lived the wrong sort of a life for a duchess. If any of it ever came to light, it would reflect badly on any man she married. Duke or otherwise.

And it wasn't as if they were in love or anything. Bedding him, finding truly amazing pleasure in his arms, didn't mean love. It certainly didn't mean they had to marry.

No, she was wedded to the idea of being a spinster and an aunt. She just had to convince Nicky it was so once she'd broken off the engagement.

Chapter Sixteen

Jimmy, his tiger, came hours before the time Freddy had set to visit Barker.

One of the grooms brought a message about his horse being in need of shoeing, a prearranged signal, while he and Minette were at dinner. Fortunately, Mother's headache required her to take her dinner on a tray, as it usually did when he was home, so they could exit his apartment with no one being aware. As they crossed the courtyard to the stables, he couldn't stop himself from glancing upwards. To his mother's suite of rooms. Narrow chinks of light indicated she was still awake.

The woman thought she was punishing him by not coming down to dinner. When he'd been young, her withdrawal had hurt. No longer. Her enmity had existed for too many years for him to care. Besides, she was giving him the hours he needed to spend with Minette. What would Mother do if she had any idea she was doing exactly as he wanted? Show up for dinner?

Unlikely. Not even to thwart him would she spend any more time in his company than necessary.

One thing she would not do was stop him from marrying Minette, despite her privately expressed disapproval.

Jimmy jumped up from the table in the saddle room, where he was wolfing down what looked like stew when they walked through the door.

With one eye on the stew and the other on Minette, Jimmy bowed. 'Yer Grace. A man arrived at the farm half an hour before I left to find you.'

'Eat,' Minette said.

Freddy nodded. 'Get something hot inside you while you can.'

'I know one thing, Guv,' the boy said, a spoonful of steaming stew hovering before his lips. 'I ain't cut out to be a soldier. Nor a farmer neither. Sooner we gets back to Lunnon the better I'm goin' to like it.' He shoved the mouthful in, chewed methodically and swallowed. 'Mind you, the vittles is good. I'll give you that.'

'Thank you,' Freddy said. He waited for the boy to clean his dish with the last of his bread. 'Now. The message.'

'Three coves showed up when it was full dark and the moon wasn't up. They's bein' very careful-like, Mr Barker says. They wasn't so leery as Mr Barker didn't see they was carrying barkers and a couple of long pops.'

'*Qu'est-ce que c'est?*' Minette said. 'Dogs?'

The boy laughed.

'He means pistols and shotguns,' Freddy said. 'Go on.'

'That's it.'

'How did they travel?' Freddy asked. 'Horse? Carriage?'

'One drivin' the carriage and a couple of outriders.' He rubbed at the bridge of his nose. 'One saddle horse, without a rider.'

'So they have enough horses for three of them to ride.' Freddy looked at her. 'It's a small force. The Regent is bound to come with a company of dragoons.'

'Perhaps a member of government isn't the target,' Minette said.

'Then who?'

'Nicky?'

Something in her voice made him look at her hard. 'Why would you think so?'

'He might be angry that she bested him.'

'Revenge, you mean.' Minette wanted revenge on Moreau for the death of her lover. The Frenchman wanted revenge on Nicky because she'd escaped his clutches. 'It all sounds rather Gothic. This is war. He might have been bested by Nicky, but if he wants to rise in Napoleon's favour he needs to do something to grab attention. That was his aim last time. The death or kidnapping of the wife of an earl won't do him a scrap of good. Though I'm sorry to say it, since Nicky's death would be a horrible blow to Gabe and to you, it won't make a ripple as far as the war is concerned.'

She worried her bottom lip with her teeth before speaking. He wanted to be the one to bite that full lip. He folded his arms across his chest to keep himself standing right where he was.

'Only three men to capture or assassinate the Prince or someone in his party?' she said finally, shaking her head. 'Why bother when there are men aplenty to take their places? Yes, that, too, would make a stir but little difference.'

'Honestly, I have no clue. Our best course is to ask them.'

Her gaze rose to meet his face. 'You will arrest them before they have a chance to do anything.'

'No point in shutting the gate after the horse has gone.'

She frowned. '*Certainement*, but I don't see what escaped horses have to do with the matter we are discussing.'

A weird feeling of tenderness he hadn't known for years lodged in his throat. Heartbreaking in its sweetness. A small chuckle escaped his lips.

Jimmy glanced up at the sound in surprise equalled only by that on Minette's face.

'It's a colloquialism,' he said, smiling. 'We need to nip their plans in the bud. Stop them before find ourselves at *point non plus*.'

'I see. Once captured you think they will tell you their plans?'

'We'll make sure of it.' Once the men were taken, Sceptre would take charge of relieving them of their knowledge. It would be up to him to find the rest of the web of spies. The key would be for no one to learn that Moreau had been arrested. 'As yet, we don't know for certain that Moreau is among these men. I will need you to take a look at first light. In the meantime, we will get some sleep. You, too, young man,' he said to Jimmy. 'You can bed down here for the night. Barker won't expect your return until morning.'

'Aye, Guv. So he said.'

Freddy took Minette's arm and walked her back to the house. Against every instinct and baser urge, he delivered her to her chamber door and stepped back. 'Get some rest. I'll make sure your maid wakes you in time in the morning.'

'What if Moreau is not there?'

'Then we wait and we watch, and hope he comes.'

He opened her door and thrust her inside, catching a glimpse of her waiting maid and walking away quickly before he changed his mind, sent her maid packing and undressed her himself.

He needed to go and consult with Barker. Arrange things for the following day to his satisfaction. Minette would not be put in danger.

* * *

The weather was fair and fine, if a little chilly, the next morning when she and Freddy rode into the clearing. Her heart was beating very fast at the thought of seeing Moreau again. At the thought of retrieving the miniature. A trickle of sweat ran down her spine. Nerves. Because retrieving that little picture under Freddy's nose was not going to be easy. She'd have to find an opportunity to go through Moreau's things without raising suspicion.

A sour-looking Barker rose from a log to greet them.

'What is wrong?' Freddy asked.

'Loped off is what is wrong,' the other man grumbled. 'Some time after you left here last night.'

Minette glared from one to the other. 'You said you would not come here last night. What is this loped off?'

'They've gone,' Freddy said.

Her stomach dropped so fast she felt sick. 'You scared them away?'

'No,' Barker said slowly. 'They'll be back, but as yet I don't know where they went.'

Freddy swung down from the saddle to face his minion eye to eye. 'You have someone following them.'

Barker nodded. 'I do.'

'What makes you think they will be back?' Minette asked.

'They left the carriage and its horses, with enough feed and water for a couple of days.'

Freddy shook his head. 'Damnation.'

'What?' she asked.

'If he's brought a carriage then I assume he means to use it to transport something or someone,' he mused. 'They must have been informed that the place is unoccupied so decided to make use of its nearness to Falconwood.'

Her heart dipped. 'And there is no Moreau conveniently waiting for his arrest.'

'Apparently not.' He turned Barker. 'I need you to send a man to London.' He went to his saddlebag and pulled out a notepad, pencil and a little book. He took a seat on the log where Barker had been sitting and set to work composing a note using the little book as a reference. The note would be in code.

'To whom do you write?' she asked.

He lifted his head and gave her an enigmatic smile. 'No one you know.'

He wasn't going to trust her with that sort of information. Of course he wasn't. The trust between them was a fragile thing and not yet complete. She certainly didn't intend telling him all her secrets. Not unless she had to. She turned to Barker. 'Did you search inside?'

'Top to bottom. Nothing except the horses. They had no intention of staying.'

She wanted to curse. They had been so certain they had their man in their net. 'What do we do now?'

'Wait for my man to report back,' Barker said. 'Keep watch for their return. Guard Falconwood.'

A mocking smile curved Freddy's lips and lit his eyes. 'In the meantime, my guests are due to arrive and I am tied to the house.'

A terrible thought occurred to her, and her hands tightened on the reins. 'You don't think I am part of Moreau's plot?'

He hesitated a fraction too long. 'I don't know.'

At least he was being honest, but it hurt. Deeply. That he would think she would betray him. 'I am not.'

'There are a few too many coincidences for my liking.' He tore a leaf from the notebook and handed it to Barker. 'Get this to our contact right away. Make sure your man is not followed.'

Barker touched his forelock and disappeared into the woods.

Freddy mounted up, his face grim.

'You do think I had something to do with it,' she said.

'I know you are at the centre of what Moreau is plotting. I know there are things you have not told me. That is all I know.'

Heat seared her face at the sound of his anger.

She felt as if she had been slapped. She urged her horse up close to him. 'If you think I would do anything to put my sister's life in danger, you really do not know me very well.'

He gave a weary shake of his head. 'You misunderstand my meaning.'

'Then explain.'

'I do not think you are complicit in Moreau's plan, but he is using you.'

A cold hand fisted around her heart. It sounded so like Moreau. 'So what are we going to do?'

'We are going to formally announce our betrothal at our ball tonight. There is nothing else we can do.'

The edge of bitterness in his tone clawed at her heart.

The guests began arriving at noon. First to arrive were Nicky and Gabe. While Nicky and Minette hugged, Freddy shook hands with his best friend, who gave him a hard look. 'Everything all right?' he asked.

'We'll talk later,' Freddy said. When they had a moment alone.

Mother, who had emerged from her rooms looking magnificent in a rose-coloured turban and an imposing gown of green silk, sailed into action. 'The butler will show you to your rooms, my lord. I have, of course, put you beside Minette, in my wing of the house. You will no doubt require time to recover from your journey. I will have tea sent up to your room.'

'You are very kind, Your Grace,' Nicky said. 'I would indeed like a few minutes to rest. Minette, will you join me? I am longing to hear all about your visit. And since there are others arriving behind us, you may show us the way. Her Grace will need the services of her servants.'

'You are all that is kind, Lady Mooreshead,' Mother said.

Gabe and Nicky followed Minette up the stairs.

The next to arrive was his cousin Arthur and his wife, Liz. The woman looked as if she had bitten into a lemon. Freddy shook his cousin's hand and kissed Liz on the cheek. 'Thank you for coming to celebrate my news at such short notice.'

'Wouldn't have missed it for the world,' Cousin Arthur said. His eyes narrowed. 'Looking a bit pulled, though, what? Shouldn't you be sitting down?'

'You do look rather tired,' Liz said with a sugary-sweet smile. 'Doesn't he, Your Grace?' she appealed to his mother.

Mother sniffed. 'Too much racketing about in the middle of the night.'

Liz gasped.

Cousin Arthur leaned closer. 'Still up to your old tricks? You will have to settle down once you are married, you know.'

Freddy gritted his teeth and passed the couple off to the butler.

And so it went on for three interminable hours. Greeting one overnight guest after another. The rain yesterday had made his leg ache like the devil. The last to arrive in a flurry of gentlemen, dragoons and boon companions was the Prince Regent. His major-domo consulted with the butler and the whole party was led up to the suite of rooms set aside for their royal visitor.

His mother sank onto one of the hall chairs. 'That is everyone, I believe.'

'Yes. Thank you for doing such a sterling job of getting them settled.'

Her shoulders tensed. 'I have never been one to shirk my duty.'

He ignored the implied criticism. 'Indeed not.'

Her face reddened. 'Your father would certainly not have approved of this dreadful misalliance.'

He sighed. 'Mother, I am marrying Miss Rideau, and there is nothing you can say or do to change it.'

'Yes, and I know how it came about. You have made us a laughing stock. My Reginald would never have behaved in such a disgraceful way.'

His fists clenched.

His mother recoiled.

Damn the woman for making him come so close to losing his temper. He sought the coldness of their usual interactions. 'I suggest you repair to your room and ready yourself for this evening.' He limped down the hallway to the library, where the captain of Prinny's guards had been instructed to wait for him.

Captain Stalbridge rose when Freddy entered. 'Your Grace.'

Freddy shook his outstretched hand. The captain was a sensible man, even if he was a Hyde Park soldier. 'Sorry to put you to so much trouble. I have a map of the house and grounds and we can talk about the disposition of your men while the Prince is here.'

'I gather we are expecting trouble.' The man looked eager.

'It is more a case of better to be safe than sorry,' Freddy said, smiling. No sense getting the man excited. That way led to mistakes. Besides, he much preferred to put his trust in Sceptre's highly trained men.

Chapter Seventeen

The gown Madame Vitesse had sent along with Nicky was the most beautiful creation. A rose-coloured gown, open at the front to reveal its white satin slip, edged in lace and trimmed with pearls and diamonds. The woman really had taken advantage if indeed she had lied to them about Moreau. The gown must have cost Freddy a king's ransom. 'Turn around,' Nicky said, having come to help her dress. 'My word, that is just lovely, and perfect for your colouring.'

A knock came at the door. When Christine opened it, one of the footmen handed her a wooden box with the Duke's compliments. She set it on the dressing table.

'Open it,' Nicky said.

Inside a nest of indigo velvet lay a tiara, along with a matching necklace of pearls and diamonds.

Nicky gasped. 'My goodness. These must have cost a small fortune.'

'According to Her Grace, these are always worn by the bride at her betrothal party,' Minette said. She had been expecting the jewels, but not their opulence. She lifted the necklace, its sparkle almost blinding.

'He must have told Madame Vitesse about them before she made the gown,' Nicky said. 'Clever man.'

That was one of the things she really liked about Freddy. He was exceedingly intelligent. About some things anyway.

Christine artfully worked the tiara into her hair and fastened the necklace around her neck. '*Mademoiselle* looks beautiful,' she said, stepping back.

'You do,' Nicky said, looking quite lovely herself in green taffeta and emeralds. She waved the maid away and once the girl had closed the door behind her came forward to take Minette's hands, searching her face with a worried look. 'You are happy about this marriage?'

'Of course,' she said, hoping she sounded happy, while inside the sadness seemed to be growing. A longing for what might have been. If Freddy had really wanted to marry her, if he hadn't been forced up to the mark, and if her life before she'd met him had been different, she might well have been happy.

An ache set up residence in the region of her heart. He was a good man, even if he was haunted by the demons of the past. He deserved a proper wife. And it was now up to her to make sure he got one. Because, in spite of all her good intentions, she had fallen in love with the man behind the icy mask.

Love. Was that what she thought it was? She'd been mistaken in her feelings before. But she did respect him and want the best for him. She was not what he deserved.

She forced a smile. 'If I look a bit peaky, it is because of Her Grace. She is a difficult woman to please and I have the strong feeling she does not approve of me. She took to her bed almost as soon as I arrived.'

Nicky frowned. 'She was supposed to be acting as your chaperone. It was the only reason I agreed not to come with you.'

'It was only three days. And we are going to be married.' Minette gave her sister a teasing smile. 'You said yourself I needed time to know him better.'

Nicky's eyebrows rose. 'Minette, you surely don't mean—'

The clock on the mantel struck seven.

'Oh, goodness,' Minette said. 'I should have gone down by now. His mother is sure to give me a scold for being late. She was most insistent I be there to greet the guests.'

'As is right.' Nicky frowned. 'You should not let his mother intimidate you. After all, you will

be the Duchess very soon. She really should remove to the dower house before you wed.'

'Can we talk about this later?' There wasn't
going to be a wedding. She certainly didn't want
to worsen the relationship between Freddy and
his mother for no good reason.

'Go, then. I'll locate Gabe and see you downstairs.'

Freddy was waiting at the top of the stairs to
take her down. 'You look lovely,' he said.

He looked good enough to eat in his black evening coat and satin knee breeches. They went well
with his dark looks. So austerely handsome. And
ducal. 'Thank you.' She touched the necklace.
'And thank you for sending the jewels. They are
magnifique.' She would have to return them after
the ball, his mother had made very certain to tell
her that. 'Any news of you know who?'

'Nothing. And we won't. The cordon around
the house is so tight not even a tadpole can wig-
gle through.'

'Soldiers?'

'They will be of help, too.'

At the bottom of the stairs, his mother waited,
wearing a gown of old gold adorned with diamonds and rubies. 'Mother,' Freddy said coolly.

His mother looked both of them up and down.
'Well, at least you won't put me to shame this
evening.'

Minette curled her fingers in her palm to stop

herself from hitting the critical face, and bit her tongue to prevent the angry words rising up in her throat from issuing forth.

Freddy smiled at her as if he appreciated her struggle, and she stopped herself from rolling her eyes in answer. They were acting like two children caught in mischief.

Then the guests started arriving and they were too busy greeting them to exchange another word for an hour. When they finally entered the ballroom the dancing had already begun and people were laughing and talking.

Lady Priscilla sidled up to her with a wary look at Freddy at her side. 'Everyone is so impressed with the room's decoration,' she murmured. 'I overheard Her Grace say it was all your idea.'

What a surprise. 'Yes. Most of the plants came from the gardens here.'

The other girl looked around her with a smile. 'It is fabulous, despite what Her Grace said. And smells heavenly. Everyone in Town will be copying it for the rest of the season.'

So Her Grace had found a way to be uncomplimentary while giving her the credit. It was almost too bad she was not going to end up marrying Freddy and getting the woman out of his house so he could have a bit of peace from her biting remarks. She just hoped the next wife he chose would manage it.

The set came to a close. 'Oh, I have to go. I

promised to dance with Lieutenant Granby.' She gave Minette a worried look. 'You don't mind, do you? I know he was one of your court, but he has been rather at a loss since the announcement of your engagement.' She blushed. 'And I find I like him.'

Minette took her hand. 'That is wonderful. He is a nice young man. I wish you both happy.'

Priscilla gave her a conspiratorial smile. 'I'm going to try to get him to go with me to the library.'

Minette laughed.

'Something amuses you?' Freddy asked.

'Very much.'

'Don't feel you have to keep me company all evening. Go and dance. Enjoy yourself.'

'When are we going to have our dance?'

His eyes gleamed with amusement. 'When hell freezes over.'

'You promised.'

'No. You promised. I'm sorry. No one will be surprised any more than they were surprised that we did not open the dancing.'

'So what will you be doing while I dance the night away?'

'Play cards. Walk the grounds.'

'To make sure all is safe?'

He inclined his head. 'One can never be too careful.'

* * *

It wasn't often Freddy bemoaned the things he couldn't do because of his foot. This evening, though, he wished he could have given in to Minette's desire that he dance instead of watch. He loved the way her eyes sparkled, how light she was on her pretty feet as she spun around her partners. He would have given his soul to have partnered her in a dance. If he'd had a soul, that was.

After an hour of standing on the sidelines, talking to guests, accepting congratulations, some of which were actually sincere, and avoiding his cousins, he needed fresh air. He also needed a word with Barker, who, with the men he had brought from London, was patrolling the gardens.

He strolled out of the ballroom, across the terrace to the stairs.

'Frederick. I say, old man.'

Damn, he hadn't notice his cousin had come this way. Too busy watching Minette and trying to look perfectly content as she whirled around the room on other men's arms. 'Arthur.'

'You have chosen a beautiful girl,' his cousin said admiringly.

'I rather think she chose me,' Freddy said.

Arthur coughed behind his hand. 'Does she know about…?' He looked embarrassed.

'About my foot, you mean.'

A wince crossed his cousin's face. 'Too bad

you took after your mother's side of the family in that regard.'

His fist clenched. He relaxed his fingers. 'Your point?'

'Well. You know. I was just wondering if…'

The man was a coward and an idiot. 'You were not wondering, Liz was. And it is none of her damned business.' He turned and walked away.

'Freddy,' his cousin said. 'You said…'

By the time he hit the flagstones at the bottom of the steps he could no longer hear his cousin's pleading. Damn it all. Wasn't it bad enough that he couldn't dance with his betrothed? Did he have to have his infirmity thrown up at him at every turn?

The urge to strike at something, someone, was a roar in his ears.

Barker stepped out in front of him, and instinctively Freddy raised his fist.

'Whoa!' Barker said. 'It's me.'

Freddy cursed and dropped his arm. 'Apologies. Let me hear you coming next time. Everything in order?'

'Neat as a pin. A mouse couldn't get near the house without someone seeing.'

Trouble was, the individual they were dealing with was far more devious than a mouse. 'You checked the guest list?'

'All in order. No one here that should not be.'

'The servants?'

'Not a Frenchie among them.'

'Hmmph.'

'What's wrong, Guv?'

Other than the lies he'd told his betrothed? Lies of omission Arthur had been pleased to remind him of. 'Not a damn thing.'

'You go on now. Enjoy your party. I've got my eye on things out here.'

Barker was right, and besides, he needed to keep watch inside the house, since they had no clue about Moreau's plans. He'd warned Gabe, who would see no harm came to Nicky, but he should be keeping an eye on Minette. Other than Nicky, she was the only person who had ever seen the man, which was a danger all of its own. 'Report to me in my rooms when the ball is over.'

Barker touched his forelock and glanced up at the sky. 'Moon is rising. Pretty soon it will be nigh as clear as day out here.'

'It is the shadows you need to worry about.'

He headed back for the house, crossing the lawn in front of the veranda, the music drifting on the breeze.

The figure of a woman was tripping across the lawn towards him, skirts lifted in one hand, her skin pearly white in the moonlight. Minette.

'Here you are,' she said gaily. She hooked her arm through his and danced along beside him. So much energy. And joy. She was enjoying this party and her joie de vivre lifted his spirits. He'd promised to squire her to balls every night if she would agree to go through with their marriage.

They were halfway across the lawn when the music stopped. A breeze whispered through the nearby shrubbery like a sigh. She halted, pulling on his arm.

He glanced quickly around them. 'What?'

'Look.' She pointed upwards. 'The moon and the stars. Isn't it beautiful?'

He gazed down into her face. 'Yes. It is.'

She frowned. 'You aren't looking.'

'Because what I am looking at is far more beautiful.' Damn, what had made him say such a thing, even if it was the truth?

A laugh shook her shoulders. 'Flatterer.'

'I never flatter.'

The music began again. Something stately and slow.

She turned to face him, 'Dance with me. Out here where no one can see us.'

'A set of two people?' he scoffed.

'No, there's a dance of two I learned in France. The Ländler. Put your hands on my waist. I dare you.'

Her voice brimmed with mischief. And something else. Affection. And, damn him, he wanted to please her on this night of their betrothal.

'You are anxious to see me fall on my face.' But he was already giving in, holding her as directed, and feeling something fizzing in his veins, something he barely recognised.

She put her hands on his shoulders. 'We step in circles in time to the music. Try it.' She moved her feet. He stumbled. Off balance.

'This is ridiculous.' He let go of her waist.

'Try again,' she said. 'Please. No one can see us.'

'A good thing, too. This is scandalous.' He clasped her once more, this time more firmly.

She laughed. 'Left foot forward, right foot forward, half turn step. Left foot forward, right foot forward, half turn step.' Somehow she adjusted for his limp, which had become more pronounced.

The rhythm came easily. It was like riding a horse. He relaxed and soon they were spinning in slow circles across the lawn in time to the music. It was magical.

'Try going straight for a few steps so we don't get dizzy,' he muttered.

She laughed up at him. 'I'll follow your lead.'

It felt a little awkward at first, but then they were gliding across the lawn, sometimes turning, sometimes not. A rosebush loomed up out of the shadows and, trying to avoid it, he lost his balance. He was going down. Taking her with him.

He twisted, landing on his back, his legs tangling in her skirts, her breasts hard against his chest. 'Damnation,' he said when he felt her shoulders shaking. 'I hurt you.'

A laugh erupted from the woman lying across him. She was laughing. He felt a chill spread out in his chest. He'd made a fool of himself.

'That was so much fun,' she gasped through her laughter. 'It is terribly wicked, you know, in polite society. The common people do it all the time, I am told.'

She wasn't laughing at him, she was enjoying the moment.

He chuckled, then laughed. Out loud. And couldn't stop. He kissed her soundly. 'God, do you have any idea how much I love you?'

He froze. Had he really spoken those words? And meant them? He gazed up at her face, and she looked down at him, her expression clear in the cold moonlight.

She blinked.

He stroked her cheek. 'I love you,' he whispered, knowing it for a truth, and kissed her lips tenderly with his heart so high in his throat it felt like tears.

She inhaled a shaky breath and he held his, hoping, like the idiot he was, that she just might—

'For Heaven's sake!' a voice said in a low whisper. 'What are you doing?'

Shocked back into the present by that hissing tone, he struggled to his feet and helped Minette to hers. He brushed them both off, trying to regain his balance, physically and mentally. 'Mother. What are you doing out here?'

'Me?' she shrilled. She looked over her shoulder. 'Half of our guests are up there, watching you cavort like a fool. Have you no shame?'

Beside him, Minette twitched at her skirts. 'I was teaching His Grace a new dance.'

'I don't know what sort of manners pertain in your family but I can assure you—'

'That's enough,' Freddy bit out.

'It is nowhere near enough. Do you think I do not know what the pair of you were doing the other evening? Dinner in your rooms.' Her voice, though little more than a whisper, shook with rage. 'Have you forgotten the vow you made on your brother's grave?'

His stomach churned. He gripped Minette's arm, intending to walk her away. This was not a conversation they were going to have.

Minette resisted his tug on her arm. 'What vow?'

'Mother,' he warned.

'The vow he swore on his brother's grave to never marry.'

'Why would he do that?' Minette asked, looking at him.

'He got want he wanted,' Mother said, her tone venomous. 'He stole the title from his brother. He doesn't deserve—'

Damn Mother, bringing this out now. 'I will not profit from my brother's death. No child of mine will inherit. My cousin and his son are my heirs.'

'You never spoke of this,' Minette said.

The triumph on his mother's face came as no surprise, but the shock on Minette's face struck him hard. 'I'm sorry.'

'You should have told me.'

Yes, he should have. But she really hadn't given him a lot of options. 'But for your little games, I would not be getting married.' *No, no.* That was not what he'd meant to say.

The hurt on her face paid him back a hundredfold.

Damn it all. He had not meant to be cruel, it was just that… They could not have this conversation now. He glanced up at the veranda. There were only two heads. Those of his cousin and his wife. They must have gone to tell his mother about their foolish dancing. 'It is time to go back inside. We have made enough of an exhibition of ourselves for one night.'

He closed his eyes and took a deep breath. It had been wonderful. He couldn't remember when he'd felt so young or so carefree. Never had he been to a ball where he had actually enjoyed himself. He held out his arm, and she placed her hand upon it. In frigid silence they followed his mother across the lawn to the terrace steps.

The emptiness inside him grew deeper as he

recalled her dismay—and that she hadn't said she loved him back.

He felt just as small inside as he had as a child when picked last for every game of cricket, or left behind when his peers had gone off on mischief. No one wanted a cripple along.

Astonishing as it seemed to Minette, Her Grace was in the dining room, playing the charming hostess at breakfast. Perhaps knowing Freddy intended to keep his vow to remain childless had cheered her up. But Freddy was nowhere in evidence. The man had said he loved her and in that shocking, astonishing moment she had realised she loved him, too. Desperately.

And she desperately wished she had said something out there on the lawn, instead of staring at him like a moon calf.

Yes, it was disappointing that he didn't want children. But after a night of tossing and turning she had decided that children were not necessary to her happiness. They would have each other. Now she was searching through the public rooms of the house, trying to find him. To tell him what had been becoming more and more apparent to her over these past few days. His declaration had taken her by surprise, left her momentarily wordless. And if she was honest, fearful that he might regret his declaration in the light of the morning.

Still, she'd been cowardly. She should have told him what was in her heart.

And then his horrid mother had arrived and she'd lost her chance.

Both the billiard room and the gun room were empty. She headed for the library, where a footman had told her several gentlemen had gathered. As she approached, male laughter sailed out of the open door. One voice lasting a little longer than the others. A deep, rich chuckle she would know anywhere.

Moreau? She froze. Moreau was in the house? In the library? How was it possible? A footman stationed outside the library door was pretending not to notice her standing as still as a statue in the middle of the corridor. With a quick breath, she set her shoulders and started walking towards the door. He was in library. She would know that laugh anywhere. How was it possible he had entered the house without anyone noticing? She had greeted everyone at the door the previous evening.

The rumble of male voices died out.

Back straight, she entered the room, took in its occupants with a swift glance. There were three men—Freddy's cousin Arthur, a thin young man with a head of cherubic mousy curls and one older man with a large lumpy red nose and a huge belly. None of them were Moreau. All rose to their feet, the fat one creaking loudly as if his corset was about to give way. He must be a friend of the Prince Regent, who also creaked when he moved.

She must have been mistaken about that laugh. Hearing things. 'Good morning, gentlemen.' She dipped a curtsey, hoping it was of the correct depth for while she remembered the other two vaguely from the introductions the previous evening she did not recall names or ranks.

'Good morning, Miss Rideau,' Freddy's cousin said. He had a hearty cheerful voice and a patently false beaming smile. 'I am surprised to see you up so early. Most of the other ladies are still in their chambers after such a rackety evening.'

Was that a sly dig she heard in his voice? Had he seen her dancing with Freddy on the lawn? Seen him fall?

The other men seemed to be waiting for her to say something. They probably wanted her to go so they could get back to their newspapers.

'Have you seen Falconwood this morning?'

'I gather he rode out early,' his cousin said. He smiled genially but there was something oily about his expression. 'You don't have to worry about my cousin, my dear Miss Rideau. He really is an excellent horseman.'

'I am not worried. I simply wanted to speak with him.'

He tugged at his neckcloth. 'I thought you might be concerned for his safety. His foot, you know. Not quite right. But he manages admirably, don't you know.'

Minette wanted to hit him for the insincerity on his face. What with his mother and this idiot, it was no wonder Freddy had withdrawn into himself. And no wonder he risked his life given the future he'd committed himself to. His admission last night of the vow he had made had given her a much greater understanding of the man he was. 'I'm not at all worried. His Grace is one of the most athletic men I know.' She glanced pointedly at the other man's small paunch.

The other two men chuckled and she heard it again. Moreau's voice. Coming from the elderly fat man. It wasn't possible. Could two so very different men have the same laugh?

She wanted to inspect him, walk around him, look at him from every angle, but she had to continue as if she had noticed nothing. She glanced at his face, trying to appear casual. While nothing else about the man looked right, his eyes were Moreau's.

Her heart lurched. With a struggle she maintained her outward calm—at least, she hoped she hadn't given her shock away—and smiled sweetly at Freddy's cousin. 'Thank you for the information. Have you gentlemen had breakfast? It is being served in the dining room.'

'Ate earlier,' the cherub said with a bow. 'Thank you for asking.'

'Feeling a little peckish myself,' Moreau said.

She gave them a vague smile. 'Excellent. Hopefully I will see you this afternoon out on the lawn? Her Grace has planned an *al fresco* tea, provided the weather holds, and we have some games for your entertainment. Shuttlecock. Croquet. Archery.' She accepted their bows with an inclination of her head and strolled out.

That man was Moreau. She was sure of it, though he had disguised everything—his face, his body. He had even managed to look shorter. But that deep, low chuckle was his. The man had ever been bold. But this? What on earth was his purpose? Had he guessed she was onto him? He must certainly recognise her. Her blood ran cold at the thought of the damage the man could do with so many important people inside the house. How could they have missed him last night when the guest list had been checked and rechecked?

Freddy. She had to talk to Freddy. Dash it all, why did he have to choose now to go riding? Perhaps she should talk to Gabe. Nicky would know of his whereabouts. She headed for their chamber on the second floor.

Halfway up the stairs the idea hit her like a bolt of lightning. If Moreau was an overnight guest, why would she not sneak into his room and take back the damning evidence of her past so she and Nicky would no longer have anything to fear?

Freddy would arrest him, and there would be no damage done to anyone.

Blast. Why could she not remember the name he had given when they had been introduced? Mr Patterson, the butler, would know, though she would have to be very careful with her enquiries. It would not do to alert Moreau she'd seen through his disguise.

Chapter Eighteen

Freddy left his horse with a groom and strode into the taproom of the Bull and Bear, where he found Barker downing a tankard of heavy wet. He nodded to the barman to pour him the same. They took their drinks to a table in the corner.

'Well done,' Freddy said. 'What do they have to say for themselves?'

'They know nothing. Not who they were working for or why. They were following orders.'

Freddy finished his drink. 'I think I will have a word.'

Barker signalled to the innkeeper behind the bar. 'We'll be going down to the cellar. No interruptions, mind.'

The man touched his forelock.

'How much did you pay him?' Freddy asked as they made their way down the stone steps.

'Enough for a day or so.'

The underground space reeked of stale beer

and damp. Barker lifted a trapdoor in the floor. 'Hidey-hole for contraband. Luckily there isn't any right now.' He lowered a wooden ladder into the darkness below their feet and grabbed a lantern from the wall. At the bottom there was yet another locked door. When he opened it and shone the light inside, three men blinked like sleepy owls.

'You can't keep us here,' one of the men said, thrusting his chin in their direction. It was the only move he could make as his hands and feet were tied. 'It ain't right. We've done nothing wrong. Report you for kidnapping.'

'That's Herb,' Barker said.

'I am sure the authorities will be delighted to make your acquaintance, Herb,' Freddy said.

'Ho, is that your game?' the same man said, obviously the leader of this little gang. 'We was asked to deliver a carriage to a farm and then to make our way back to Lunnon. Which is just what we were doing.'

'You were asked to act as a decoy for a French spy. In other words, you are traitors.'

The man cursed.

'Tell me about the man who hired you. What did he look like?'

'A proper good 'un,' Herb said. 'Paid half up front. I figured that even if we never got the other half we'd done very well out of the arrangement.'

'Where and when were you to collect the other half?'

'We were to see the cove in charge of the Fools' Paradise. A hell in Whitechapel.'

Barker cracked a laugh. Freddy glowered at him. 'I know it.'

'That's it. In a nutshell.'

'What did he look like? This man who hired you?'

'Not much to look at. Ordinary. Dressed like a cit. Not a nob, but not down at heel. Sat in the shadows so it was hard to see his face.'

'How tall was he?'

'He never stood up. We left first.'

Freddy cursed inwardly. 'And he gave you no hint as to why he wanted you to undertake this delivery?'

'I asked 'im, but he said weren't none of my business if I wanted the money. I got mouths to feed, I 'ave. There ain't no crime in delivering a carriage, now, is there?'

'It is a crime to help a French spy.'

'I didn't know that then, did I? Wouldn't have done it else. I'm as loyal to my country as the next man. He never sounded like a Frenchie.'

'So there is nothing more you can tell us that will help us find him. Listen well. If I find out you lied, that you knew even a smidgeon more of information, I'll have you clapped in irons and off to Newgate quicker than a cat can lick her ear.'

One of his companions squeaked like a mouse and wriggled.

Freddy lifted the lantern to shine on his face. 'Well?'

'I did 'ear somefink,' the fellow said.

Their leader made a growling noise. 'Ratty, I told you not to follow 'em.'

Freddy could quite see why he was called Ratty. His sharp nose and large yellow front teeth gave him a rodent-like appearance.

'I didn't,' Ratty said. 'Honest. I just 'appened upon 'em on my way 'ome.'

The leader made a sound of disgust.

'What did you hear?' Freddy asked.

'Promise you'll let us go?' Ratty pleaded.

Freddy shrugged. 'No promises. But if the information is useful…'

'Tell 'im, you nodcock,' Herb said. 'If you knowed one of 'em was French then you shoulda said.'

Not that Freddy thought it would have made a bit of difference to Herb, but he would give him the benefit of the doubt. This time.

''E met another cove outside the tavern,' Ratty said. 'Said as how some bird in a forest would never look right under his nose and to have a ship standing ready.' He shook his head. 'Couldn't make any sense of it. Then they started talking foreign like.'

'Who did he meet?' Barker rapped out.

Another shrug. ''E was a Frenchie. Or I think he was. Spoke foreign when he answered. No idea what he was sayin'.'

'*Some bird in a forest* wouldn't happen to be Falconwood, would it?' Freddy asked.

'Yerst. 'Ow did you know?'

'Not your concern, my lad,' Barker said.

A chill slithered down Freddy's spine. 'Right under my nose.' He started for the door, Barker following.

'Hey!' Herb yelled. 'You said—'

Barker locked the door behind them. 'I'll be back for you lot later.'

'What is it?' Barker asked as the climbed the steps to the taproom.

The man had a nose for trouble. 'If I'm right, though I hope to God I'm not, he is in my house.' And everyone he cared about—Nicky, Gabe, Minette—was in there with him.

Heart high in her throat, her pulse racing, Minette stole into the room assigned to the man the butler had identified as a Lord Peckridge. He'd been on the guest list as a distant relation of Freddy's cousin's wife, Liz. The chamber was one of the smaller guests rooms on the third floor in the oldest wing in the house, as far from the public rooms as it was possible to be without entering the servants' quarters. Peckridge was clearly considered one of Falconwood's least important guests.

The room had a bed, a nightstand, a desk, an armchair beside the fire and a wooden chair beside the desk. Against one wall was a clothes press. There was no dressing room for the man's valet—he would be quartered up in the attic with the other servants.

Where to look? She must not linger long. Even though he had expressed the intention of going to breakfast, his servant might return. Or the man himself. Peckridge indeed. Her blood ran cold. But for his laugh she would not have seen through his disguise. And he had been walking among them for hours.

It was not a disguise he had used when she had travelled with him. Then he had usually been a displaced aristocrat or a rebel peasant. It was not important now. Not until she had the portrait in her hands. Then she would reveal him to Freddy.

She started with the desk. There was nothing in its drawers but the obligatory writing paper, pens and ink. The clothes press held linens. The nightstand held a candlestick and a book. Rousseau. Suitable reading material for an English gentleman. Even more suitable for a French revolutionary. The washstand, the usual gentleman's toiletries.

And that was it. Where were his personal papers? Jewellery? Could the valet have them locked away somewhere?

She took a deep breath, tried to calm her rapid breathing. Think. Where would he hide items he wanted no one to find? She slipped a hand under the pillows. Cold metal. She lifted it to reveal a pistol. It wasn't loaded, but the ball and shot were in a small leather pouch alongside. Clearly he was so sure of his disguise he didn't expect to be discovered or it would have been loaded and ready to fire. Useful as it was to know he had a weapon in his room, it wasn't what she had come to find. Carefully she returned the pillow to its original place, smoothing the creases.

She got down on her hands and knees and peered under the bed.

Nothing but a pair of slippers set side by side.

Old memories careened through her mind. Times she'd tried not to remember. She used the pattern on the carpet to establish their exact location, then carefully lifted the slippers clear. With her fingernails she scraped the surface of the carpet around where the slippers had sat until she found an edge. Slowly she lifted a square patch of carpet free and the board beneath it. In a hollow between the floor joists, she discovered a small leather satchel.

Moreau had always been secretive about his hiding places. Though she hadn't ever told him, she had always been able to discover them in the inns where they had stayed. He had liked to hide things under the floorboards, though none of those rooms had been carpeted.

Desperate to lock the door, she didn't dare to in case he or his man came in. She had to hurry. With shaking hands she pulled the bag from its hiding place and set it on the floor beside her. It was locked, of course, but it didn't take her a moment to open it with a hairpin. Inside, she found a notebook and pencil. She flipped the pages. It was full of tiny writing, none of which made any sense. Code others would find of interest.

She pulled out a small leather-covered box. Inside it was a signet ring. A gold fob. A set of collar studs set with emeralds and a matching stick pin.

And beneath a layer of white velvet, the miniature. Just the sight of it made her flush hot then cold. What could she have been thinking to pose in such a lewd manner? But she'd loved him and had thought it a great joke to give him such a gift. Before she'd discovered the truth.

Fear a hard lump in her throat, she slipped it into the valley between her breasts, hiding it between her stays and her chemise.

She packed everything else back exactly as she had found it. Moreau would notice the smallest difference, though hopefully he'd be arrested before he noticed the missing memento. She returned the valise to its hiding place, covering it with the board, the carpet and finally the slippers. She let go a sigh of relief and rose.

A creak as the door opened.

Heart rising in her throat, she took one big step. It brought her up against the desk. She slid the drawer open at the same moment Moreau, in his disguise as Peckridge, stepped in.

Bushy grey eyebrows rose towards his hairline. A smile broke out on his face. It looked more like a leer on that horrible face, but she remembered it well now she was positive of his identity.

'Well, well, my little Netty. What a pleasant surprise. I should have guessed you of all of them would sniff me out.'

'Pierre,' she said, her heart contracting as she forced a smile. To her he would always be Pierre Martin, no matter that he had used the name Paul Moreau in all his dealings in England. 'I certainly never expected to see you at my betrothal ball.'

He opened his arms. 'I have missed you.'

She quelled a shudder and steeled her spine against the trickle of fear creeping through her veins. 'Did you, Pierre, when you abandoned me to my fate?'

He frowned. He shifted, his body growing in height and breadth, though his face remained purely Peckridge. 'You could not possibly believe such a thing of me, my sweet. You break my heart.'

He looked so forlorn, even within his horrid

disguise, she believed him implicitly. That was what made him so very irresistible. His charming sincerity. She also knew he would kill her without a second of thought if she posed the most minute of threats.

His gaze dropped to the desk. 'What are you seeking? You know I would give you all that I have.'

More allusion to their time together sent a shudder through her body. Was he saying he wanted her back? Or was it all a trick to set her at ease before he struck?

She gave him a hesitant smile. 'Your disguise is so good I wanted to make sure I was right. I didn't want to make a mistake in so public a place.'

'Hmm.' He glanced in the mirror, touching his face. 'What gave me away?'

'A small thing. Nothing anyone else would notice.'

'It is good, I admit. I studied the man for weeks. Your Duke should take more care to familiarise himself with his distant family.' His gaze met hers in the glass. He smiled. A quick baring of his perfect white teeth. Another thing she had liked about him. 'Congratulations on your betrothal, by the way. You were always one of the most intelligent females I have ever met.'

'Thank you. So that's what you were doing up north. Establishing a new identity.'

'Indeed. My original plan to capture Falconwood was to use this cousin to get close to him. Your engagement and the invitation to your ball brought things to a head in a much more satisfactory manner. Your Duke has been making a thorough nuisance of himself these past few years. Fouché would be very generous with anyone who could bring him to France for questioning.'

Her heart seemed to stop beating. Of all the people she had assumed Pierre might be here to kill, Freddy had not been among them. Fear was a cold, hard lump in her belly. 'I would have expected you to be more interested in the Prince.'

A burst of the so-familiar laughter filled the room. 'That fat fawn? That tearful, womanising dilettante? You think I'm fool enough to want to replace him with his brother, the Duke of York? A real man and a soldier? The emperor would have my head in a basket and rightly so. No, the loss of your Duke and his secrets will be a setback from which the British will never recover.'

'You plan to kidnap him.'

'Naturally.' He turned away from the mirror, walked over to the bed and retrieved his pistol. He loaded it with methodical ease.

This was not good. She eyed the distance to the door. But he was in between. And the window was closed.

He rammed the shot home and glanced up. 'You haven't yet told anyone of my identity, I presume?' He shook his head. 'Of course not. You were not sure.' He glanced around. 'And there was something you wanted, hmm? A picture perhaps?'

Nausea rose in her throat. He had planned to use it against her somehow. She repressed the urge to press her hand against her bosom, where the miniature suddenly seemed much too large for so small a space, where she was sure he would see it should he happen to look more closely. She had to think of something. Anything. To stop him.

Her heartbeat quickened as she slipped into a version of the games he had taught her when she had thought he was working for the loyalists. When she had handed him their lives, thinking she was saving them. Until she'd discovered his true colours by accident. One day while he'd been out, she'd found a letter from Fouché congratulating him on his success in trapping a leader of a small band of royalists. A heartbreaking shock she'd never revealed and instead had tried to warn his potential victims. And then, with professions of undying devotion, because he'd thought her besotted, he'd used her as bait to trap her sister. It seemed he still thought her besotted. The man's ego knew no bounds at all.

She gave him a winsome smile. 'I am so glad to see you again, safe and whole. I worried about you in Spain, and me stuck here in England with no way to reach you. I thought you had abandoned me entirely.'

He frowned. 'Me, abandon you? You left me completely in the lurch at Boulogne. I was lucky not to lose my head over that debacle. All this time I have been languishing in Madrid, you have been enjoying the delights of English nobility.'

The man had no idea about loyalty or familial love. To him it was all about advancement, power, money.

She widened her eyes as if in shock. 'You think I wanted to come here to live with a sister who left me to my fate in a burning building? You were my only friend in the world.'

A protective friend, she'd thought, and a lover, at least for a time. Until she'd discovered the depths of his betrayal. He had broken her heart, but she had made him pay.

'Why did you leave with your sister?' he asked, his face puzzled. 'You knew I would return.'

'They didn't tell you, did they?'

Doubt filled in his expression. 'What the devil are you talking about?'

'The men who were supposed to be watching over me left me with that boy, David, and went off to the tavern.' She'd gambled with them, deliberately cheated and lost all her money to them, and all the while had teased them with sexual innuendo until the only thing they had been able to think about was swiving. Since they hadn't dared touch Pierre's mistress, they'd gone off to find women of their own.

She certainly wasn't surprised his men hadn't told him the truth. Why would they risk his wrath when they never expected to see her again? 'David will confirm my story if you ask him gently enough and don't make him afraid. The poor lad didn't stand a chance against Mooreshead when he showed up. I had no choice but to go with him.' The lies tripped off her tongue as easily as they had when she had been Pierre's dupe, enticing unsuspecting loyalists into his net. She felt ashamed. She'd told the same lies to Nicky when her sister had asked what had happened to her. Told her she'd spent the entire time hiding with nuns until Moreau had discovered her only weeks before Nicky had. 'Ask David, if you don't believe me.'

His grimaced. 'Dead men don't talk.'

Her heart dipped. David had been sweet. 'You killed him?'

Moreau's jaw dropped. 'Not I. Your brother-in-law.'

She shook her head. 'He was alive when we left. I swear it.'

It was hard to see his real expression through the disguise, but she had the feeling he was beginning to believe her story. 'My men must have killed him,' he said slowly. 'To hide their dereliction.'

'I would never have left, but Mooreshead said you told them where to find me to save your own life. I thought you had betrayed me.' He'd certainly betrayed her, but not then. By then she'd known exactly what Pierre was. And what he had made her into.

'Mooreshead.' He spat the name out. 'He lied, *chérie*.' He put a hand to his heart. 'You should know I would never willingly let you go.'

He'd betray his mother for a *centime*, if it came with a smidgeon of advancement. She had to get out of here, get rid of the portrait and tell Freddy she'd found Moreau. 'I'm sorry,' she said softly. 'I should have known better. I hate England. Hate their nobility. I thought once I married Falconwood I would have access to all his secrets. I was planning on passing them along. Who would suspect a duke's wife of being a traitor? He has not been easy to catch, however. I missed your help. I missed you.' She didn't have to pretend to sound miserable, she was desperately sorry to be back in his clutches.

Somehow she had to get away and warn Freddy.

'My little brave one,' he cooed at her, as he had so often in the past. He closed in on her, put his arm around her waist and for a moment she thought he would kiss her. She tried not to tense.

He laughed. 'Damn this disguise. I am an unpleasant-looking fellow, am I not?'

Obviously she hadn't succeeded.

'You will return to France with me,' he said. 'Together we will show Falconwood to Fouché, who will extract all his secrets. The Emperor will reward us handsomely, I am sure, when Britain is brought to her knees.'

'I would like that very much.'

'I missed you, *chérie*. It is good to work with you again. This will make things so much easier.

He believed her story. The ego of the man. But then he had always thought she was blinded by his charm. Always. Even when he had left her staked out like a chicken to bait a wolf in Boulogne. Even though it had been so very hard to hide her hatred for him by that point. And he was desperate. 'Was it so very bad in Spain?'

'He put me in the army. As a private. It was hell.'

'How on earth did you get away?'

'I found evidence of a plot against us. Sent the information to Fouché and was forgiven.'

'A real plot?' she asked with a twinkle in her eye.

'Hmm, not so much.'

They laughed as they had laughed together in the old days at their cleverness, only her eyes had been blind to some of that laughter having been directed at her. For believing in him.

'What is your plan? It will be hard to spirit away a duke from his home.'

'Now you are with us it will be very much easier. You will go to the Duke tonight, drug him and let us into his room when the house is asleep.' He tipped her face up to meet his gaze. 'You will do this for me?'

She nodded. 'And we take him to France? Alive.' It was a relief to know he didn't intend to assassinate Freddy out of hand.

'We do. Tonight. There will be a carriage waiting for us.'

The carriage from the farm. Thank God. Even if he did manage somehow to leave Falconwood with Freddy, that carriage was being watched. It would be stopped.

'You have everything arranged.' She filled her voice with admiration. If he would trust her enough to let her go from his room, she could warn Freddy. 'It is perfect. I cannot wait to return to France.'

The door swung open. Freddy stood on the threshold, his pistol levelled at Moreau. 'No one is going anywhere.' His gaze flickered over her, dark, unreadable and so very cold.

Ah, mon Dieu, how much had he heard? Surely he did not believe...

She pressed a hand to her chest, felt the hard lump of the miniature against her sternum. If he found it, would he believe her innocent?

It hadn't taken a great deal of Freddy's ingenuity to discover which of the gentlemen was the cuckoo in the nest. Peckridge was the only man no one had ever met before and Arthur had been quick to point out that his wife's cousin was known to be a solitary eccentric man, and it had come as a surprise to find him attending a ball, though, of course, he had to be invited.

He was the only one no one could vouch for.

Neither had it taken long to ascertain that the man had gone up to his room after breakfast. With Barker at his back and their men covering all possible exits, Freddy stood with his pistol pointed at the couple embracing by the window. Like old friends. Or lovers. There was no mistaking the familiarity between them or the words he'd heard before he'd opened the door.

Worse was the guilt written across Minette's face. The pain in his chest almost sent him to his knees. He cut himself off from it, keeping his gaze fixed on the Frenchman. Keeping his heartbeat steady. His mind clear. 'Ah, just the man I am looking for.'

A bitter look twisted Moreau's lips as he glanced down at Minette, who remained held close to his side. 'You betrayed me?' He sounded so wounded Freddy's teeth ached with the pressure of his jaw.

'No. I figured it out for myself,' Freddy said. 'We caught the men who brought the carriage.'

Chagrin passed across the other man's face. 'It

is a bad workman who blames his tool, but these English peasants, they have no imagination.'

Minette remained in the circle of his arm, so very close to the pistol he held loosely in his hand. One wrong word and the situation might get very nasty. 'You can confirm this is Paul Moreau?' he asked her.

She stared at him wide-eyed and nodded slowly. 'He is.'

Moreau preened. '*Chérie*, you told him about us? That was very brave of you, before the wedding.'

'Not really,' she said softly, regretfully. 'I only told him about Pierre. I never mentioned that my Pierre and Paul Moreau were the same person.'

Pierre. The pieces fell together with an unpleasant little click inside his head. Her Pierre and Paul Moreau were one and the same. She had loved this man. Possibly still did. And now, if he had any sense, he would doubt where her loyalties lay.

Damn it, from the look on her face she was clearly hurting. He couldn't think of that now. He had to make Moreau believe his words. 'It seems you have a penchant for misshapen men, my dear.'

The Frenchman bristled. Used his free hand to remove his bulbous nose and pull off the bushy eyebrows. He spat out wads of padding in his cheeks, becoming a handsome man in his late thirties. '*Voilà*, not misshapen at all.'

Odd bits of glue dripped from his face, making it look as though it was melting. And the damned pistol stayed where it was, firmly grasped in the hand about her waist.

'Step away from the lady,' Freddy said.

Moreau tilted his head. 'You plan to arrest us, I presume? See justice done. Not take us outside and shoot us?'

'I'm a gentleman,' he said coldly. 'What is done with you is not up to me. I will hand you over to the authorities.'

The expression of fear on Minette's face clawed at his vitals.

'Put down your weapon,' Freddy enunciated slowly. 'Miss Rideau, step aside.'

Moreau hesitated.

Freddy cocked his pistol. 'I will shoot you.'

The man swore, glanced down at Minette and back at Freddy. 'I suppose you would not care which of us got hurt.'

'No.' He prayed like hell the man wouldn't test him on that particular point. 'Why would I?'

Moreau sighed. 'You overheard our conversation.' He tossed the pistol aside.

'Freddy?' Minette said.

'Not now. Barker, see to him.'

Barker and two of his men were across the room in a flash, picking up the Frenchman's weapon, holding him by the arms.

'What the hell is going on?' Gabe said, strid-

ing into the room. 'By Jove, you got him. And in
the house, too. That was a close-run thing.' He
glared at Moreau. 'Mooreshead, *à votre service.*'

'I know who you are,' Moreau ground out, all
his smiles and charm gone. 'You stole one of my
very best agents.'

Minette sent him a look of appeal. 'Tell Nicky
I'm sorry. I never meant to cause her harm. None
of this is her fault.'

'Get her out of here, Gabe,' Freddy said, 'while
I finish with this one.'

Minette looked startled. Shocked.

Moreau stared at him. 'So she has your *couilles*
in her sweet little hands, does she?' His lips
twisted in a bitter smile. 'You played me well,
Falconwood. But since you care about her, I will
make you a trade. Let me go and no one will ever
know her part in this.'

The man was a cur. A trapped cur bargaining
for his life by saying she was involved in his plan.
That not only had she been planning to run off
with him, she'd made it possible for Moreau to
enter his house. That she'd been involved since
the start. Freddy's stomach fell away. The Home
Office boys would be very interested to hear it,
because it would put him in very bad odour and
reflect badly on Sceptre. Something that would
please them no end. He could imagine Blazenby
taking full advantage of the situation to advance

his career. He looked at his friend. 'Get her out of here, Gabe. Now.'

Gabe hustled her out of the room.

God, he hoped he had his temper under control by the time he was ready to talk to her, because right now he wanted to hit something he was so damned angry.

Moreau watched her go, his face puzzled. He straightened his shoulders. 'Doesn't it bother you that she played you for a fool? That she was planning to help me?'

The hollow in his chest widened. 'I doubt she'll want to go where you are going.' He gestured to Barker. 'Tie him up and gag him.'

Once he was sure his prisoner could not possibly escape he went in search of Minette.

Chapter Nineteen

He found her pacing in Gabe and Nicky's drawing room, her eyes sparkling with anger. Why did she think she had the right to be angry?

Seated beside Gabe, Nicky followed her with a worried expression.

The moment Minette saw him she stormed towards him. 'What you heard. I wasn't—'

He cut her off with a chop of his hand. Rude, yes, but he had to know. 'Tell me one thing. Why did you go to his room?'

She gasped, looked indignant, then defiant. 'Why do you think?'

Gabe made as if to stand but subsided at Nicky's murmur of protest, watching them through narrowed eyes.

'I think you are an idiot,' Freddy said.

'Falconwood,' Gabe said with a growl in his voice.

He shot his friend a glare. 'If you wouldn't

mind, both of you, I would like to speak to my betrothed alone. We have some matters we need to discuss.'

Looking troubled, Nicky rose. 'I think that is a fair request.'

'Listen to me, Freddy,' Gabe said. 'Hurt one hair of her head and you'll have me to deal with.' The man was barely holding on to his temper. Freddy knew exactly how he felt. His was rapidly slipping from his grasp.

'Gabe,' Nicky urged.

Mooreshead gave him one long last hard look and gently escorted his wife out.

The door closed softly behind them.

'Well?' Freddy bit out. 'Did you think me so incompetent you had to try to capture him yourself?'

Minette stared at him. Took in his fury. Snapped her mouth shut. Was that what he believed? That she thought him incapable, the way his mother did? Thought him less than a man? Not good enough to produce the next heir?

She hurt for him. Badly. And wished and wished she'd spoken of her feelings out there on the lawn.

The weight of the miniature against her heart made itself known when she moved towards him. Brought her up short. If she let him continue in this misapprehension, for which he would no doubt hate her, he would never have to know how careless she'd been with her virtue. Never have to see the picture that would not only have ruined her but destroyed her sister in the eyes of society.

The man had offered her his heart. Told her he loved her. She owed him the truth. He would never expose her folly, not even when he turned away in disgust, glad of a lucky escape. At least she would know she had kept a shred of honour. 'He had something of mine. Something I had to get back before he was arrested. He caught me before I could leave.'

He stilled. 'Did you get it?'

She swallowed and nodded, fumbled in her bodice, and drew forth the miniature. She held it pressed close to her chest for a second or two then held it out, the back towards him, the ugliness of what she was staring her right in the face. She dropped her gaze to the floor, dreading seeing his anger turn to disgust.

'You risked your life for a trinket?'

Her heart ached at the flatness his voice. The distance. 'Not a trinket,' she said, forcing herself to speak what was in her heart. 'It is a portrait of Paul and me in what might be described kindly as *in flagrante delicto*.' Her faced heated. If it was possible to go up in flames and have the ashes of combustion blow away on the wind, now would be the right time. 'It was a jest between lovers. Our faces painted onto a lascivious picture by an artist in the market square. A jest in very poor taste.' When he made no move to take the picture, she let her hand fall.

'When I heard he was back in England I was terrified he might use it as blackmail. To get me back under his control. He would know I could not bear the idea of anyone seeing it, especially you. Worse, though, would be the *ton*'s reaction. Nicky and Gabe sponsored me, introduced me to society. To have it become public knowledge that they'd taken such a woman into their midst would have ruined them socially. Look at the way Sparshott behaved over the matter of a kiss. Moreau would know what would happen. And he would use that knowledge to gain his freedom. Those rivals of yours in the Home Office would be only too glad to see Gabe brought down. I could not let it happen. Surely you can understand?'

Bleak-eyed, he kept his gaze on her face. 'I do understand, though I regret you did not trust me to retrieve it for you.' He strode to the window, staring out as if he could not bear to look at her any longer.

Perhaps knowing that it was Moreau who had been her lover had destroyed his regard, his love. And how could she blame him? She had never been honest with him.

She crossed the room to stand at his shoulder. 'I am sorry, Freddy. My intention was not to cause you pain.'

His fists clenched and then opened. He placed one hand flat on the window frame, as if to stop himself from striking out. But not at her. Never at her.

He gave her a hard glance. 'You have no reason to apologise,' he said in a low, dark voice. 'He might have killed you when you were supposedly under my protection. Seeing you there, so close to that damned pistol... It would have been my fault. My damned fault.'

The pain in his voice squeezed a fist in her chest. 'It was my decision. I thought I had time. I did not mean for him to find me.' She glanced down at the miniature clenched in her hand. 'I had to be sure.'

He glanced her way, shadows deep in his eyes. Sadness. 'If you had trusted me more, you would have waited for my return.' He shook his head. 'But I do not blame you. Not one bit. And I certainly will not hold you to our betrothal,' he added softly. 'I know it is not going to work. Cry off, but give it a week or so. The *ton* will not be pleased at having been dragged out here for nothing.'

Oh, no! How could she tell him she loved him now? He would think it was all about his title and not about him. Oh, why hadn't she spoken of what was in her heart when he had? Now he was giving her what she'd thought she wanted.

Or was she being a fool yet again? Perhaps he hadn't meant what he'd said. Perhaps he was glad he'd found the way out of a marriage he had never wanted. He knew the truth of her relationship with Moreau now. A man of his standing would certainly have trouble explaining a wife who had taken England's enemy to her bed. Something Moreau would no doubt delight in relating to anyone who would listen, even if he no longer had the proof.

'It is likely for the best,' she said, half hoping he would disagree. And the other half, the honourable half, hoping not.

He nodded.

Impenetrable cold clenched around her heart as he turned and headed for the door.

'Freddy,' she said.

He hesitated. So slightly she almost didn't catch it, but that tiny hesitation provided the courage she needed.

'What if I don't cry off?' she asked. 'What then?'

He stopped, turned back, his expression impenetrable. 'Then you'll be tied to a man you will end up hating because we will never spend another night under the same roof.'

He walked out.

A clock chimed one in the morning. Freddy stared at the note he'd written, but instead he saw Minette's face, her pained expression at his rejection. He hadn't expected it to hurt her. He'd expected relief. Damn it all, what had made him say what he had out there in the darkness on the lawn? The laughter? He couldn't remember laughing like that since his brother had died. No. Hell, no. He was still pretending, lying to himself. His brother hadn't died. He'd killed him. Intentionally or not, the accident had been his fault. Being sorry didn't change what had happened or make it any less his fault.

What if she did insist on going forward with the wedding? Out of pity? For that was all it could possibly be. He could not in all honour walk away.

The pain of longing struck his heart.

And then what? He went cold inside. He'd never resist the temptation of having her under his roof. Past experiences proved he would not. God, he'd made love to her twice already and, despite being careful, she could even now be carrying his child.

They would have to wait to know for certain, before they called off the engagement. Even he wasn't villain enough to abandon a woman carrying his child. Where the hell was his famous cold reserve when it came to Minette? His control. He'd have to talk to her in the morning before she left with Gabe. Make it clear that she must not cry off for a month or two. Just in case. A bubble of hope rose in his chest. What if she was pregnant?

Dear God. He closed his eyes. If she was, it would be a dream come true, and his worst nightmare.

He blinked his thoughts away, forced himself to focus on the task at hand. The resignation Sceptre had insisted upon. He'd been exposed and was no longer useful. Brief and to the point. He signed it. Folded it. Melted wax in the candle, surprised to see that despite his inner turmoil his hand remained steady. One drop. Two. He put the candle and the wax aside and pressed his seal into the blob.

Done.

Over.

What the hell was he to do now?

A whisper of sound behind him. He spun around.

Minette. In her nightgown, her unbound hair a soft fall over her shoulders, her face pale, her eyes wary. God, she look so lovely standing there in a gown so sheer he could see the outline of her form, the thrust of her breasts and hardened nipples, the dark triangle at the apex of her lovely slender legs. He rose to his feet, aware of the pounding of blood in his ears. And farther south. 'What the deuce are you doing here?'

'Don't you want to know what I have decided?'

For a moment he couldn't make sense of her words. He had never been in any doubt what she would decide. No woman would take the kind of rejection he had delivered and think about it. Unless the worst had happened.

His heart leaped as if to greet her, pull her close.

He backed away lest he be tempted to do something they would both regret. 'Tell me in the morning. There is one more thing we needed to discuss.'

'I am here now,' she said softly, with an enquiring tilt of her head.

Damn it all. 'I am asking you to wait awhile before you announced that we do not suit. There is a reason to wait.' His lips felt stiff and awkward. It was hard to form the words, but he could leave nothing to chance. 'Obviously, if you are with child as a result of our... We'll get married.'

She gave him a dark look. 'Are you sure you wouldn't prefer me to pass it off on some other man so you won't have the trouble?'

He flinched. 'No. That would be dishonourable.'

'Honour,' she scoffed, as if she doubted she had a scrap. 'Perhaps you would rather I leave for the country, discreetly abandon it on an orphanage doorstep or give it to some poor family who would be willing to raise it as their own for a large enough sum of money. I am sure you can afford it.'

A way out. She was offering him an escape.

A way not to break his vow. His child raised by strangers. And what if that child—? 'No!'

She recoiled.

He'd been too forceful. 'If it is my child, I will do my duty by it.' Too blunt. Too, too blunt. And cold.

A shrug of her shoulders rippled the soft fabric at her feet. 'How very noble.'

'Damn it all. What more do you want of me?'

Her expression softened, she stepped closer. 'I want you.'

He stepped back, maintaining the distance between them, his body shuddering with the effort to retain the distance when he wanted to ravage her lush mouth, feel her lovely curves pressed against him, bury himself inside her. Ease the pain of his miserable past. Such a coward.

She reached out a hand. He ignored it. 'I'm not expecting your child.'

The faint hope inside him died, though he had not even realised it had existed, not in any rational way. Disappointment swept through him, followed swiftly by relief. Blessed relief. Life would be so much simpler. 'How can you be sure?'

'There are certain herbs a woman can take. Rape was always a risk in France and the nuns taught us how to avoid unwanted children from such an event.'

She sounded so matter-of-fact it shocked him

to the core. What must her life have been like in France? 'And you continue to use the herbs?'

'They have other beneficial effects.' She coloured. 'Less painful monthly visits.'

His own face heated. This was not a conversation he should be having with a woman who was not his wife. 'So you are saying, if we married, you could continue taking them?' She would be the one in control. He would have to trust her not to make any mistakes. And he would have his cake and eat it, too.

So very tempting.

And convenient. Keep to the letter of his vow, if not the spirit. The freedom to blame any errors, deliberate or otherwise, on her. He shook his head. 'Too risky.'

'I was looking for you when I recognised Moreau by his laugh,' she said.

'He's gone. There is no more to be said about him.'

Her expression turned stubborn. 'I thought I was hearing things at first. When I saw him in that disguise. But I knew I was right. The opportunity was too good to miss.' She crossed the room to peer at his collection of rocks, picking them up and putting them down as if it would help put her thoughts in order. 'I had to get that miniature for Nicky's sake. He would not have hesitated to find a way use it against us once he realised he was caught.'

'And you have it.' He kept his voice cold and his gaze firmly fixed on a place above her head, but it did not stop him from seeing her beautiful body as she strolled around his room, touching his things so intimately he knew he would never see the items again without thinking of her. 'There is no more to be said.'

'Vilandry was an utter pig. Nicky let him use her in order to protect me.'

She put down a lump of granite and turned to face him. 'She suffered years of that man for my sake. She thought I was too young to realise, but I knew. One of the maids let it fall that he liked very young girls. If Nicky hadn't agreed when our uncle proposed the match, he would have taken me instead. He used the threat of it to keep her in line.'

Bile rose in his throat. 'Then it is a good thing he's dead.'

A painful smile curved her lips. 'It is. I didn't know it until much later but Moreau had visited Vilandry. Saw Nicky and wanted her. When he learned Nicky and I had escaped the fire, he searched for her. It took him a while but he found me. And I led him to Nicky.'

The guilt in her voice pained him greatly. 'It wasn't your fault.'

'I try to tell myself that,' she said.

'No matter how many times you repeat the words, they never quite ring true, do they?' Over

and over he'd told himself he wasn't responsible
for the death of his brother.

She smiled sadly. 'You understand.' She picked
up the tail feather of a grouse and stroked it across
her palm. 'I spent more than a year with Pierre,
as he called himself, helping him catch loyalists without realising what I was doing. It was
such a grand adventure, spying, reporting back,
finding little pockets of resistance, people who
needed help. I thought we were fighting for the
king. But slowly, slowly, his talk became more
revolutionary in tone. And, fool that I was, I followed his lead. For a while. He was handsome
and outrageously daring. After a life of trying
to be a perfect young lady I had embarked on a
grand and courageous adventure. He was my rock
in my new strange world. He taught me things.
About my body no decent girl should know. He
encouraged my wantonness, the results of which
you know.' She glanced at him sideways from
beneath lowered lashes. 'And that you seemed to
like, too, though I thought for certain you would
be displeased.'

Displeasure was the furthest thing from what
he was feeling right now, with her strolling scant-
ily dressed around his room, her fingers brushing across surfaces he hadn't so much as looked
at in years. The thought that she would never do
so again was a jagged pain in the emptiness of
his chest. 'You loved him.'

'I loved a man who never existed, but I do not believe I was ever in love. I was his pet. I wanted to please him so he would keep me close. I feared being abandoned. It had happened too many times already.'

And Moreau had known it. Used it against her. Did she think he was also abandoning her? The thought tightened his throat.

She drew in a hitching breath. 'He used me, Freddy. And I never suspected a thing. First to trap the local loyalists and then as a lure to force Nicky to do his bidding. By then, of course, I knew the truth of who he worked for and I mitigated the damage as best I could. When we left Boulogne I was happy to be free of him. Happy his plot against Nicky had failed.' She paused in her wandering to look at him.

'It was only later I remembered the gift I had purchased for him months before. Realised the harm it could do if it was made public. I didn't care for myself, but it would have ruined Nicky and Gabe by association. I could not allow it. Not after what she sacrificed for me.'

'The miniature.'

She opened her hand and set it on the desk. 'A portrait of the most salacious sort. They were sold in the market. I had our faces painted in, his and mine, as a joke.' She shrugged.

He glanced down at the scene. A woman sprawled without shame and a man giving her pleasure with his hand, the faces easily recognizable.

He was glad she was telling him her story. It cleared up his lingering questions about Moreau, but he could not let it matter. He deliberately did not glance at the picture again. 'Destroy it and forget it. It is over.'

She wandered to the window, opened the curtains a fraction and stared out into the night. 'I think if two people really love each other there should be no secrets between them.'

His heart gave a lurch. Stuttered, then raced. He pulled her around to face him. 'What are you saying?'

'When you told me you loved me, you caught me by surprise. I was afraid. I'd said it once before to Pierre in a moment of passion, and realised I'd been mistaken in his feelings for me. I thought that by saying nothing I wouldn't give you the power to break my heart.' She huffed out a breath. 'I am such a coward.'

He cupped her cheek with his hand. 'You are the bravest person I know. How you managed to survive alone in France... How you faced Moreau and his damned gun. I was proud of you.'

She gave him a sad smile. 'Not proud enough to go through with our wedding.'

His heart contracted painfully. 'It wouldn't be fair. I can't give you want you want. What every woman wants. I can't take the risk.'

'Children.'

He nodded. 'And I cannot control myself when you are near. I want you too much.'

Her expression lightened a fraction at his admission. 'I can live with not having children as long as we can be together.'

'You think that now, but what if you change your mind? What then?'

'I would forgo them to be with you. But, Freddy, my dearest, not having children cannot bring your brother back. You are punishing yourself for no reason. His death was an accident. You know it was. You would never have cheated. You have far too much pride. Too much honour.'

She was right. In a way. 'I made a vow. I can't go back on my word.'

'Your father was wrong to extract such a dreadful promise.'

'He didn't. He was horrified when I told him. But when I realised Reggie was dead I knew I couldn't do it. Couldn't be the heir. Not and bring another child into the world like me.'

'I don't understand.'

'You saw my foot. It is a hereditary condition, passed down through my mother. My children are likely to be born with it, too.' She didn't react with revulsion, as he'd expected. Her face showed only puzzlement. 'Do you think I'd let a child go through life with such an impediment?' He gestured downwards.

'You said it didn't hurt.'

'It hurts when your family hates the sight of you, can't bear to watch you limp around so they hide you away in the nursery. Reggie wasn't so bad, most of the time, but Mother couldn't stand the sight of me. I swore to myself I would never put a child of mine through the misery of growing up a cripple.'

'Oh, Freddy.'

There. There was the pity he'd fought to avoid. 'If I don't have children, it can't happen.'

'No child of ours would be treated so poorly.'

Red filmed his eyes, anger along with frustration. 'You don't know that. Can't know.'

'You wouldn't hold a deformity against a child any more than I would. And we would defend them from anyone who tried. Look at you. It makes very little difference to your life. You walk, ride, play cricket occasionally.' She smiled hesitantly. 'You even danced.'

Something inside him cracked open. Warmth and light seemed to fill all the dark places inside him. A grin forced its way to his lip at the memory. 'I did. Not all that well.'

'You would get better if you practised.'

A laugh at her prosaic statement would not be stifled. He sobered. 'Mother would never forgive me for going back on my word.'

She looked at him solemnly. 'Your mother has much to account for, but this is your life, *mon cher.*' She frowned. 'You say this problem comes from your mother's side of the family. Is it possible she blames herself? That she feels guilt?'

The truth hit him like a blow to the head, making his ears ring. Always he had hoped, even if he hadn't fully admitted it, that by doing exactly what his mother wanted, trying to please her, she would find it in her heart to forgive him for not being perfect. For not being his brother. Perhaps even gain her love. But how could she, if she could not forgive herself?

He'd been so heartsick, thinking he might have harmed his brother on purpose, he'd let guilt rule his life. Yet he'd always known, deep inside, he would not have cheated, and had known Reggie would have. He hadn't been the sort of fellow to accept coming in last. Only it wasn't the sort of thing one said about a dead man.

Devil take it, he'd been such a fool.

And he didn't have to be alone—if what Minette was hinting at was true. If.

'I love you,' she said softly, as if sensing his doubt.

A storm raged inside him, hope at war with the dread of being wrong, of once more being rejected by one he held most dear.

'I love you, Freddy.' She opened her arms.

He walked into her embrace. 'I love you,' he said hoarsely, his heart feeling too large in his chest. 'I need you.'

'Yes.' She twined her arms around his neck went up on her toes and kissed his mouth. 'I need you, too.'

For the first time in his life he felt as if he had come home. He had a place where he belonged.

He carried her to the nearest flat surface. His desk. He set her on it. Standing between her thighs, kissing her until he thought he would go mad for wanting to be inside her.

He stroked the silken skin of her calves. The lovely, lovely turn of her ankle.

Chapter Twenty

∞

He wanted her so badly. Not the joys of her body, though, God help him, he wanted that, too, but the radiance of her spirit that had brought light into his increasingly dark world.

If he gave in to this, let himself hope and then lost her, it would finish him.

She cradled his cheek with her fingers. Cool skin. A searing touch. 'Freddy, darling, you don't deserve to be shut out in the cold.'

She understood. What barriers he had left were sundered by the realisation that she really did understand. He caught her wrist before she could draw back, pressed his lips to the centre of her cool little palm. 'I love you. I will always love you.'

'I love you, too.' A small laugh stirred the air across his cheek. He shivered with pleasure. She pulled back to look at him, her eyes full of mischief. 'I thought you were so annoying the first time we met. On that ship. You were so handsome. I wanted you to see me yet you treated me like a child. I wanted to shake you and make you look at me.'

'I saw you,' he croaked, his throat so dry it hurt to speak. 'I was terrified by how much I saw you. I thought the best thing was to keep far away.'

'I missed you.'

The words soothed him like balm on a raw wound. 'You are sure? You really do want to marry me?'

'With all my heart.'

'I will get a special licence.' Urgency filled him. 'Tomorrow. I won't wait any longer to make you mine.'

'I am yours. You don't have to wait.' She twined her arms around his neck and kissed him with all the heat of a passionate woman.

He pulled her tight against his body, feeling her curves and hollows against him, cupping her lush bottom in one hand, a high plump breast with its hard little peak in the other, and tangled his tongue with hers.

It felt right. As if she was the part of him he'd been missing all his life. He'd been broken but hadn't known it. With her he was whole. A new man. A better man.

Her breathing became urgent, ragged, her fingers digging into his back, her hips arching against his now painful arousal.

He broke their kiss on a groan. 'I want you so badly.'

A small smile of satisfaction lit her face. 'Good.'

His body jerked at the erotic note in her voice. He shrugged out of his robe. While she nimbly attacked the buttons of his shirt, he toed off his slippers and shucked off his pantaloons. It was a mess of hard breathing and groping hands and so sexy he couldn't stop his smile. Free of all but his shirt, he gripped her shoulders and kissed her again. Her hands slipped under his shirttails and, no longer cool, stroked his back and his buttocks. He glanced around desperately for a place they could lie down in comfort. She gazed at the jutting evidence of his arousal beneath his shirt. She slid off the desk and lowered herself to her knees, grasping his buttocks in her hands.

'Minette,' he gasped. 'Oh, devil take it...'

She cast him a saucy glance from under her lashes. 'You don't like this?'

The proximity of her mouth so close to his aching flesh, the heat of her breath, left him blind with lust. 'You honour me. You make me so damned happy.' Being this vulnerable with a woman had never been an option.

'It is all I want. You happy.'

Unable to think of a reason to protest, he pulled his shirt up over his head. She leaned back on her heels to look at him. Her gaze travelled from his

face and down to his ugly foot, before returning
to his face. With any other woman he would have
plunged the room in darkness. He stood silent,
waiting for her judgement. If she turned away
now...

'You are such a beautiful man,' she said softly.

'Hardly that.'

She caressed the backs of his thighs. 'Pure
muscle. Like a racehorse.' She licked her lips.

'Please,' he said. Never in his life had he
begged for something he wanted. Never had he
shown such weakness. But he didn't feel weak. He
felt stronger than he'd ever felt before. Because of
her he was free to be himself. 'Minette, please.'

She smiled and leaned forward, taking him in
her mouth. Heat. Wetness. Suction. Her tongue
teasing.

He widened his stance, keeping his balance.
She reached up to stroke his belly, and he tun-
nelled his fingers into her lustrous hair. The sight
of her moving rhythmically, the sensation of that
movement, sent heat ripping along his veins. She
brought him to the brink far too quickly. Black-
ness and bliss beckoned.

He eased her mouth from his body with a careful hand and brought her to her feet. She smiled
knowingly, her mouth rosy and moist. So luscious.

'I need to be inside you.' His voice was barely
more than a hoarse whisper. 'Now.' He swal-

lowed. 'I would please you as you have pleasured me.'

She gave him a tender smile. 'Always so generous.' She touched a finger to his lips. 'I am not sure I deserve you.'

Too full of emotion for words, he swung her up into his arms and carried her to his bedroom. He stumbled a little but he didn't care. He set her down on his bed and kissed her smiling mouth while his hand found her breast, the peak beading beneath his touch. She moaned into his mouth, arching up into his hand. So responsive. He climbed onto the bed and stretched out beside her, admiring the swells and hollows revealed through the sheer fabric of her nightgown, skimming his hand over them, learning her contours with his hands and his gaze. Never would he forget this moment. 'You are so beautiful. And mine.'

'As you are mine.'

Hers. They belonged together. And if they had children she would love them, no matter their faults. He drew her nightgown upwards, above her hips, and slid it off over her head. She didn't hide from him or blush. She lay before him like a banquet prepared only for him, her gaze taking in his state of rigid arousal in a pass down his body. He delicately parted the sweet hot folds of her cleft. So wet. So ready.

'Please, Freddy. I want you. Now.'

A demand he could not resist. He nudged into

position and eased himself into her, inch by amazing inch, feeling her delicious heat draw him into her depths. For a moment he couldn't move for the extraordinary gift of the pleasure she gave him. She lifted her legs around his waist, pulling him deep, arching up to meet his thrusts, urging him on with little cries and moans that drove him far too close to the brink when she was nearly there. He must not let her down, not in this.

He nuzzled her throat, curled down to take first one nipple then the other in his mouth, suckling and teasing with his tongue. She cried out her pleasure at his touch. And then she was coming apart around him, so beautifully, so intensely. He followed her into bliss.

The lay in each other's arms, a sated, trusting tangle of limbs. The beauty of it gave him a lump in his throat and a prickling behind his eyes. She sighed and shifted. 'That was…' He waited, breath held. 'Amazing.'

Yes. It was. Truly amazing. Unlike anything he'd ever experienced. Carefully he withdrew from her and held her within the circle of his arms, knowing she was his to protect and he was hers to command. For all time.

He bent and kissed her cheek then her lips.

'No going back after that, my darling,' he said, hearing the sound of his smile in his voice and liking it.

'Oh, indeed not,' she said, smiling up at him. 'From here we go only forward.'

Forward to a future he had never dared imagine.

He kissed her long and lingeringly, wrapped her in his robe and carried her back to her bed.

Epilogue

⟨⟨⟨⟨⟨⟨⟨⟩⟩⟩⟩⟩⟩⟩

As Freddy had promised, he obtained a special licence the very next day. Their wedding was held in the drawing room of Falconwood Hall the following morning, with the vicar from the village officiating. The only witnesses were Gabe and Nicky and Barker, who had returned from town to report on the disposition of Moreau earlier that morning, along with the Falconwood servants, who seemed touched at the invitation, if a little intimidated.

Now Minette and Freddy stood on the steps, waving farewell to Nicky and Gabe, who had kindly decided to leave the newlyweds to their own devices. Barker had gone off to the inn in the village.

'Would you care to walk in the grounds with me, Your Grace, since the weather is fair?' Freddy asked.

Suspicious at the note of anticipation she heard in his voice, Minette raised an eyebrow.

He grinned.

The man clearly had something in mind. 'Certainly, Your Grace.' She frowned. 'Is it required that we are so formal in private?'

He gave a shout of laughter. 'Not at all, beloved. I couldn't help it, I feel like I am living in a dream and keep having to remind myself we truly are married.'

'Not a nightmare?'

'Not at all.' He grinned at her, making her toes curl. She had never seen him so carefree, and there was an air of mischief about him. 'A dream come true.'

She pulled him down so she could kiss his cheek. 'You make me so happy, *mon coeur*.' He did. Her heart felt so large it barely fitted behind her ribs, and a feeling of total well-being permeated her.

'I'm sorry Mother refused to attend the ceremony,' he said, his face turning grave. 'But you were right. It is her loss. I assume she is settling into the dower house.'

'I understand so. She has already received calls from some of her cronies.'

'Perhaps she will come round.' In truth, Minette doubted it. The woman had held on to her grief too long to let it go now. Indeed, it seemed to her that Freddy had barely avoided the same fate. Much longer and his heart too would have shrivelled to nothing beneath the weight of guilt and regret.

They walked arm in arm through the formal gardens at the side of the house and onto the lawn at the back. Snatches of music wafted on the breeze. It seemed to be coming through the open French doors leading onto the terrace from the ballroom.

'What is going on up there?' Freddy asked, far too nonchalantly to be innocent.

A wife ought to humour her husband. 'How strange. It sounds like an orchestra.'

'I think we should go and see.'

They crossed the lawn and mounted the steps to the veranda. The music was indeed coming from within. An orchestra had set up in the same place they had been on the night of the betrothal ball, but this time she and Freddy were alone in the vast room. All the decorations had been taken down. Gilt chairs were placed at intervals around the walls, but oddly all the chandeliers were alight. The room glittered.

She frowned. 'Is this your doing, *mon cher mari*?'

'How did you guess?'

'Well, if it was anyone else, I believe it would go hard with them. Such extravagance to light

all these candles when there are only a few occupants in the room.'

'I can see you are going to be a fearsome Duchess.'

'I do not like unnecessary waste.'

He was laughing.

She looked around her, and then she realised.
'Your promise. You are keeping your promise.'

'I am.'

He made a gesture to the orchestra, and the
music changed. It was the tune they had danced
to in the garden. He held out his arms. 'I promised I would dance with you on our wedding day.'

She managed a mock frown. 'Rather clever of
you to make sure there was no one here to see us.'

'You are not accusing me of cheating, I hope.'
He put a hand on his heart. 'You will give me time
to become accustomed to displaying my clumsiness for all to see. And I will, I promise you. I
will never let it stand in my way again.'

She couldn't speak for the lump in her throat.
The man had so much courage.

He opened his arms, and she stepped into
them.

He began to move, gliding her around in circles down the length of the ballroom, a good bit
steadier than he had been on the grass in the dark.

'This, *mon cher*,' she said reprovingly, 'is not
a dance we can do in public. We would be ban-
ished from the *ton*.'

'I have to say, that is quite a relief,' he said, and twirled her under his arm. 'I don't see me mastering the Roger de Coverly in the near future.'

'Oh, I wouldn't be too sure of that.'

'I love you, Your Grace,' he said in a low, dark murmur in her ear.

'I love you, dearest Freddy,' she said, smiling up at him and adjusting her step just a tiny bit to accommodate a slight list to the left.

And then he stopped and pulled her into his arms and kissed her.

The orchestra kept on playing.

* * * * *

Don't miss Sarah Morgan's
next Puffin Island story

Some Kind of Wonderful

Brittany Forrest has stayed away from Puffin Island
since her relationship with Zach Flynn went bad.
They were married for ten days and only just
managed not to kill each other by the
end of the honeymoon.

But, when a broken arm means she must return,
Brittany moves back to her Puffin Island home.
Only to discover that Zac is there as well.

Will a summer together help two lovers reunite or
will their stormy relationship crash on to the
rocks of Puffin Island?

Some Kind of Wonderful
COMING JULY 2015
Pre-order your copy today

0315/MB507